Whiskey on the Rocks

A Whiskey Mattimoe Mystery

Nina Wright

Midnight Ink
Woodbury, Minnesota

First Edition
First Printing, 2005

Author's photo by Laura Ahrens
Book design by Donna Burch
Cover art © 2005 by Bunky Hurter
Cover design by Lisa Novak
Editing by Connie Hill

Llewellyn is a registered trademark of Llewellyn Worldwide, Ltd.

Library of Congress Cataloging-in-Publication Data
Wright, Nina.
    Whiskey on the rocks : a Whiskey Mattimoe mystery / Nina Wright.
        p.   cm.
    ISBN 0-7387-0749-X
    1. Women real estate agents—Fiction.   2. Michigan—Fiction.   I. Title.
PS3623.R56W48   205   2005049606
813'.6—dc22

This is a standard work of fiction. All names, places, characters, and incidents are either invented or used fictionally.

All mail addressed to the author is forwarded but the publisher cannot, unless specifically instructed by the author, give out an address or phone number.

Midnight Ink, an imprint of Llewellyn Publications.
A Division of Llewellyn Worldwide, Ltd.
2143 Wooddale Drive, Dept.0-7387-0749-X
Woodbury, MN 55125-2989 U.S.A.
www.llewellyn.com

Printed in the United States of America

FORTHCOMING BOOK BY NINA WRIGHT

Whiskey Straight Up

DEDICATION

For my father on his next birthday.

And in memory of Lucille, the most difficult dog
I've learned to love. So far. . . .

ACKNOWLEDGMENTS

Gratitude beyond words to Richard Pahl, Kate Argow, Bonnie Brandburg, Diana West, Laura Ahrens, Pamela Asire, Barbara Winzeler, Philip Williams, Barbara Sayers, and Paul Epstein. You sustained me.

Hearty thanks to Nancy Potter and Rita Thomas for helpful feedback on early drafts.

To fellow writers Theodora Aggeles, Melissa Buhler, Rebecca Gall, and Greg Neri; you make me laugh, you make me cry, you make me better. Write on.

ONE

"He was lying there like you are now. Only he was dead."

I stared at Noonan as she worked the muscle in my left calf.

"You were massaging a corpse?" I asked.

"For a minute. Jenx thinks he couldn't have been dead very long before I noticed."

I shuddered. Noonan's strong hands stopped their magic.

"I'm sorry," she said. "You've had enough death in your life lately. You didn't need to hear that."

"Life is full of death. Either we keep moving, or we . . . stop moving." I hoped the words sounded wiser to her ears than they did to mine. Spouting New Age aphorisms is the safe conversational choice in this resort town. It's not my style, however.

"That is so wise," Noonan agreed, moving on to my ankle. I moved to the next topic.

"Did Jenx call the county coroner?"

Noonan nodded, shooting me an uneasy glance. "Do you want to go there? I only brought it up because you asked what was new, and a dead guy on this table two hours ago is about as new as it gets."

Before I could jackknife into an upright position, she added, "I changed the sheets."

"Don't you always? I mean, between live clients?"

"Sure, sure. Health Department code."

Noonan repositioned herself at the foot of the table to get a better grip on my sole. As she pressed her thumbs into the ball of my left foot, I flashed on Jenx and the coroner.

"Those two in this studio. Whew. They hate each other!"

"They have trust issues," Noonan corrected me. "Jenx thinks Crouch is political."

"He is. He's elected. But he's also a forensic pathologist."

"And Crouch thinks Jenx is a dyke."

"She is—and proud to be one. But she's also the Deputy Chief of Police."

"And Crouch is a Fundie."

Fundie is local-talk for Fundamentalist. What we used to call "Born-Again," only I've concluded that most of our Fundies grew up that way. They're not redeemed. They're not much fun, either.

"So Jenx and Crouch got into it?" I said as Noonan rolled me onto my stomach again with more grace than I could manage on my own. Lucky me. A bonus round. I love it when she stretches the massage to fit the conversation.

Noonan said, "No name-calling, but you could feel the negative energy. It poisoned my space. After they left, I had to do a spiritual cleansing."

I hoped she'd done a chemical cleansing, too. After all, there had been a corpse on this table. And not a corpse we knew.

"Did Crouch say what killed him?"

"It looked like a heart attack, except for his age. Thirty-four, according to his driver's license. He was in great shape. Fantastic muscle tone." I detected a hint of sexual arousal in Noonan's voice. She went on quickly, "Crouch will do an autopsy."

"What's the dead guy's name?"

Noonan massaged my shoulders with renewed energy.

"That part . . . is weird. He told me his name was Dan, and he was from Grand Rapids. Passing through on his way to Chicago. Business trip. He said he stopped in Magnet Springs for lunch and saw my shingle. Thought a massage would do him good."

"What's the weird part?"

"When Jenx checked his driver's license, it gave his name as Gordon Santy. And—get this—he's Canadian. From New Brunswick. Isn't that on one of the coasts?"

"Atlantic. Maybe Dan was his nickname, and he had business in Grand Rapids."

"Maybe. What I wonder is, if he was Canadian, why did he sound just like us?"

That made me laugh, which made my ribs hurt. They're almost healed from the accident, but when I'm lying on my stomach and I laugh—which I don't think I've tried in five and a half months—I realize I'm not completely recovered yet.

Noonan sounded defensive. "Canadians have an accent. They say 'oot' for 'out.' And they say 'eh' a lot. Haven't you noticed?"

"I guess I don't watch enough CBC."

She sighed. "Have you ever known anyone named Gordon who was called Dan?"

"I don't think I've known anyone named Gordon. And the men I knew named Dan never told me their real names. I assumed they were Daniels, but I didn't check their IDs."

In silence Noonan kneaded my back, my buttocks, and my thighs. Neither of us spoke for several minutes. By the time she had finished, I was blissed out. Her voice jarred me back to reality.

3

"You're funny, Whiskey. And that's cool because humor can heal. But humor can also deflect. I'm telling you this because I think you're still in pain."

I struggled to sit up, clutching the sheet to my chest.

"My ribs still hurt a little, but only when I laugh, and only when I'm getting a massage."

"See what I mean? You're being funny, and I'm talking about Leo."

"Yeah, you are. Haven't you had enough death in this room for one day?"

"You should talk about Leo. You'd feel better if you did."

"I feel fine! If you're suggesting I get a dose of New Age mood therapy, no thank you. I get that every day talking to almost anyone in Magnet Springs."

Noonan regarded me solemnly. "Okay, Whiskey, but please don't wear your armor all the time. It will smother your soul."

The lingo again. Before I could summon an appropriately trite response, she added, "And deaden your heart."

I thought of a punch line about the dead heart that had been on Noonan's table, but decided not to use it.

My name is Whiskey Mattimoe, and I own the hottest real estate agency on the West Coast. The West Coast of Michigan, that is. Right across the Big Water from Chi-Town. Sunsets R Us. We got dunes, we got beaches, we got nice, clean air. In short, we got *The Good Life*. And compared to the good life on the other West Coast, this one's afford-able, mostly. Sure, the value of lakefront property soared like a bottle rocket in the '90s, but it's stabilized, for now. You'd be amazed what a million dollars can buy, and Michigan property taxes aren't bad. You'd pay less in Arkansas or Oklahoma, but what would be the point? Our taxes are bargains next to California's or New Jersey's, and who in their right mind moves to New Jersey?

Six years ago, I married Leo Mattimoe, founder of Mattimoe Realty. Before that I was an agent—real estate, not secret or IRS—and a part-time refurbisher of old properties for investment purposes. I know how to use power tools.

Leo and I were electric together. We had plans. We bought, we sold, we rented, we resold. We made money. We made love. And then suddenly Leo was dead. Leo is dead. I'm still grappling with that one. It wasn't in our plans.

Leo was fifteen years older than me, which made him all of forty-eight the night his heart exploded. I think of it as a cardiac "blow-out" because he was driving when it happened, when his aorta burst without warning.

We were coming back from Chicago following an ill-fated attempt to breed Abra, Leo's Afghan hound, a stunning, high-strung creature with exquisite bloodlines and exasperating manners. I still call her Leo's dog because she has too much self-esteem to belong to anyone else. Least of all me. Every time I gaze into those chocolate eyes, I have an attack of survivor guilt. She'll never forgive me for failing to die in Leo's place. Sometimes I have trouble forgiving myself.

Nesbitt, the young Chicago stud Leo chose as Abra's mate, was a handsome dude, but he couldn't put a round peg in a round hole. Two whole days, and he never grasped the geometry, even with the help of human hands. Or maybe he didn't like his blind date. If a blonde bimbo exists in canine form, it's Abra.

We were heading home to Magnet Springs on that balmy late-April night, the rear windows of our Saab rolled down and the lush air rushing in. Leo was disappointed. Back in his first marriage he'd bred Irish Setters, and he longed to raise more big, glossy show dogs. Abra seemed relieved to be rid of that putz Nesbitt. I'm sure she didn't want his spatially-impaired genes mixed up with hers even though he was a hunk.

The last thing I remember was Leo changing CDs to play our favorite song, "Once in a Lifetime" by the Talking Heads. I squeezed his hand. He squeezed mine back. Then I must have fallen asleep.

I don't remember the impact or the paramedics or the ambulance ride, or anything that happened in the ER, but I can still hear Abra's agonized wail close to my head. She wasn't hurt. She was mourning Leo before I knew he was gone.

I learned the rest of the story by reading the police report. We were within five miles of home on a rural two-lane highway when the Saab sailed off the road and wedged itself deep in a ditch. Abra wriggled out a back window to wait in the road like a pale apparition. The guy who came along told the 9-1-1 dispatcher he thought at first she was an aggressive, long-haired goat. He tried to drive around her, but she kept lunging at his car. She wouldn't let him leave the scene. When she set up a howl and pointed her nose to the side of the road, he got out to investigate. I had a concussion, a broken collarbone, a broken arm, and three broken ribs. Abra played Lassie and saved my life. I don't think she meant to. She meant to protect Leo's remains. Now that he's gone, she lives to humiliate me.

TWO

My office is two doors down from Noonan Starr's Star of Noon Massage Therapy. Very convenient since I buy my body treatments in bulk. Basically, if I want a massage, and she's not busy, Noonan obliges me free of charge. All Magnet Springs merchants barter for goods and services. I have less to offer than most since I buy, sell, and rent real estate, but I give lots of free advice and, whenever possible, discounts on rental properties. Noonan lives in one of my fix-ups on the east side. I love everything about her except her latest business venture, the Seven Suns of Solace. It's a New Age tele-counseling service. That's telephone, not telepathy. I think she advises clients about their karma. Noonan says I should subscribe, but I get a free face-to-face sample, like it or not, with every massage.

Odette greeted me with "Did you hear about the dead man?"

"I not only heard about him, I got his massage."

"You'll also get his business. His wife's, that is. She's coming to town tomorrow, and she wants to stay awhile."

Odette Mutombo is the best real estate agent I ever hired. She's tireless, thorough, resourceful, and ambitious, so I knew she wasn't joking.

"Jenx referred her to us. The lady wants to rent a room or a cottage, or whatever you got."

"Why on earth?"

"She wants to find out what happened to her man."

"I thought that was Jenx's job."

Odette gave her trademark shrug, a quick lift and drop of her narrow shoulders accompanied by a tilt of her ebony head. "Maybe the lady doesn't trust Yanks. She's Canadian. And very, very upset."

After three years of listening to Odette Mutombo talk, I still love the musicality of her accent. Odette and her doctor-husband Reginald are from Zimbabwe by way of London, Paris, and Boston. Both speak a round-voweled, syncopated version of English that ought to be taught in school.

"We don't have anything available, do we?" I said. "We're a week away from peak color."

Leaf-peeping is one of our four major seasonal events, the others being winter sports, water sports, and blossom-spotting. It was already the last week in September, and our trees were wowing audiences from near and far.

"Ordinarily, we would not," said Odette. "But the Reitbauers just called, wondering if they should rent their home before they sell it. I said that sounded like a fine idea."

"And we could help the new widow," I said. "I'm sure she'll be grateful."

Odette sniffed. I knew what that meant. It was her polite way of letting me know that I didn't know what I was talking about.

"The new widow is rather rude, I think. But you can judge for yourself when you meet her. She'll be here at ten tomorrow, and she will only do business with you. I don't think she likes my accent."

"Not possible. What's her name?"

"Ellianna Santy. She's about thirty, I'd say. Tall, blonde, blue-eyed—or maybe green. Very well dressed."

Odette has an uncanny ability to read people over the phone. From their voices, she gets clues about age, eye color, lifestyle, and more. I call it telephone telepathy. It makes money.

"Will there be children with her?" I said.

"No. But she is bringing a companion."

"Who?"

"Her brother."

Odette looked away.

"Something wrong?" I asked.

The shrug again.

"Come on, Odette!"

She gazed at me with lids half-lowered. "I don't like *her* accent."

I called the Reitbauers in Chicago and negotiated a fair weekly rental rate on their cedar-sided Cape Cod, called Shadow Play. Situated in a pine glen on a dirt lane less than a quarter mile from Lake Michigan, it's one of those ubiquitous "within-walking-distance-of-the-beach" properties. Only this one really is.

As I thanked Mrs. R. and disconnected, Mattimoe Realty's front door swung open to reveal the compact form of Magnet Spring's Deputy Police Chief, Judy "Jenx" Jenkins. At five feet, five inches tall, Jenx is a tornado in uniform. She's fast, she's loud, she's blunt, and frankly, she's electric. According to local lore, Jenx in high dudgeon can screw up our legendary magnetic fields. I haven't witnessed it myself, but I've heard the tales. Let's just say about Jenx that the Force is with her. Unofficially, she's Magnet Spring's acting police chief since her boss Big Jim is spending leaf-peeping season at a rehab clinic up north. Most Main Street merchants would bet their inventories we'll never see Big Jim again.

"Yo, Whiskey!" Jenx boomed before the door could slam behind her. "We got a corpse next door!"

That made my skin prickle. I thought Noonan had got it out of there. Being massaged on a table that recently held a dead man was unnerving enough. Hearing that he was stashed nearby canceled all therapeutic effects. I told Jenx so.

She made a rude, raspberry-like sound. "I meant he *was* next door. Now he's at the county morgue in Ritchie. Crouch has probably peeled his face off already."

"Good afternoon to you, too, Deputy." Odette's mellifluous tones emanated from her cubicle. "Could I offer you a cup of coffee—or would you prefer a barf bag to go?"

"I don't drink coffee, Det. And I don't puke, either. Thought you knew that by now." Jenx adjusted her holster.

"And I thought you knew by now that I answer only to my Christian name. Whiskey can spell it for you. Phonetically, if necessary."

"Come on. I give all my friends nicknames—Hen, Noon, Big Jim, Det…"

"All your *friends*, yes. That should spare me."

I interrupted the fun. "Jenx, I understand you told the widow to call us?"

"Yeah, what a head case. Called back three times to recheck the facts as we have them. Her husband's heart quits on a massage table, and she calls *me* a loser."

From her cubicle, Odette harrumphed. Jenx ignored her.

"Sure, he was young to go that way, but shit happens. Think of Leo."

I was, actually. "So she's coming in to see about the disposition of the body?"

"And to see where he died, who he talked to, and so on."

"She wants to interview people?"

"I get the feeling Widow Santy had no idea her husband was in the States."

"You mean—?"

"I mean, she now thinks he had a girlfriend in town."

"Did he?"

"Don't know yet. That's one of the reasons I came by. To see if either of you ever saw this guy."

Jenx produced a Polaroid photo of a handsome, square-jawed man who appeared to be dozing.

"It's hard to tell with his eyes closed," I said. "Most men I meet I never see asleep."

"He's not asleep," Jenx said.

"I knew that."

"Let me see." Odette emerged from her cubicle. She studied the picture. "Generically handsome Caucasian male, between thirty and thirty-five."

"Thirty-four, as a matter of fact," confirmed Jenx.

"Never seen that one before." Odette handed back the photo. Returning to her cubicle, she added, "His eyes are brown, I think. And he's six-foot-two."

Jenx released a low whistle. "You're damn good, Det. And not just on the phone."

Before they could restart the name game, I said, "Have you shown the photo around town?"

"I'm starting here, working my way down Main Street. Maybe somebody saw him with somebody, either today or another day. Noonan said he came to her place alone."

"Yeah, well, he wanted a massage, not a room. Speaking of rooms, why didn't you refer the widow to Red Hen's?"

Jenx's partner Henrietta Roca owns the largest inn in Magnet Springs, a sprawling Prairie-style mansion overlooking Lake Michigan.

Jenx cocked her head at me. "Noticed the tourists lately? Seen what's happening to the trees? Hen's booked solid for the next three weeks."

"What made you think I'd have something?"

"Your business changes all the time. Somebody sells, somebody rents, somebody buys. I figured you'd come up with something."

"If handsome Gordon Santy from Canada died of a heart attack, that's tragic. But why does it matter if he had a girlfriend?"

"It doesn't," said Jenx. "*If* he had a heart attack."

At 5:30 Odette left to show a new listing. I headed for Shadow Play to check the property before offering it for rent the next day. Mrs. Reitbauer said they kept an extra key under a flowerpot at the base of the biggest tree in the yard. Not helpful. At Shadow Play all the trees were huge, and all the trees had flowerpots. We're talking densely packed pines. I couldn't see the trees for the trees, let alone decide which was the tallest. After ten minutes of circling the yard and craning my neck, it dawned on me that Mrs. R. might have meant girth, not height. And so I found the key.

Gaining access to a house these days is rarely as simple as turning a key in a lock. The kinds of homes I sell come with alarm systems—often very sophisticated alarm systems. Shadow Play was no exception. Fortunately, Mrs. R.'s instructions in that department were easier to follow. Inside I readily located the lighted keypad and entered the prescribed series of digits. Colored lights flashed along the panel, followed by a high-pitched hum, followed by a click—then silence and the glow of a single tiny green bulb. I was clear. The Reitbauers had spared no expense in protecting their hideaway.

I might as well admit something right now about my attraction to real estate: this biz lets me indulge my talent for snooping. No apologies. I pay attention. It's one of the keys to my success. Technically I wasn't snooping that evening at Shadow Play; I was following the client's instructions. Mrs. R. had faxed me a list of valuables that she wanted removed to a safe in the master-bedroom closet.

So I had to look around. Very closely. One day soon I hoped to list this place for sale. Hardly a cottage, it was almost three thousand square feet and exquisitely decorated. The floors in the front half of the house were bleached hardwood; the rest were wall-to-wall white Berber. I noted murals and custom-made wallpaper, plus recessed lighting in the tray ceilings. Mrs. R. collected watercolors, apparently. Every room was a testament to her taste: mostly garden scenes with pale flowers under watery skies. It wasn't my style—too floral—but it was a classy style. One of the watercolors must have been truly valuable. A miniature painting of pansies and violets was on Mrs. R.'s list of objects to be stowed away.

I walked through a second time admiring the home's best features, which included floor-to-ceiling windows overlooking the flagstone terrace. The better I knew the place, the faster I could move it once I got the go ahead. Shadow Play would be a quick sell when the Reitbauers were ready; I knew people who were in the market for just such a second home.

Mrs. R. was "selective" about tenants. She had inserted a clause in the property management contract, reserving the right to approve or disapprove of any prospective tenant I recommended. She said she understood that Mrs. Santy was a special case since the police had requested our help. Of course, I would still interview the widow, ask for references, and run a credit check before administering the Shadow

Play "entrance exam": Mrs. Santy would have to be able to work the alarm system. No point renting this place to a technophobe.

I completed my second walk-through, admiring the home's overall design. Shadow Play combined shade, seclusion, and just enough brightness, thanks to the terrace's southern exposure. The sooner the Reitbauers were ready to part with it, the happier I'd be. Selling a place like this is a lot simpler than managing its rental, and vastly more lucrative. I double-checked the sophisticated lock on the bedroom safe, reactivated the home's alarm system, and departed.

I didn't mean to be impatient with the Reitbauers. Postponing the inevitable was something I understood. It had been five months, one week, and three days since Leo died, and I still hadn't gone through his things. Even worse, every day I put off as long as possible going home. It wasn't just that I dreaded walking all alone into that big house we built together. It was also that I dreaded Abra. She still rushed past me to the door, her head and tail held high in expectation. When she saw that I had once again failed to bring home her man, the expression she turned on me broke my heart anew.

A ruddy setting sun turned Lake Michigan blood red as I drove along the coast toward Vestige. Leo and I intended the name of our modest estate as a nod to another era. This land and our crumbling barn had once belonged to a vast farming dynasty, long ago sold off and subdivided. Now it's a vestige of something else: the dreams that Leo and I shared.

I did what I do whenever I pull up the driveway. I tried not to look at the sign out front, hand-carved by my late husband, but that evening my peripheral vision detected a small blur due south. The blur had waving arms, churning legs, a bobbing white-blonde head, and glasses. It was moving toward me. Fast.

"Hey, Chester," I said as I stepped from my Lexus RX330, a modest-sized SUV. He was panting dramatically. Chester does everything dramatically, or it wouldn't be worth doing.

"She got out!" he announced.

"Who did?"

"Abra! I've been trying to catch her ever since I got home from school!"

Chester is eight years old, small for his age, and also my next-door neighbor. He's obsessed with Abra, and she makes the most of it.

"How could she get out?" I began and instantly saw how. The side entrance to my garage gaped open.

True confession time: unlike my clients, I don't activate my alarm system every morning. I don't even lock the door leading from my kitchen to the breezeway that connects with my garage. Usually, I lock the garage itself, but apparently that morning I hadn't. If motivated, Abra can open most doors. Afghan hounds are uncanny that way. The worst of them, that is. Leo didn't name her Abracadabra for nothing.

"Where did you see her last?" I asked. Chester pointed toward the edge of the bluff overlooking the lake.

"I think she wanted to go for a swim."

That was unlikely. Abra hates the water unless, of course, I want her to stay away from it.

"How long ago was that?"

He pressed a button on his dauntingly complex sports watch and reported, "Three minutes and forty-eight seconds."

"Let's go." I dropped my purse, my briefcase, and my rapidly cooling take-out dinner back into the car. Fortunately, I was already wearing my Nikes.

Chester and I jogged around the house to the edge of the bluff. I looked out over the wide wooden stairway down to the water. Leo had designed it to include two decks above the dock level. On the lower deck stood Abra. I swear she was waiting for me. The wind lifted her glossy blonde tresses as she stared at us impassively.

Like a bad actor, Chester pointed and declared, "There she is!"

She responded with a toss of her head that distinctly said, "Screw you." Then she bolted for the water. I was sure she was testing us.

Chester glanced at me worriedly. "Can she swim?"

"All dogs can swim. You've heard of the dog paddle? But this one won't go in."

"She looks like she's going in. And that current is really strong!"

"She won't go in."

"Look!" He pointed again. "She's getting ready to dive!"

"She won't go in." My voice held less conviction that time. I could hardly believe it, but Abra was bounding down the dock like a stunt diver making her approach.

Anyone who has seen an Afghan hound run knows they're poetry in motion: the long ears trailing behind them like a woman's sleek, straight hair, their pom-pom feet barely touching the earth as they cover yards in a single stride. Now she was airborne. I felt my jaw drop as Abra arced over Lake Michigan, the surf crashing beneath her.

"You said she wouldn't do that!" cried Chester.

The blasted animal lives to prove me wrong. No belly-flop for her. She entered the water as gracefully as she'd left dry land. From where we stood, she barely seemed to break the surface, and then she was swimming. That dog doesn't paddle. She cruises. Holding her proud, pointed nose high, she moved determinedly away from us.

"Where is she going?" Chester said.

"Maybe she needs some exercise."

"But it's deep out there, and look how high those waves are!" His voice had taken on a querulous quality that set my teeth on edge.

I regarded him frankly. "What do you want me to do about it?"

He pointed at the dog again. "Save her!"

"Oh, get real."

And then . . . he started to cry. He's only eight, after all, and his mother won't let him have a pet of his own.

"Look how far out she is," he moaned. "The waves are crashing over her head!"

Damn if he wasn't right. The next thing I knew I was on the edge of the dock, calling frantically. Begging, really. Abra never glanced back. Since I was shouting into the wind, I doubt she even heard me. Chester was sobbing. Thank God it was a balmy evening, and I'd learned to swim before I'd learned to walk. In seconds, the Nikes were off, and I was in the water. The very cold water. Nobody swims in Lake Michigan in late September without a wetsuit. Unless they're nuts—or goaded by an emotionally needy child.

Like Abra, I don't dog paddle. I don't cruise exactly, but I do have a powerful crawl. Arm over arm into the oncoming waves I went, cursing the Affie with each stroke. Catching up to her was a challenge. We were both panting hard by the time I seized her rhinestone-studded collar and yanked her drenched blonde head to my chest. She didn't resist. She'd known I would follow and save her, so she had spent herself.

THREE

"SHE WAS CHALLENGING YOU to rise above your self-inflicted pain. Abra is a message from the Universe. You should meditate on that."

I stared at Noonan over my steaming double-mocha-super-latte.

"You should *sit* on that," I wanted to say. I didn't, though. Noonan is not only Magnet Springs' genius massage therapist, but she is also one of its sweetest citizens. And a dream tenant. So I nodded non-committally and continued to sip my favorite wake-up beverage. The way my ribs ached, I knew I'd need another free massage soon.

After rescuing the dog who does not deserve to live, I had shivered all night. Two long soaks in a very hot tub did nothing to dispel my chill, which was surely due as much to fury as exposure. Odette stopped by around eight o'clock to report that her evening's appointment had led to an offer. She found me blow-drying the bimbo, my own head still dripping. Leo used to insist that Abra had a delicate constitution. So, in deference to him, I made reviving her job one. She was the perfect canine Camille, playing the scene as if she'd washed up on her own. In Abra's eyes, I was merely doing what any human should.

Odette is my witness to the dog's ingratitude. She is also the reason every Main Street merchant knew the story by morning. In the Goh Cup, our local coffeehouse, every customer greeted me with "How's Abra doing?" Never mind that my eyes were red and swollen, my nose was leaking, and my naturally wavy hair was a mass of lumps. I hadn't taken the time to blow-dry myself. I'd even forgotten about the carry-out spinach lasagna until I sat on it in my car that morning. But no one worried about me.

"Drink deeply from the well of truth" was Noonan's exit line. What the hell did that mean? I glanced at Peg Goh, proprietor, who winked. Thank God, I thought. A fellow cynic. Then she said, "I'm just glad Abra's okay."

A few hours later, I was in my office at Mattimoe Realty, struggling with paperwork and a nonstop runny nose. Odette knocked and entered before I could discard the dozen dirty tissues spread before me.

"They're here!" she announced, surveying the sticky landscape of my desk. "The grieving party from Canada. Well, the male portion. His sister is with Jenx."

"What does the male portion want?"

"He'd like to discuss possible rental properties."

"Shadow Play," I said, reaching for the appropriate file.

"He will require a selection." The glint in Odette's eye was unmistakable.

"Did you explain that there is no 'selection' for last-minute visitors during leaf-peeping season?"

"Oh, yes. He insists on seeing the proprietor."

"I thought Canada was a kinder, gentler nation," I sighed.

"Perhaps. But this Canadian is not." Odette reached past me into my center desk drawer and extracted a small mirror. "He is, however, very handsome."

Accepting the mirror, I shuddered at my red nose, rumpled hair and pouchy eyes.

Odette said, "He's not patient, either, so work fast." She paused at the door to evaluate me. "If the lights were out, you could almost get away with it."

The Canadian proved to be beyond handsome. More like movie-star magnetic. Young, too—no more than thirty-five. I tamped down my hair as I approached, hoping to at least make the lumps symmetrical. Dressed in expensive though casual clothes, he was taller than I, which meant well over six feet. The word "strapping" sprang to mind. He cast cool blue-gray eyes in my direction.

"Ms. Mattimoe? I'm Edward Naylor, Ellianna Santy's brother." His manicured hand pressed mine lightly. "I understand you manage rental properties."

"That's part of what we do. We're a full-service real estate agency."

The gallon of Lake Michigan I'd swallowed last night had turned my usual contralto purr into a tenor growl. I cleared my throat and added, "I understand that Jenx—I mean, Chief Jenkins—referred you to us."

"Yes. Ms. Mutombo said you have a property in mind. I'd like to see several."

I glanced at Ms. Mutombo, who offered her lightning-quick shrug before disappearing into her cubicle.

"I'm sure Ms. Mutombo also explained that you've arrived during peak tourist season. Our inns and B&Bs have been booked for a year. To be honest, Mr. Naylor, it's a fluke that we have even one unit to offer on such short notice."

He paused as if weighing what I'd just said.

"Then I suppose you should show me what you do have."

"Does your sister want to come, too?" I hoped not.

He shook his head. "Ellianna is leaving this matter to me. She has enough to deal with. Losing Gordon was a shock."

The woman had my complete sympathy. She also had a damn good-looking brother, who wasn't wearing a wedding ring. This was the first time since marrying Leo that I'd had that reflex: to glance from a guy's eyes to the third finger on his left hand. Why did it make me queasy? I knew I wasn't ready to act on such an impulse, but was it too soon to have it? My ribs throbbed. God is punishing me, I thought. Till I realized I had collided with a file cabinet while reaching for my jacket without taking my eyes off the Canadian. Fortunately, he was checking his Rolex.

In the car, I savored something else about him: his scent. Edward Naylor smelled the way I thought Ralph Lauren would. Or Robert Redford before he got old: Woodsy. Manly. Rich. Edward wasn't much of a conversationalist, but I didn't hold it against him. He was here on a tragic errand, after all. His thoughts were probably with his sister, who was with Jenx at the county morgue.

At Shadow Play, my prospective client remained quiet. Reading people is my business. I could tell that Edward Naylor approved of the Reitbauers' taste. He didn't need to say so.

When I explained their rental terms, he replied, "Ellianna plans to stay no longer than a week. I'm sure this will be adequate."

Then it was time to administer the rental entrance exam—i.e., the security system aptitude test. *Please don't let him turn out to be a techno-boob*, I prayed. It would be too embarrassing to watch this hunk fumble a keypad. As it turned out, I barely had to show him how it worked.

"You must have a system like this in your own house," I said.

He didn't reply. Or if he did, I didn't hear him because I got lost in the dimple in his right cheek. When I recovered, I reminded him to fill out the rental application form so that I could contact references and run a credit check. "Blah, blah, blah," I heard myself say; what I really wanted to talk about was him.

"Ellianna will fill out the form," he said. "She's the client, eh."

Eh? Noonan had said Canadians talk like that.

Edward Naylor continued, "I have to return to Fredericton in a day or two."

"What do you do there, if I may ask?"

"I run a small business."

A restaurant? A law firm? A male escort service? I strained to imagine this gorgeous man doing anything besides acting or modeling. Maybe he's a kept man, I thought, who turns the lights on and off for some fortunate older woman.

Edward Naylor was aloof, but I expect that of the supernaturally beautiful. His sister, on the other hand, turned out to be supernaturally bitchy. I retracted whatever sympathy or empathy I had felt for her as a fellow widow. Ellianna Santy didn't play well with others. She saw herself as the star of the moment, the sun in the solar system, and so forth. As gorgeous as her brother, she lacked his ability to not piss people off.

Odette had correctly predicted Mrs. Santy's general appearance: blonde, willowy, rich. Her uncertainty about whether the eyes were green or blue was justified since they turned out to be turquoise. Edward was darker. I didn't see a family resemblance.

"What do you mean, you need to check my 'references'?" Mrs. Santy said. "Chief Jenkins is my 'reference,' or have you forgotten?"

"Actually, Chief Jenkins referred *us* to you."

She stared at me as if I were too far down the evolutionary scale to comprehend. Thank God her brother jumped in.

"I'll help you fill out the form, Ellie," he said, placing his broad hand over her slender white one. "It won't take long."

"It had better not. I have business to conduct. If everyone in this town is as dense as the people I've met so far, we'll be here for weeks."

Edward eased her toward the table where Odette had laid out the necessary documents and writing instruments.

"What does one have to do to be served a beverage in this establishment?" Mrs. Santy demanded.

Odette smiled helpfully, indicating the water cooler and coffeemaker. "One need only serve oneself," she said and faded into her cubicle.

As soon as the Stunning Sibling Team had finished their paperwork and paid one week's rent plus deposit, I gave them Shadow Play's key and security code. According to the clause in our contract, I should have gotten Mrs. R.'s written approval, but I figured these people were her kind of people. All about money and attitude. Besides, Mrs. R. knew what I was doing.

Edward gave me a polite smile and handshake; Ellianna didn't. I half-hoped she had bad credit so I could bust her. Then again I didn't want to have to act ugly in front of her better-behaved brother. Given the circumstances of their visit, and the volume of my business, I doubted I would even check Ellianna's background. Now if Edward were the client, I'd leap at the chance to investigate him. Is he single? Affluent? And what about this "small business" he runs in New Brunswick?

After they left, I phoned Mrs. R. to make sure she approved the arrangement. She said she did, so I faxed her a copy of the signed contract.

Then Noonan flung open our front door. Her spiky hair looked pricklier than usual, and her round eyes were red.

"She accused me of killing her husband!"

I didn't need to ask who she meant.

"That woman is wicked!" Noonan said. "Why would I *kill* anybody? I'm a healer!"

"Everyone knows that." I put my arm around her muscular shoulders.

"Mrs. Santy said I got him so excited he had a heart attack. I told her I don't give that kind of massage!" She blew her nose angrily.

"Of course you don't! You're a trained professional."

I had heard of paid sex-providers who also described themselves that way, but Noonan seemed to take comfort.

She said, "I told Mrs. Santy her husband was dead before I even started. You know what she said to that?"

I couldn't imagine.

"She said, 'Then someone must have worn him out first.' What was that supposed to mean?"

"He had a woman in town," Odette interjected, joining us.

I said, "I don't know. He looked like a nice guy in Jenx's photo."

"He was dead in Jenx's photo," Odette reminded me. "His wife thinks he was having an affair here. Having met her, I can only hope it's true."

Noonan said, "He told me he was driving to Chicago."

Odette shrugged. "Maybe he was. Maybe he wasn't. Maybe he was nothing like he looked."

"I liked his looks," said Noonan.

"Me, too," I said, remembering Jenx's photo. "We should all look that good. Alive."

FOUR

MRS. SANTY DIDN'T BOTHER me. Much. I deal with unreasonable, high-maintenance types every day. It's not as if she'd accused *me* of anything . . . other than being a realtor. But my reaction to her handsome brother was unsettling.

I left the office early for the second day in a row. Early in this biz is before 8 PM. Since Leo died, I tried to make the least of the dinner hour. He and I used to make the most of it: he cooked, I assisted. Mostly by pouring good wine and holding up my end of our conversations about the future. We thought we had a lot of that.

These days, I was in the habit of stopping by Mother Tucker's. No relation, just my favorite restaurant run by two good people. Walter and Jonny St. Mary are a long-committed gay couple retired from previous lives in Chicago. Now they feed the tourists and lonely working folk of this town.

"Will it go away soon?" Walter asked as he poured me my second glass of a very fine Riesling. He was referring to the hubbub over Gordon Santy's untimely demise.

"If Crouch can confirm he had a heart attack, and the widow can't find a smoking . . . whatever." I giggled, feeling the tingle of Walter's wine.

"Ah, yes. The other woman scenario," Walter sighed. "I hear Mrs. Santy is a shrew. Is her beautiful brother straight?"

Caught in mid-swallow, I stared at him. It hadn't occurred to me that the gorgeous, aloof Edward might be gay.

"I don't know. I just thought he was Canadian. Does he seem gay to *you*?"

"I haven't talked to him." Walter's lustrous white hair gleamed in the bar light. It occurred to me that I might have been attracted to Walter if I hadn't known he was gay. I chugged the rest of my wine.

"Hit me again."

"Slow down, Whiskey," Walter said. "This stuff isn't potent, but it is precious. Jonny and I paid sixty dollars for the bottle. It's not meant for guzzling."

"Then switch me to the cheap stuff."

Walter kissed my cheek. "Go home, dear. You have a dog to feed. And Jonny has your dinner ready."

This was the routine we'd fallen into: I'd have a couple, three glasses of expensive wine, and then Jonny, the chef half of the team, would pack me a deluxe go-box of the nightly gourmet special.

"What am I having?" I asked Walter.

"Broiled lake perch almandine with locally grown corn on the cob and garlic mashed potatoes. Peach pie for dessert. If you want it *à la mode*, you'll have to stop at Food Duck for a pint of vanilla."

"No *à la mode* necessary."

"The Canadians felt the same way. They had what you're having."

I cupped my chin in my hand and smiled at Walter. "What do you think of them—really?"

"Scenic but chilly. Like the country they come from."

The phone at Vestige started ringing as I was entering my security code. That morning I'd taken the time to activate the alarm. Abra wouldn't win another free pass to the outside world if I could help it. When I entered, she ignored me, as usual. But the aromatic lake perch in my go-box had her attention.

I grabbed the phone on the fourth ring, a split second before the machine could pick up.

"What do you want to hear first—the bad news or the not-so-bad news?"

I recognized Jenx's voice.

"You're calling me with news that's not so bad?"

"And bad news, too. What order do you want it in?"

"Hit me with the hard stuff."

"Shadow Play's been burglarized. Mr. Naylor called it in. The alarm system failed. He claims he set it, but it never went off. Somebody broke in while he and his sister were at dinner."

"What was taken?"

"We'll need your help to answer that one. Some of Mrs. Santy's jewelry, for sure. I assume the Reitbauers left you an inventory of household contents."

They had.

"Any damage?" I asked.

"The back door's broken, but I haven't noticed anything else. I just got here, though."

I sagged against the kitchen wall. "What's the not-so-bad news?"

"Mrs. Santy might not sue you."

Jenx suggested I come to Shadow Play as soon as I could. I took three greedy bites of Mother Tucker's perch filets before stuffing the box in the fridge and taking Abra out to relieve herself. I let her pull me around the house; then we went back inside. But she craved more action. As I was leaving, she slipped out the kitchen door with me. I tried to tackle her in the breezeway. Abra bounded over to my car and placed her paws on the passenger door. Although I managed to set the alarm, Naughty Dog got to go for a car ride.

I was surprised to see young Officer Swancott at the scene. In the glare from his patrol car's headlights, Brady was posting crime scene tape around Shadow Play's bashed-in back door.

"Do you have to do that?" I said, rolling down my window. Abra leapt across my lap and out. "Damn that dog!"

Brady said, "No problem, Whiskey. I got Officer Roscoe with me. He'll bring her in."

Officer Roscoe was Brady's assistant, a dignified German Shepherd trained by the Michigan State Police. When Brady whistled, Roscoe appeared from around the corner of the house and stood at attention. Brady barked a command. Roscoe dashed off to execute it.

"Thanks," I said. "But does this have to look like a crime scene?"

"It is a crime scene."

"I know. But that yellow tape is bad for business."

Brady pondered the situation and then yanked the tape down. I asked where I could find Jenx.

"Inside," he said. "Interviewing Mrs. Santy and Mr. Naylor. Let's go in this way."

He opened the previously sealed door, and we followed Mrs. Santy's anxious voice into the master bedroom. Three faces turned our way. Jenx's looked as smooth and mulish as ever, but the other two were strained.

"I thought you said the alarm system was state-of-the-art," Mrs. Santy began. To her brother she added, "She told you the same thing, eh?"

Eh again. Before I could reply, Jenx said, "Thanks for getting here so fast, Whiskey. Mrs. Santy is missing a watch—"

"Not a 'watch,'" Mrs. Santy snapped. "A Piaget. If that means anything to you people."

"We get it," I said.

Jenx continued, "Mrs. Santy hid her other jewelry before they went out, and the intruder didn't find it."

"My other jewelry is antique—priceless family heirlooms." The Canadian beauty fixed her icy eyes on me. "You'd be in deep, deep trouble if they were gone."

Edward Naylor laid a calming hand on his sister's arm. He spoke softly. "Ms. Mattimoe, I didn't notice anything missing from the house, but I did observe that the safe is damaged."

He indicated the Reitbauers' built-in closet vault. The safe was intact, but the keypad was smashed.

"Somebody must have pounded on it," I observed.

"Obviously," sneered Mrs. Santy. "A junkie, probably. We might as well be in Detroit."

Outside Abra let loose her freakish howl, somewhere between a wild dingo sound and a dying human sound.

"What is that?" cried Mrs. Santy.

Jenx glared at me. "You brought *her* along?"

"She brought herself, actually. I had very little to do with it."

"Jesus, Whiskey, this is a crime scene."

"I know, I saw the tape."

Before Jenx could reply, Mrs. Santy started screaming and didn't seem able to stop. We all looked where she was looking, through the window to the floodlit terrace. Abra stood in the center, something dark and shapeless dangling from her mouth.

"Shit," hissed Jenx. "She went and stole somebody's purse again!"

"Maybe not," I said lamely. "Maybe she found it in the street."

"Somebody, get that goat out of here!" shrieked Ellianna Santy. Then she fainted.

What makes people mistake my dog for a goat? By the time Jenx, Brady, and I reached Abra, Officer Roscoe was on the case, attempting to subdue her with one of those fancy police moves he had learned in East Lansing. Unfortunately, Abra mistook his professional vigor for sexual ardor. This dog's no Nesbitt, she must have thought, for she eagerly assumed the position. Her response confused Roscoe. Apparently they didn't cover that contingency in Canine SWAT School. Human Officer Swancott snatched the handbag from Abra's grinning mouth and ordered Roscoe back to the patrol car. He sailed in through the open passenger-side window. With difficulty, I wrestled the whining Affie into my vehicle, sealed the windows, and activated the child-proof locks. She continued howling and making bedroom eyes at Roscoe, but he ignored her. Clearly, he was still on the clock.

Inside Shadow Play, Brady and Jenx had donned surgical gloves and were examining Abra's find. They glanced up when I entered.

"Can I just go ahead and pay the fine this time?" I said, cringing at memories of Abra's purse-snatching past and the court hearings that followed. "I thought she was rehabilitated."

"She might be," Jenx said. "This time she might be on our side."

"I doubt it." I peered over Jenx's shoulder at what looked like an expensive leather purse, none the worse for Abra's mauling.

"Check out the ID." Jenx flipped open an eel-skin wallet to display a Michigan driver's license.

I studied it. "So?"

Brady said, "Probably our thief. This was in the bag, too."

He produced a gleaming gold wristwatch, edged in diamonds.

Jenx whistled. "I take it that ain't cut glass."

"Probably worth about thirteen thousand," I said.

"Dollars?" Jenx said. She whistled again. "But does it keep better time than my Timex?"

"There's something else," Brady said. From the purse he carefully withdrew a square wood-framed watercolor, about five inches by five. Instantly I recognized it from my walk-through last night. It had adorned the master bathroom wall next to the vanity; I remembered because it was one of the few paintings in the house I had liked: cottony clouds floating in an azure sky.

"I thought Mr. Naylor said nothing was missing," I said.

"He probably didn't check the bathroom," replied Jenx, "or else he didn't notice. This isn't very big."

"But it's valuable," Brady announced. "It's a Warren Matheney. See?" He pointed to the artist's signature. Jenx's eyebrows arched.

"Geez," she whispered.

"So what?" I said.

The officers stared at me. "You don't know Warren Matheney? 'Cloud Man'?"

"Should I?"

They exchanged glances. Jenx said, "You ought to get out more, Whiskey. Warren Matheney had a show at the West Shore Gallery last month."

"I'm not into watercolor. Is he supposed to be good?"

"Like the best in the Midwest," Brady said. "He's been on *Oprah*."

"And the cover of *People* magazine," Jenx said. They looked at each other again. I had the feeling, and not for the first time, that most people knew things I didn't.

Brady added, "Cloud Man's popular because his paintings help people relax. Stare at this a minute."

I did. Brady was right; the picture was soothing. Kind of like white noise.

"So you're saying this is worth something?"

"I take it you haven't seen the news this week," said Jenx. "Warren Matheney was found dead in his Chicago apartment."

"He'll never paint again," Brady said. "So his stuff just got super expensive. I'll bet this little number's worth at least a hundred grand now."

"Get out of here!" I snorted.

"Brady should know," Jenx said. "He's doing his master's in art history, aren't you, bud?"

"Nights and weekends. On-line through Northwestern."

"But if that picture is worth that kind of money, why didn't Mrs. R. have me put it in their safe?"

"Maybe she forgot she had it," Brady replied. "The Reitbauers have a lot of nice stuff. And they haven't stayed here much. That's an early Matheney. Circa '78."

"How can you tell?" I said.

Brady pointed to the picture. "Those are cumulus clouds. From his cumulus period. Matheney moved on to cirrus and then nimbostratus. He was flirting with cumulonimbus when he died."

We heard a low moan from the bedroom.

"Should someone look in on Mrs. Santy?" I said.

Jenx said, "Her brother's in there."

"I hate to sound like a nag. But shouldn't you be chasing the person whose purse this is? Before she gets away?"

"Oh, she's long gone by now," yawned Jenx. "We called the sheriff."

"His boys are better at pursuit," Brady explained. To Jenx he added, "Want me to do a look-around? Canine Officer Roscoe could use the exercise."

FIVE

NONE OF US KNEW Heather Nitschke. She was the leading suspect, the assumed owner of the leather bag. Hers was the name on the Michigan driver's license brought to us by Abra.

The sheriff's office ran her ID through the system and, like us, drew a blank. Ellianna Santy showed no interest in the recovered Matheney; neither she nor her brother had noticed it on the bathroom wall. Nor did Mrs. Santy seem grateful to see her Piaget again. She declared that the Reitbauers and I should give thanks that she didn't plan to sue for emotional distress. Jenx volunteered Brady and Roscoe for overnight guard duty. I promised to notify the Reitbauers, make sure the back door was repaired or replaced, and dispatch a security technician to reprogram the alarm system. When Abra resumed howling, Mrs. Santy was still seething.

"Why can't they stop that ungodly sound?" she asked her brother.

I took a long look at Edward Naylor and felt a fleeting kinship with Abra. We were both horny. And hopeless.

Back home, Abra and I tried to exit the vehicle at the same time through the same door. It wasn't pretty. As I recovered my balance, a shadowy figure flew from the breezeway straight at me. I screamed. Abra yelped. Chester screamed back.

When the hysteria had subsided, he said, "I have a suggestion: Next time you remember to lock the door and turn on the alarm, don't forget to check the windows."

"I left a window open?" I said.

Chester flashed three fingers.

"Why didn't the alarm system tell me that?"

"It did, but you didn't listen."

"You broke into my house!" I pointed out.

"Sometimes I have to. If you lock the door."

"What are you doing here, Chester?" It was after 9:30 on a school night. "Are you locked out of your house again?"

Unlike me, Chester's mother always secures their house. Sometimes she secures it so well that her own son can't get in. I guess she forgets which side of the door she left him on. In her defense, Chester's mother is extremely busy. In fact, she's a superstar. She's Cassina—the sexy yet spiritual harpist-slash-singer frequently seen on TV and the covers of supermarket tabloids. Chester had mentioned that she was about to launch a world tour promoting her latest CD, *Cumulus Love*. At least I think that's what it's called. Chester left a copy of the CD here somewhere, but I haven't played it. I'm not into harp music. Cassina has one of those ethereal voices that's supposed to remind you of heaven.

She and her entourage are often on tour. Usually she leaves Chester behind in the care of some nanny, but live-in help is short-lived at their house, which locals call The Castle. I conclude that Chester's mother, like her son, is VHM (Very High Maintenance).

Rumor has it that Cassina wears out the hired help faster than most people wear out their socks.

Even when Cassina is in Michigan, she's usually not home. She prefers to hang out at some kind of studio-slash-retreat near Traverse City. Occasionally Chester accompanies her, but more often she leaves him next door with one hired stranger or another. Chester has developed the habit of admitting himself to Vestige, whether I'm here or not, whether he's locked out or not, whether I've locked up or not. Abra loves him. I . . . like him, but I sometimes wonder if his mother locks him out on purpose. He gets attention over here, and he craves attention.

Chester explained that Cassina and Company were in Traverse City, "laying down tracks." He was sure they'd be back by Friday.

"I guess they forgot to call The Service," he said. The Service is what Chester calls the army of nannies, maids, gardeners, cooks, and chauffeurs Cassina hires. Abra was cleaning his glasses without bothering to remove them from his nose. Most Afghan hounds aren't into licking, but this one loves to taste Chester's face.

"Do you want to phone your mother about her . . . oversight?" I said.

Through smeary lenses, his eyes were earnest. "I'd rather not, thank you."

"So—do you want some Mother Tucker's take-home?"

"If you have enough to share."

I did. And I'm handy enough in the kitchen to reheat Jonny's food the way he intended. The three of us sat around the kitchen table chewing contentedly. Then I cleaned up while Chester walked Abra, or, rather, while Abra dragged Chester in circles out back. I left a brief message on Cassina's voice mail that her son was here; I didn't expect a response.

Back inside, his face flushed from fresh air and exercise, Chester announced, "I have an offer for you, Whiskey. A business proposition."

"I'm listening."

"Abra and I get along great. Right?"

"Right."

"But Abra and you—well, you've got issues. Right?"

"*Issues*? I wouldn't put it that strongly," I lied.

Chester said, "She went to jail because you couldn't handle her!"

"Abra went to court-mandated therapy because she has criminal tendencies. Those purse-snatchings would have happened no matter what. The dog-shrink said so."

Actually, the dog-shrink had said Abra was "acting out" her anger over Leo's death. I believed she was "acting out" her anger over my survival.

"What about the other night?" Chester persisted. "She almost drowned!"

"I saved her! You're forgetting that part."

"Because I told you to!"

"What's your point?"

"I'd like to offer my services as Abra's keeper."

"You mean, like a zookeeper?"

"Like a guardian. I'll train her and protect her from danger."

"Does that include suicide attempts?"

"There'll never be another one while I'm on the job. I'll keep her safe."

"But can you keep Magnet Springs safe from *her*?"

"I'm just one kid, but I'll do my best. What do you say?"

Abra was sitting next to him, staring at me. I thought I detected a threat in her eyes.

"I suppose the decision should be Abra's," I said.

At that she leapt into the air, performed a canine double-axle, and landed on Chester's head.

"You're hired. What are your rates?"

"I'll draw up a contract," he said, rolling on the floor with his new charge.

"A contract?"

"I'm a professional, Whiskey. Just like you."

That reminded me: I needed to call the Reitbauers and inform them of the break-in. I got the answering machine featuring a message from Robert Reitbauer, who sounded a good deal older than his wife. I explained what had happened, emphasizing that no one was hurt, and everything was recovered.

I had barely returned the phone to its cradle when it rang. Mrs. Reitbauer sounded like a teenager although she was almost thirty. We had never met face to face, but I knew people who had met her. No one I knew had met her husband, the cement baron.

"Whiskey? It's like a trauma. You said one of my watercolors got stolen?"

"Yes, but it was recovered. No damage."

"Which one?" she asked.

"The Matheney."

She gasped. "No way!"

"Yes. The tenant got her watch back, too. A Piaget. And no one was hurt."

Mrs. R. said, "You gotta catch the creep who stole my painting!"

That seemed a tall order for a realtor. I told her the police were working on it.

"Cool, that's cool. I'm like so relieved. Oh—did you need something?"

I explained that our contract gave me the authority to act on her behalf in managing the property. However, I wanted to know her preferences regarding replacing the back door, repairing the closet safe, and so forth. She told me to do whatever I thought was right and send her the bill. Then she clicked off.

Something was wrong, and it had nothing to do with the break-in at Shadow Play. My house was silent. My house, whose current occupants included a rambunctious eight-year-old boy and a hyperactive Afghan hound. The great room was empty. Then I heard something outdoors. Something familiar, yet foreign. What was it? I rushed to the nearest window overlooking the lake. Nothing there . . . except that faint sound again. Laughter. A *child's* laughter.

He crossed into view then, strolling across the illuminated terrace with the dog at his side. They both looked at me. I waved. Chester smiled. Abra turned her back on me and took a shit.

The next day was the kind of hellish circus that only realtors in resort towns can understand. Leaf-peeping season arouses in visitors fantasies of living, at least part-time, in our part of the world. Thus, on that lovely fall day, Mattimoe Realty was overwhelmed with inquiries. Some walked in the door; others telephoned. All tried the patience of my very patient receptionist with questions like "Do you have anything with four bedrooms, a sundeck, a Jacuzzi, a fireplace, and—oh, yeah—lake frontage . . . for less than $200,000?"

We welcome inquiries. It's how we make sales and eventually money. Since agents work on commission only, we try to separate prospects from dreamers, and we identified mostly dreamers that day. Still, Odette and my other agents landed a few live ones. The earliest and likeliest were whisked away to view properties.

I had secured my house and dog and delivered my houseguest to his private school in town. Hunkered down in my back office by eight, I called my property manager about replacing or repairing Shadow Play's door and reprogramming the alarm. He called back around noon to report that everything had been repaired, except the moods of the tenants. Oddly, he assumed that Edward and Ellianna were married. When I asked why, he couldn't explain other than to say that they acted pissed off.

I worked right through lunch. The next time I checked my watch, it was almost three. Chester had assured me that he could get a ride back to Vestige from a classmate's mother.

"Today I begin my work with Abra," he had announced, sounding like a happy mad scientist.

"Shouldn't we wait till we have a contract?"

He grinned broadly, revealing two missing baby teeth. "I trust you, Whiskey."

Now my stomach was growling, so I headed across the street to the Goh Cup. It was busy for a Thursday mid-afternoon. Most of the overstuffed chairs and sofas were occupied by pink-faced tourists enjoying a pick-me-up, probably before descending on our office. Owner-operator Peg Goh greeted me. She's an unfailingly cheerful woman in her late fifties.

"Morning cup o' java finally wear off?"

I ordered an iced coffee and one of those spinach pies Peg's famous for.

"Oh, I almost forgot," she said as she rang up my order. "Jenx is looking for you."

"Why didn't she try my office?"

"Too many tourists in your foyer. Jenx is sick of them."

"Aren't we all?"

Peg whispered, "I think Jenx has something to tell you that she doesn't want leaf-peepers to overhear."

"I locked up this morning! That dog couldn't have got out again!"

Peg patted my hand maternally. "This time I don't think it's about Abra."

I raised Jenx on my cell phone. She was four blocks away and would pick me up in her patrol car. I ordered an extra iced coffee and waited in the alley.

"Something doesn't make sense," Jenx said in greeting. "Maybe you can explain it to me." She took the paper cup I offered. "I hope that's a Coke."

"Iced coffee. Sorry. Where are we going?"

She swung the car west on Main.

"The Broken Arrow Motel. Heather Nitschke was there. Till last night."

"How do you know?"

"Investigation, Whiskey. It's what we in law enforcement do."

I rolled my eyes.

Jenx continued. "According to her driver's license, Heather Nitschke's from Hillsdale. So I started checking motels. Third place I tried— jackpot! Desk clerk says Heather's been there three days."

"Alone?"

"Yup." Jenx read my mind. "We cleaned up that place. No prostitution out there for almost two years."

"That you know of."

"Desk clerk says Heather was real chatty. Told her she was trying to patch things up with an old boyfriend, but she didn't want to stay with him."

"I don't suppose she got the boyfriend's name, or where he lives?"

"That'd make my job way too easy."

"What is it you think I can help with?"

"Heather didn't come home last night. Hasn't been there since yesterday morning, says the desk clerk. I want your opinion as to a few items in her room."

Jenx patted her side. "I got a warrant from Judge Verbelow. He asked how you are, by the way."

Judge Wells Verbelow had presided over Abra's purse-snatching case two months earlier, one of several episodes in my recent life I was trying hard to forget.

"The next time you see the Judge, tell him Abra has a keeper."

"A what?"

"A trainer. A guardian. Chester."

We had reached Broken Arrow Highway, the major artery tracing the coast. It's dotted with restaurants, antique malls, farmer's markets, and motels. Our destination was a rundown affair with twenty units, all but one occupied by leaf-peepers lucky to find last-minute accommodations and willing to ignore roaches. Jenx introduced me to the desk clerk, an overweight twenty-year-old with bad skin and orange hair. She led us to Heather's room, Number 17. Brady had already strung a piece of yellow crime scene tape across the door, which the desk clerk didn't like any better than I had.

"My boss hates that," she mumbled. "It'll scare off business."

"Leaf-peepers don't scare easy," Jenx said.

The drapes were drawn in Number 17. Jenx flipped the wall-switch, and a fluorescent ceiling light buzzed awake, bathing the room in a sickly yellow glow. The bed, with its worn chenille spread, had not been slept in. Though sad, the scene appeared orderly.

"What are you wondering about?" I said. This kind of snooping didn't feel like fun.

"Over here." Jenx led me into the bathroom, where she switched on another humming light. "Does that look right to you?"

SIX

INDICATING THE BATHROOM SINK lined with cosmetics, hair-care products, and a curling iron, Jenx said, "I don't use make-up, so I don't know. But that seems weird to me."

I stepped closer. Taped to the mirror above the sink was a close-up of Julia Roberts, torn from a magazine.

"Don't tell me Heather's in love," said Jenx.

"No, this is about make-up. Do you have Heather's driver's license?"

"At the station. Why?"

"I'm thinking maybe Heather's photo looks like Julia Roberts. And maybe the person staying here isn't Heather."

"I was afraid it was something complicated. Need a ride back?"

I reminded Jenx that she had brought me. Busy though I was, I wanted to stop by the police station for a look at Heather's driver's license. Jenx said that Heather/Julia had been paying cash for the motel room, one day in advance.

At the station, Brady announced, "Heather Nitschke of Hillsdale didn't know her wallet was missing. She's had the flu since Sunday.

That was the last time she opened her purse—to buy a couple scrips at her pharmacy. Somebody lifted her wallet."

In her driver's license photo the real Heather Nitschke didn't look much like Julia Roberts, except for the bouncy brown hair and wide mouth.

Jenx said, "If our gal wanted to make herself look like Heather from Hillsdale, why didn't she tape the *license* to her mirror?"

Brady took a stab at that one. "Because beauty's in the eye of the beholder?"

"What the hell does that mean?"

"Maybe our Heather wannabe thinks the real Heather looks like Julia," I said.

"No way," said Jenx. "Julia's cute. The real Heather isn't."

I remembered something from the Broken Arrow Motel.

"The lighting in that room is terrible for doing make-up. A driver's license photo would be hard to copy. So maybe the fake Heather found a larger photo—of someone she thought Heather sort of looked like. Or someone she wanted people to remember."

Brady said, "The hair's the same."

Jenx checked her pocket notebook and dialed a number.

"Acting Police Chief Jenkins again. I'm wondering if the customer in Number 17 reminded you of anybody? Somebody famous, maybe?" Jenx's eyes narrowed. "Why do you say that?"

She thanked the other party and hung up.

"The Broken Arrow desk clerk didn't hesitate. Number 17 looked like *Pretty Woman*. Want to know why?"

"The hair?" Brady suggested.

"And the laugh. And the fact that Number 17 told the desk clerk *everybody* says she looks like Julia Roberts."

Since my side trip had yielded no news for the Reitbauers, I decided to get back to work selling real estate. At 4:50, our foyer still held one tourist family leafing through our listings. Odette was perched on the front edge of the receptionist's desk, arms crossed, foot tapping. The receptionist had left for the day, and the other agents were in the field. Odette was stuck doing PR that wouldn't pay.

"We're just wondering if you have one like this—for a lot less money?" The leaf-peeping mom pointed to a three-story stucco beauty with multiple cedar decks.

"How much less?" Odette said.

Ma and Pa Leaf-Peeper exchanged worried looks. Ma said hopefully, "Say, half that much?"

"A house like that for half as much. . . ." Odette squeezed her eyes shut as if visualizing the myriad possibilities. She reopened them. "No."

"Perhaps you'd like to take this home and talk it over." I handed Ma Leaf-Peeper the current edition of *Coastal Michigan Properties*, the real estate industry's local monthly. "We have a web site, too, so you can go online and browse at your convenience. It saves time."

Especially ours. After they left, Odette reported that the day had been good. She's a genius at separating dreamers from prospects and matching them with properties. Today she'd received offers on three different listings.

"I shall close them all," she declared. "And to prove how confident I am, I'll take you to dinner."

"Not Reginald?" I asked, referring to her psychiatrist husband.

"He's at a conference in Vermont, peeping at someone else's leaves. I stayed home to make money."

Remembering my temporary roommate and new employee, I told Odette I should probably feed Chester first. Like me, she doesn't lead a child-centered life since her only daughter goes to boarding school, but I asked her advice, anyway.

"How often do you suppose eight-year-olds need to eat?"

"How often do you eat?"

"Whenever I can."

Odette shrugged. "It's probably the same for him."

"But he needs healthier foods, right?"

"Theoretically. No booze, at any rate. If you can keep that dog alive, you'll probably do all right with a kid."

I promised to meet her at Mother Tucker's at seven.

Chester may be VHM, but in some departments he's self-sufficient. I arrived home to find him finishing a frozen dinner I'd forgotten I had.

"You sure that was still good?" I asked, looking through the trash for the carton it came in.

"Positive. They're good for at least six months after the expiration date if they were never thawed and refrozen. I figured you don't open the freezer enough for that to happen." He wiped his mouth with a napkin I hadn't known I owned, either. "Want dessert? We had carrot cake at school for Tripper's birthday. I got to take home what was left because the other kids have nut issues."

"*Nut* issues?"

"Food allergies."

"Why didn't Tripper take his own cake home?"

"He hates carrots. His mom's a Vegan."

Since I love carrot cake, I sat down with Chester. The cream-cheese icing was melting in my mouth before I realized what was missing.

"Where is she?" My eyes darted around the kitchen.

"Relax, Whiskey. Abra is in the isolation portion of her training. She needed a time-out."

"You locked her up somewhere? Why don't I hear her howling?"

Chester's eyes twinkled. "Because I know how to handle her."

"How? You've never had a dog! You told me you've never even had a goldfish!"

What if he'd accidentally *killed* Abra? What was I thinking, entrusting Leo's legacy to someone with no animal-handling experience?

Chester said, "I went online: Dogs-Train-You-dot-com. It has everything we need to know. The professionals use it."

I tried to keep my voice calm. "Tell me what you've done with Abra."

Chester collected our dessert plates and stood on tiptoe to set them carefully in the sink. Then he led me to the guest room. Tucked neatly under the slate-gray velour bedspread was Abra, apparently sound asleep.

"Can you believe how she covers herself up? She gets in bed just like a person," Chester said admiringly.

I started to say that that was precisely the sort of thing I wanted her trained *not* to do. Instead I said, "But she's not a person, Chester. Which is why she needs a keeper."

Chester shushed me, so I lowered my voice. "That doesn't look like a time-out. It looks like a nap."

He motioned me back into the hall. When I glanced over my shoulder, I could have sworn that Abra was grinning.

"Lesson One from Dogs-Train-You-dot-com," he said. "Figure out what calms them. It's called their Sucker."

I'm the sucker, I thought. "Do you mean 'succor'? As in comfort?"

"Right. Succor. So, when Abra's having a Hyper Day, we give her succor."

"With Abra, every day is Hyper Day," I reminded him.

"Not for long! That's why you're paying me."

"How much am I paying you, Chester? Where's our contract?"

"In the computer. I'll print it out later." He smiled at me. On the other side of the guest room door Abra snored.

Mother Tucker's was packed with leaf-peepers. At the bar, Odette was chatting up Walter, who was in the process of opening a very fine bottle of Pinot Noir.

"You like this one, don't you, Whiskey?" Odette indicated the wine.

"It's her Red of the Month," Walter said.

I toasted Odette's good work and then congratulated Walter on his own business success.

He wiped his brow. "Tourists. They want it all, and they want it *now*. And, of course, they want it perfect."

Odette and I commiserated. Walter added, "Those Canadian clients of yours are the worst. She's a bitch, and he's not much nicer."

Over the rim of her glass, Odette said playfully, "Whiskey thinks he's nice enough."

"He's straight enough," Walter said.

"Last night you didn't think so," I reminded him, trying to sound indifferent.

"Well, something happened in here about an hour ago."

Odette said, "He turned you down?"

She was teasing, and Walter knew it. "Not me. He was sitting at the bar when Rico Anuncio came in."

Odette and I groaned. Rico Anuncio runs the West Shore Gallery, where Warren Matheney had his recent exhibit. Since Rico is a tall, blue-eyed blonde who speaks only English, we suspect he wasn't born with that name.

"We weren't busy yet," Walter continued. "Rico tried a few times to start a conversation with your client."

"What happened?" asked Odette.

"At first, not much. Naylor barely responded. I didn't pay attention until he raised his voice. He told Rico, 'Kindly contain your sexual deviance, sir.'"

"Oh, no!" I hooted.

"Oh yes. Apparently that's how Canadians decline an invitation. Anyway, that was the end of it. Rico backed off fast enough. He muttered an apology and moved to a table. Then Naylor said to me, 'Don't you hate it when *they* do that?'"

Odette and I almost choked with laughter.

"And that convinced you he's straight?" I said.

"Yes. But that's not the punch line."

"Go on."

"Then he added, 'Maybe they should call this town Faggot Springs.'"

Walter refilled our glasses as we wiped tears of laughter from our eyes. When the phone behind him rang, he excused himself to answer it.

"You might have a shot with Mr. Naylor, after all," Odette said. "Cheers!"

She clinked my glass, and we drank. Walter reappeared, looking stricken.

"That was Jenx. There's been a murder at Shadow Play."

SEVEN

EVEN AS I FELT the wine goblet slip from my hand, I couldn't make my fingers close around it. Fortunately, Odette's lightning quick reflexes extend beyond her ability to calculate commissions in her head. She intercepted the glass on its way to the floor.

"Who's dead?" she said.

Walter shook his head. "Jenx didn't say, and there was too much background noise to continue the conversation."

"You mean sirens?" I said.

He looked puzzled. "I mean the background noise in here. Happy hour is no time to talk on the phone."

Odette said, "If there was a murder at Shadow Play, we might have to knock twenty percent off the asking price."

"Please!" I glared at her in disgust. "Ten percent, max."

Walter said, "Jenx tried calling you at home, Whiskey. She said that's how she knew you were here. Does your voicemail say, 'If I don't answer, I'm drinking at Mother Tucker's'?"

"Whiskey hired that harpist's kid," explained Odette.

Walter said, "Why not just get voicemail?"

I said, "Does Jenx need to see me?"

A food server was asking Walter more important questions, so I waited.

"Sorry, yes, that was the message."

I asked Odette, "Care to substitute a crime scene for our dinner date?"

She declined, so I went alone. An ambulance was pulling out of the drive at Shadow Play. Since its siren was off, I deduced that help had come too late for somebody. Brady Swancott was once again stringing yellow crime scene tape around a bashed-in back door.

"This is turning into *Groundhog Day*," I said, referring to the Bill Murray movie.

"Except that was a comedy," Brady said.

"Right. Who's dead?"

"Everybody's Favorite Canadian."

"You mean—?"

"The dead guy's wife got whacked."

"How?"

"Looks like she interrupted a burglary. The way she was beaten, I'd say the killer was high on PCP or meth or something. Either that or she pissed him off. Her head's a bloody pulp, bludgeoned with a marble bookend. Real messy. She was dead way before he stopped."

My legs decided that it was time to sit. Without warning I plopped onto the wooden steps at Brady's feet.

"You okay?" he asked.

"Compared to Mrs. Santy, I'm peachy. How's her brother taking it?"

"About how you'd expect. I think he's in shock. Naylor came home from Mother Tucker's with take-out and found her on the bedroom floor. She was sick with a migraine headache when he went out. When he got back, she had no head left."

"Please—." I felt Walter's red wine rising in my throat and clamped my hand over my mouth.

"Yo, Whiskey!" Jenx's steel-toed boots appeared next to my knees. "Is she going to hurl?" I assumed the question went to Brady. When he didn't answer, I grunted.

"Is that a yes or a no?" Jenx said. "Breathe, damn it!"

I took her advice and concentrated on working my lungs for a while. I hadn't felt this queasy since high school biology.

Jenx squatted next to me. "Whiskey, we got some real bad news to break to your client. Do you want to do it, or should I?"

"I have to make the call." I cleared my throat. "Same person who was here last night, you think?"

"Not unless whoever looks like Julia Roberts is built like Vin Diesel. Our killer's a guy."

"How'd he get in?"

"That's part of the bad news. The alarm system failed, second night in a row. We called the company. They got no sign that anything was wrong. If I were the Reitbauers, I'd cancel my contract."

If I were the Reitbauers, I'd fire Mattimoe Realty. Even if we couldn't have done more, it looked like we should have. Saving this account seemed as unlikely as keeping the leaves on the trees.

"Give me the rest of the bad news for the Reitbauers."

"After we get the sheriff's department out here to run forensics, they'll need to hire a cleaning service. I'm talking biohazard removal. The bedroom's splattered with blood, body fluids, and brain tissue."

I tasted Walter's red wine again and selfishly hoped this trauma wouldn't put me off Pinot Noir.

Jenx said, "I'm not supposed to recommend anybody, but I can give you the name of a firm in Grand Rapids. They'll have to remove the carpets, wallpaper, and so forth. She was killed in the bedroom, but the guy tracked up the whole house."

"So much for white wall-to-wall Berber," said Brady. "Looks great in showrooms, performs poorly in crime scenes."

Jenx added, "I hope your client has good insurance and a good interior decorator. This house is going to need a makeover."

"Anything stolen?" I asked.

Brady said, "The Matheney, again. Officer Roscoe's on the case. I told him to make like Abra and sniff out purses and so forth. He's scouring the area as we speak."

"But doesn't that mean whoever was here last night came back?" I said. "They didn't get the painting the first time, so they tried again, harder?"

Jenx said, "Only one set of bloody footprints, and they belong to a guy."

"Couldn't he have had an accomplice?"

"You mean 'Julia Roberts' waiting in the getaway car?"

"Yeah."

"Except there's no sign of a getaway car."

"Anything else missing? That we know of?"

Brady said, "According to Mr. Naylor, a set of ivory candlestick holders is gone. So's Mrs. Santy's jewelry."

"The Piaget again?"

"And the family heirlooms."

"Mr. Naylor's in shock, but he took inventory?"

"I guess he knew what to look for," said Brady.

Jenx said, "One problem solved: I just talked with Hen, and she'll put him up tonight."

"I thought Red Hen's House was packed with leaf-peepers."

"It is. We have a guest room in our personal quarters. He can sleep there."

Edward Naylor didn't know it, but he was about to rely on the hospitality of Magnet Springs' most conspicuous lesbian couple. I assumed they would "contain their sexual deviance" during his visit.

"Can I talk to him?"

"You don't want to see him tonight, Whiskey."

My cell phone buzzed.

"How's the crime scene?" Odette asked.

"If you just ate, you don't want to know."

"That's why I'm calling. Jonny's Chilean sea bass is too spectacular for you to miss. Your take-out is waiting at the bar. I told him to add something suitable for the child."

I bid Brady and Jenx good night and walked stiffly to my car. As I opened the door, something rattled the bushes on my left. My chest tightened. A gray blur glided past. I screamed. Officer Roscoe froze in his tracks.

From the porch Brady shouted, "You all right, Whiskey? He didn't mean to startle you."

The canine officer sniffed my feet.

"Abra couldn't come out and play tonight," I told him. "She's in training."

He whined sympathetically and trotted away.

I arrived home with the two boxed dinners from Mother Tucker's to find Abra using Chester as a beanbag chair while they both watched TV. As usual, she ignored me. But her pose triggered a potent repressed memory: Abra pressed against Leo as he lay on the couch after dinner.

Jonny's second meal was what Chester dubbed a "Gourmet Whopper": three ground-sirloin patties on a homemade Kaiser roll, smothered in grilled mushrooms, onions, and two kinds of imported cheese. Chester felt too tired "to digest so much saturated fat." He suggested we give a few pieces to Abra as treats at the end of a hard day of training.

"About this online program, Chester. Did you call it Dogs-Train-You-dot-com?"

He nodded.

"But isn't that what Abra is doing already?"

"It's about animal psychology, Whiskey. We have to let her *think* she's in control."

"But she *is* in control. Look what she's doing right now!"

Abra was helping herself to the Gourmet Whopper. Her choppers were full of chopped sirloin.

"I'll handle this," said Chester.

What happened next was not pretty. Chester snatched what remained of the burger and stuffed it in his mouth. Chewing hard, he dropped to all fours in front of Abra, who began to lick his lips. Her goal, apparently, was to transfer Chester's food from his mouth to hers. I tried not to imagine his celebrity-harpist mother and her entourage looking on.

"That's wolf behavior," he said, wiping his face with Mother Tucker's napkins.

"Well, I wouldn't recommend it for humans."

"Domestic dogs do it, too. When I feed her like that, I'm Top Dog."

"But are you current on your shots?"

After that excitement, I felt as ready as I'd ever be to phone the Reitbauers. Reaching their machine, I left this message: "I'm afraid there's been another break-in at Shadow Play. I'd prefer to give you the details in person, so please get back to me as soon as possible. You can call me any time tonight."

I repeated my various phone numbers and hung up. The string of events was rapidly adding up to a business disaster.

Chester appeared in my home-office doorway. "Everything all right in the real estate game?"

I had to smile. "Thanks for reminding me it's a game. Everything all right with you?"

"Uh-huh. Oh—by the way, Cassina called."

"Your mother?" I asked stupidly. "What did she say?"

"She's okay."

"Good. . . . Uh—where was she calling from?"

"Traverse City. They're still there, still recording. The sessions aren't going too well."

"I'm sorry to hear that. . . . Any idea when she might finish?"

He shrugged.

"Okay then. . . . Well, good night." I studied him, wondering whether he needed a hug or something. For all his big ideas, Chester seemed very small.

"Good night." He hesitated. "Dogs-Train-You-dot-com doesn't *require* it, but I was wondering if Abra could sleep in my bed. I think we might bond better that way."

I couldn't imagine bonding more closely than sharing pre-chewed food. But I agreed, rejecting a nasty mental picture of slate-gray Egyptian-cotton sheets layered in long blonde fur.

"About your contract, Chester. Can I see it?"

"As soon as I revise it a little. Don't worry, Whiskey. You can afford me."

The Reitbauers didn't call back. When I hadn't heard from them by 8:30 the next morning, I phoned again, from Mattimoe Realty. I reached the maid. She informed me that Mrs. Reitbauer was, even as we spoke, on her way to Magnet Springs via her husband's private plane. That was not good news.

An hour later, Noonan knocked on my office door.

"I heard what happened," she gasped. "Tuesday the husband dies at my studio, and Thursday the wife gets whacked at Shadow Play. This is a real bad latitude for that couple. Oh—and I just spotted Mrs. R. walking into Best West."

Meet the competition. Best West Real Estate is the second-largest realty in this part of the state and catching up fast. Best West has a nifty new advantage: its owner/broker was recently elected mayor of Magnet Springs. The town held a special election last June after our once-esteemed city leader was indicted for tax fraud. Gil Gruen of Best West ran unopposed. Many Main Street merchants encouraged me to run, but it was too soon after Leo's death. I'd read somewhere that new widows should avoid making major decisions for at least a year. Embarking on a political career seemed significant. Plus, Abra had begun snatching purses and getting caught. That didn't speak well for my leadership skills.

Thanks to Noonan's tip, I was more or less prepared for what happened next. My receptionist buzzed me to say that the owner of Shadow Play was in the lobby—with the mayor.

"Good morning, Mrs. Reitbauer . . . Gil. . . . ," I said, focusing on my client. "Mrs. Reitbauer, come back to my office, where you can be comfortable."

"That won't be necessary, Whiskey," Mr. Best West drawled. Gil Gruen was dressed in his usual costume—a Western shirt, tight jeans, alligator cowboy boots, and a Stetson. Indoors, he stowed the last item under his arm. Although we'd endured twelve years of Lanagan County public education together, Gil acted as if he'd been raised on the Ponderosa with Little Joe. His cowboy realtor persona was born the day he founded Best West.

"Get down off your high horse, Whiskey, and stop wasting Mrs. Reitbauer's time. She came all the way from the big city across the lake just to hand-deliver you a letter."

He nodded at Mrs. R., who wore enough make-up and attitude to pass for a runway model. She extracted an envelope from her purse and gave it to me without making eye contact.

"What's this?" I said.

Still looking the other way, Mrs. R. said, "Sorry, Whiskey, but this, like, isn't working. Okay? That's a letter of agreement to cancel the whole rental deal-thing. My husband and I don't want to do this anymore."

"You don't want to rent Shadow Play? Or you don't want me to manage the rental?"

"Both. The whole scene is like a downer. We just want it to be over."

"I see. Then let's talk about listing your property for sale. Mattimoe Realty sold another house in Shadow Point this year—for fifteen percent above appraisal."

Mrs. R. looked at Gil and then at me.

"No, Whiskey. I want to dissolve our contract. Then I've got to go. I'm getting my nails done at eleven."

Gil said, "It's in your best interest, Whiskey."

I turned on him. "Why are you even here? You wouldn't be soliciting her business, would you?"

He looked stunned. "In *your* lobby? While she's *your* client? Shame on you! I'm here purely as the mayor of this fine town. I just want to make sure our part-time resident gets the courteous treatment she deserves. Mrs. Reitbauer confided in me that you scare her a little."

"What?!" I looked at the stylish, raven-haired Mrs. R., who wasn't looking at me. She was studying her already perfect nails. "We'll be more comfortable in my office," I told her and started in that direction. Behind me, I heard a chair being dragged across my lobby floor.

"Sit yourself down, ma'am, while I expedite this on your behalf," purred Gil. "I'm sure the cute little gal who answers Whiskey's phones also makes a decent cup o' joe—and will be happy to pour you one while I talk to her boss. Ain't that right, Missy?"

I could feel my feminist receptionist's wrath. It was almost as hot as my own.

I said, "Mr. Gruen, may I remind you that Mrs. Reitbauer is *my* client? I will personally make her a cup of coffee, a cappuccino, a cocktail, or whatever she prefers. But I shall do it in *my* office. Good day, sir."

Mrs. R. spoke up. "Whiskey, just sign the damn cancellation letter so I don't have to sue you for negligent management."

"Mattimoe Realty has not been negligent," I said with exaggerated calm.

Gil interjected, "I'm not sure the West Michigan Realtors Board will see it that way. As mayor of Magnet Springs, I've asked them to look into the string of violent crimes that has occurred under your management."

EIGHT

"You win some, you lose some. Make sure you win more than you lose."

That was Leo's summary of how to stay in business. I needed to win one soon. Although I trusted Odette to close her deals and my other agents to do the same, I wanted a victory of my own. It hurt to watch Mrs. R. fire us and then, one minute later, hire Gil Gruen on the sidewalk in front of our office. Through the open window we could hear the mayor's plan for turning a murder scene into a money-maker. He was confident that Mrs. Santy's grisly death would add thirty percent to Shadow Play's resale value.

"The newly rich get turned on by tragedy," Gil told Mrs. R. "The more violent, the better. You might want to leave a couple bloody handprints on the wall. . . ."

I needed a drink but opted instead for a dose of caffeine and Peg Goh's common sense. Plopping onto a stool at her counter I said, "Give me the strongest thing you got."

She did and then listened to my tale of woe. Peg shook her head.

"Gil's wrong. Nobody wants to live in a haunted house. They only want to gawk at it. And there will be a lot of that. I'll bet the Reitbauers' neighbors will think about selling once the new traffic pattern sets in."

Why hadn't I thought of that? People moved to Shadow Point because they craved privacy. Drive-by ghouls would drive them right out. I rushed back to the office and had my receptionist run a reverse look-up on the Reitbauers' neighbors. Happy prospecting ahead.

Jenx called shortly after noon.

"Good news, for a change: Edward Naylor wants this nightmare to end. He's going to take both bodies back to Canada as soon as Crouch releases them."

"When will that be?"

"Maybe as early as the end of business today. Crouch is doing Mrs. Santy's autopsy now. Her husband's body is already cleared for departure." I could hear Jenx shuffling papers. "I'm going to the coroner's office later to get the report. Always a pleasure to witness his distaste for lesbians. But he prays for us."

"He told you that?"

"Oh yes. When Crouch came to Noonan's studio to see Santy's body, he announced that he prays for *all* lost souls. And he looked my way."

"Last night did Edward Naylor mention anything about—oh, I don't know—a lawsuit?"

"Not to me. He was a quiet, cooperative guest. Even managed to thank us for our hospitality."

"You did him a favor."

"Maybe you can do your local police a favor. Brady wants to borrow Abra this weekend."

"That would be doing me a favor."

Jenx explained that Brady thought Abra could teach Roscoe a thing or two about purse-snatching.

"Are you trying to corrupt him?"

"If Roscoe sees how she steals them, maybe he'll learn how to retrieve them."

I reminded Jenx that Abra's purse-snatching days were over. She was in recovery.

Jenx said, "She grabbed that purse at Shadow Play, didn't she?"

"I'd prefer to think she retrieved it."

In any case, I agreed to bring Abra to the station. Always happy to be of public service, especially when it earns me a dog-free day. I felt a pang when I remembered that Chester had his own training program in progress. It wasn't exactly guilt gnawing at me. After all, Chester is eight years old, and I'm an adult. An adult who's going to end up paying him to be my houseguest. My real concern was how to amuse Chester if I couldn't foist him off on Abra.

As the afternoon wore on, Mattimoe Realty hummed with tourists dazzled by fall colors and Lake Michigan's broad, sandy shore. Jenx called again at 4:30; I hadn't yet taken a break.

"You can look for Magnet Springs on the news tonight," she said and hung up.

What the hell was that about? I cursed her in three languages—the only foreign words I know—and went back to work.

Odette burst into my office without knocking.

"Guess who just called?"

"Please tell me it wasn't my mother."

"It wasn't your mother. It was Mr. Reitbauer."

"Is he suing us?"

"No! He apologized for canceling the contract. But he said he defers to his wife in such matters."

"His child bride, you mean."

Odette perched on the corner of my desk in that eager, bird-like way of hers. "I picked something up in his voice, Whiskey. . . ."

"Your telephone telepathy again?"

"I don't think the caller was really Mr. R."

"Why not?"

"First, he didn't *feel* like Mrs. Reitbauer's husband." Odette cocked her head as if recalling some psychic vibration. "Second, I know the voice on their home answering machine, and it doesn't match his. The taped voice is older."

My desk phone buzzed again. Jenx said, "Do you or do you not want the scoop on how the wrong corpse left the country?"

Five minutes later I was sitting next to Jenx's desk, peering at her through a manila canyon. She doesn't like to file; she prefers to stack folders as high as gravity permits and then shuffle as needed.

"Check this out." She passed me a Missing Person bulletin fresh off the wire. I studied the blurred black-and-white photo of a handsome, square-jawed, thirty-four-year-old man named Daniel Gallagher Jr., from Grand Rapids, Michigan. Missing since Tuesday.

"Good-looking guy," I said, returning the paper to Jenx.

"If you're into that," she agreed.

"Wait." I grabbed the bulletin back. "I thought this was Gordon Santy."

"We all did."

I sank back in my chair. "Noonan said he said his name was Dan!"

"We can thank our favorite forensic examiner, who released the body based on Mrs. Santy's identification."

"But if it wasn't Gordon Santy, why would Mrs. Santy say it was?"

Jenx's eyes flashed. "You'll have to ask the boys from East Lansing."

"Who?"

"The state police. It's their case now. This morning the Lanagan County prosecutor turned it over to them. Too big a crime for our small jurisdiction. Make that *two* crimes that are too big. And two bodies now on their way to Canada."

Jenx fired a rubber band across the room.

I said, "The first corpse didn't look like a homicide, but the second one sure did. Why did Crouch let both bodies go?"

"In both cases, next of kin identified the remains. Crouch was satisfied, and so was the MSP." She added, "Mr. Naylor's threats to involve the Canadian Consulate probably speeded things up."

"Will Daniel Gallagher's widow get back his remains?"

Jenx said, "Do you have any idea how hard it is to get a corpse back from Canada?"

I shook my head.

"Me, neither," she admitted.

Before I left the station, Jenx reminded me that I'd have to feed Chester. So I picked up two dinners at Mother Tucker's. When I arrived at Vestige, I found Cassina and eleven sulky people in my great room. They were watching Chester put Abra through a series of "pack moves," none of which, fortunately, involved the oral exchange of chewed food. There was a lot of pushing and rolling and barking, however. Chester had mastered a convincing repertoire of howls and growls. At the end, Cassina's black-clad entourage applauded uncertainly. Then one of her people approached me.

"You're Whiskey Mattimoe?" the sallow young man asked. "Cassina would like a few words with you about her son. In private."

I had expected him to call her the Great Cassina and was disappointed when he didn't. I said, "Would she like a cup of coffee or a glass of wine?"

He regarded me sternly. "Cassina drinks only Tahitian shark-fin tea."

I went off to the kitchen in search of a corkscrew and a bottle of Pinot Noir. I would imbibe even if the diva didn't. A moment later, Cassina glided into the room. Her hip-length wavy hair was an unnatural flame red. Her translucent skin was alabaster, her immense almond eyes the deep moist green of a forest. This was my first face-to-face encounter with a genuine superstar. Although I had waved to Cassina as she climbed in and out of limos, we'd never met. Now here she was in my understocked kitchen. Draped in a flowing gauzy gown like the kind she wore in concert and barefoot with emerald rings on all ten toes, she didn't look like a neighbor. Or an Earthling.

From behind her back Cassina produced a fifth of Glengoyne, arguably Scotland's finest single malt whiskey. The Late Great Leo preferred bourbon, but my first husband Jeb Halloran loved Glengoyne; he called it "the cool burn." Without smiling—without, in fact, showing any emotion—Cassina handed me the bottle.

"Based on your name, I assume you love the stuff."

"Actually, I got my nickname because of my husky voice. And my first husband's sick sense of humor."

Cassina murmured, "Ex-husbands, ex-lovers—they should all rot in hell."

She stroked her veil of hair and added, "Chester seems happy here, though it's bizarre how you let him push your dog around."

I started to explain about Dogs-Train-You-dot-com but decided there was no point.

"You can do what you want," she said. "It's your dog."

"Actually, it's my husband's dog. He's dead, but not in hell."

"Are you going to open that?" she said, pointing to the Glengoyne.

"Thanks, but I rarely drink whiskey."

"I meant for me," she said. "I need a fucking drink."

NINE

I can't say that the Great Cassina and I bonded over that bottle. She did, however, drink her fair share. By the time she would let her people take her home, they had to carry her. Fortunately, it was just across the lawn and into a first-floor bedroom. I, on the other hand, had but a wee sip of Glengoyne to honor my Scotch-drinking ex.

What Cassina wanted: It wasn't to thank me for taking care of Chester. I must have been doing a decent job, though, since she tried to hire me to "keep him" during her upcoming World Tour. I was going to pay Chester to be Abra's keeper, and his mom wanted to pay me to be his.

When I explained that I was a realtor, not a child-care provider, Cassina disagreed. Then I insisted that I was just plain unfit. She snorted and said, "You think *you're* unfit?" When I confided that I couldn't even stop my own dog from breaking the law, she cried, "We all break the law!"

In the end, I offered to help her find another sitter; she said that wouldn't be necessary since I was her choice. Out of curiosity, I asked how long her World Tour would last. She replied, "Either six months or forever."

Then she began blaspheming someone named Rupert—who might have been her agent, her manager, her lover, Chester's father, or all four—and passed out. She briefly revived as her people slipped her through the back door like a pizza delivery in reverse. Cassina tried to sit up, cursed Rupert again, and fainted. The pale young man who had arranged our "meeting" pressed an envelope in my palm. Before I could speak, someone caught Cassina's mile-long hair in the closing door, and she roared like a leopard with an arrow in its flank. Abra raced into the kitchen, made three rapid circles around me and then started bouncing like a pogo stick. Chester appeared. When he threw back his head and howled, she froze in mid-jump and sank to the floor, her tail thumping.

Chester peered at me through smeary lenses.

"She still has a love-hate relationship with performing," he explained.

"Well, she's a novice." I patted Abra's blonde head.

"I meant Cassina. That's why she gets weird sometimes."

"Oh, sure. That makes sense." It didn't, though, and we both knew it.

"Will I live with you while she's on her World Tour?" Chester wrapped an arm around Abra, who nestled against him. They both looked at me hopefully.

I swallowed. "I probably can't afford you. How much is this training costing me, anyhow?"

"Don't worry about it. Open the envelope," he said.

As I stared at the contents, Chester said, "Let me guess. . . . Three days' care and accommodations, plus the guilt of forgetting me and failing to return your calls. I'm going to say Cassina paid you . . . twelve hundred dollars."

I gaped at him. "Chester, I can't take this."

"Everybody else does."

"But I'm not a nanny. Or a sitter. I'm not what your mother seems to think I am."

"You're taking care of me, aren't you?" He produced a brush and began grooming Abra. She always ran away when I tried that.

"Well, sure. But this was . . . an emergency."

"That's the only reason you let me stay?"

"Of course not," I lied.

"Why else?" he asked. Abra emitted a low moan of pleasure as he brushed her throat.

"Well, Abra adores you. And we know she needs training." I was stalling. "But you can train her without living here. Right?"

Chester grinned, and I noticed he had lost another tooth.

"You're missing a canine—I mean, an incisor."

"It was loose. Abra knocked it out while we were playing."

"I hope you didn't swallow it."

"Abra did. It happened last night when we shared the burger. She already passed it. Want to see?"

"No thanks." I sat down to match his eye level. "I can't keep your mother's money, and I can't keep you. But I do want you to work with Abra."

He said, "Give Cassina's check to charity. She won't take it back. You might as well make somebody happy."

Leo used to say that.

Good-natured Brady Swancott forgave me for bringing Chester to the police station the next morning. He's a family man, after all.

"I have a son just your size," he said, patting Chester's white-blonde head.

"Is he six?" asked Chester.

"Yes he is!"

"I'm eight."

"Oh." Brady looked at me, unsure what to say next. "Well, you'll catch up."

"Probably not. I was a preemie. But I'll always be smarter than your son."

Wordless, Brady patted Chester's head again.

"Please don't do that," Chester said.

Brady didn't approve of the greasy fast-food breakfasts I had brought.

"Definitely not regulation canine-officer chow." He arced the paper bag into the waste basket. When Abra dove in after it, he said, "I guess we can make an exception."

Always busy on Saturday mornings, Mattimoe Realty thrums in leaf-peeping season. When I arrived at 8:15, Odette was on the phone and two other agents were chatting with eager-dreamer tourist families. Odette tossed me the *Magnet*, our local news weekly. The headline read: "Magnet Springs Murder: Canadian Widow Slain While Looking Into Husband's Sudden Death."

"They say all publicity is good publicity," Odette said.

I closed my office door and sat down to read. Who needs caffeine when you can contemplate a fresh unsolved murder? The article was thin on details, for which I was grateful—especially since the missing facts included my name and my firm's. I had barely finished my second read-through when I heard Odette's rapid-fire three-tap knock.

"It's already started," she announced. "The new traffic pattern at Shadow Point. Carol Felkey called to say that she can hardly get in or out of her driveway! The story's on every TV station in the tri-state area. People yell out their car windows, 'Is that Murder House?'"

Odette rubbed her hands together. "I smell money waiting to be made!"

Then Jenx called.

"Let's hope history won't repeat itself. Dan Gallagher's widow is on her way to Magnet Springs. She wants to know what happened to her husband."

"Well, she can't stay at Shadow Play," I said.

"I should warn you, she's a Fundie. On the phone she asked me to pray with her. Something tells me she won't be happy at our house."

I offered to put the widow up at Vestige if nothing else could be found.

"There's a room at the Broken Arrow," Jenx said. "Our fake Heather Nitschke never came home. Glad I kept that crime scene tape on the motel-room door. I'll tell the desk clerk to expect Mrs. Gallagher."

Jenx asked if I'd ever heard the name Holly Lomax. I hadn't.

"Her prints were all over Shadow Play and the motel room: She's twenty-nine years old, with at least that many arrests for prostitution."

"And you thought the Broken Arrow Motel was reformed."

"Lomax failed to check in with her parole officer in Grand Rapids last week."

I said, "Grand Rapids was Dan Gallagher's hometown. Maybe a coincidence?"

"Most of life is."

Jenx invited me to join her and Mrs. Gallagher for coffee later.

"Her husband died on your turf. She might want to meet you."

I pointed out that Noonan owned the massage table.

Marilee Gallagher was nothing like the late Ellianna Santy. She wasn't Canadian or blonde or beautiful. She also wasn't a bitch. When I stopped by the police station, I thought Jenx's office was empty. The door was ajar with no one in sight. Then I heard whispering. Stepping cautiously inside, I glimpsed a puffy brunette hairstyle bobbing low on the far side of Jenx's desk. A moment later, the attached face and body appeared. Marilee Gallagher struggled to her feet.

"Oh!" she exclaimed when she spotted me. "I was just on my knees having a word with the Lord. I'll bet you're looking for Chief Jenkins. She's checking her fax machine."

Marilee Gallagher gave me a radiant smile. A large woman with lovely dimples, she possessed a perfect heart-shaped mouth and sparkling teeth.

I thanked her, turned to go, and crashed right into Jenx.

"Mrs. Gallagher, this is Whiskey Mattimoe, a local real estate broker."

"Pleased to meet you, Mrs. Mattimoe."

I asked her to call me Whiskey, but she was uncomfortable saying the word since her church outlaws liquor.

"Why would your mother do that to you?" she asked, her eyes shining with sympathy. "Was she . . . an alcoholic?"

I explained that the nickname was based on several weird factors, beginning with my real name. My dear mother is a teetotaler. Nothing stronger than decaf for her. Sweet Irene Houston christened her baby girl Whitney. She chose the name after reading it in a romance novel. I never liked it, and eventually it became a joke. I'm not black, I was never beautiful, and I have no musical talent whatsoever. What I do have is the raspy voice of someone who lives in a bar. Or someone with a three-pack-a-day habit. Never mind that I rarely drink the hard stuff, that I haven't lit up since I turned thirty, and that I've sounded this way since I hit puberty. That's when a kid named Jeb Halloran dubbed me Whiskey, and the name stuck. A few years later, I married Jeb Halloran. That didn't stick.

Marilee Gallagher still wasn't "at peace" with my nickname. So Jenx sadistically encouraged her to call me Whitney—the birth name I loathe as much as Jenx does hers.

"Why don't we *all* use our first names then?" I said brightly. "Chief Jenkins loves to be called Judy, or—even better—Judith."

Jenx's eyes narrowed as if prepared to fire lasers.

"My sister's name is Judith," chirped Marilee. "I always wished my mother had saved that name for me."

Suddenly, she shrieked and went spinning away from us as if flung by an unseen dance partner. At the same instant, everything made of metal on Jenx's desk jumped, and all the phones at the station started ringing. I glanced at the acting police chief, whose eyes now bulged.

"Easy, Jenx," I whispered.

"Oh my," Marilee said again, from the corner where she had landed. "I do believe I felt the Holy Spirit in me!"

What she had felt was a disturbance in our local magnetic fields. Such occurrences are legendary, dating back to the earliest days of Magnet Springs' history. In recent years, though, the phenomenon has been linked exclusively to Jenx. I'd never seen her so exercised about her birth name and said so.

"It's not about that," she hissed.

"I haven't felt like this since the tent revival in Kalamazoo," Marilee cried. "Let us pray!"

"Let us not," said Jenx. She handed me the paper she had been holding when I ran into her. The fax from the New Brunswick Department of Transportation, Motor Vehicles Services, featured the photocopied driver's license of Gordon David Santy, age thirty-four, of Fredericton. Although the driver's photo was blurred, I recognized him at once. Gordon Santy was Edward Naylor.

TEN

"What happened to the driver's license you took off the corpse?" I asked Jenx.

She glanced at the widow across the room. "Released to next of kin. *Presumed* next of kin."

Jenx exhaled loudly, and I felt a shift in magnetic pressure.

"Careful," I whispered.

When Marilee Gallagher said, "Amen," we moved toward her. She smiled, radiating pure good will. How the hell could we tell her?

"Your husband's dead," Jenx blurted, helping Marilee to her feet. "And his remains have left the country."

"I thought it was something like that," she said calmly.

"Why?" I had to ask.

"The Holy Spirit filled me with Truth and Light."

Jenx said, "What can we do for you, Mrs. Gallagher?"

"Call me Marilee, please. Well, first I'd like to see your reports. And then I'll need a word with the medical examiner."

"Anything else?"

She poked around inside her purse and came up with a business card. "Please call my insurance agent and find out how the heck I'm going to collect Dan's life insurance when you've lost his body."

A few minutes later, I was sipping instant cappuccino and contemplating a plate of Pepperidge Farm Milanos. Marilee likes comfort foods. The cookies and coffee mix had come from her handbag.

"This will cheer us up," she declared. Her fussing, clucking, and purring made me feel like I was the new widow. I offered my condolences.

"I'm sure it hasn't quite sunk in," she said. "The Holy Spirit took away my pain. Cookie?"

Jenx returned with a fat manila folder and a legal pad.

"Whiskey has a dog," she began.

"Let's leave her out of it," I said.

"High-strung and contrary," Jenx continued. I wondered if she meant me or Abra. "But I think she can help. Being recently widowed, she knows what you're feeling."

Marilee turned to me. "Your dog is a widow?"

"No. I am."

Then it hit me: maybe Abra felt like a widow, too.

Jenx said, "Whiskey lost her husband last spring. She's having a real hard time."

"I'm handling it just fine!" I said.

"Shall we pray?" asked Marilee.

"No," said Jenx.

"But thanks for asking," I added.

I wanted to know how Jenx thought Abra could help. She reminded me about the training session in progress with Officers Swancott and Roscoe. Then she reviewed the crime scene report following her call Tuesday to Noonan Starr's Star of Noon Massage Therapy Studio.

"Dan was having massage 'therapy'?" Marilee asked. I started to explain, but she asked me not to.

When Jenx showed her the photocopy of the driver's license found on the corpse, Marilee gasped, "I took that picture of Dan at his birthday party!" She observed that his height and weight statistics were wrong. "Didn't the coroner measure him?"

"Of course I did."

We turned to the rotund bald man filling the doorway.

"Such discrepancies are routine," he said. "People self-report personal statistics at license bureaus. And people lie."

"Thanks for coming, Dr. Crouch," said Jenx.

"It's my job, Officer Jenkins."

"Acting chief," she reminded him as he waddled past.

Crouch extended a doughy hand to Marilee and said, "I'm sorry for your loss."

She thanked him and asked what he could tell her.

Crouch began, "The word *autopsy* literally means 'see for oneself.' What I saw when I examined your husband was an apparently healthy thirty-four-year-old man who died of asystole."

"What does that mean?" Marilee said.

"His heart stopped."

"Why?"

"I'm not sure. That's why I've ordered drug screens. Are you aware, Mrs. Gallagher, that your husband used cocaine?"

Marilee's rosebud mouth went slack.

"I saw no evidence of chronic abuse," Crouch went on, "but there were traces of the drug in his nasal passages."

I thought Marilee might cry or pray; instead she reached for Crouch's hand and squeezed it in both of hers.

"My husband was the man the Lord sent me," she said. "I don't know what he was doing in this town or why he had that fake ID. But whatever your science says, I won't love him any less."

"Amen," Crouch agreed. Then he invited Marilee to worship with him and his wife.

"Will I get Dan's body back?" Marilee asked, offering Crouch a cookie.

He passed the question to Jenx.

"We don't know yet," she said. "The state police have the case. I can refer you to them."

Crouch told Marilee, "Whoever took your husband's remains might cremate them to destroy evidence."

She looked worried. "Our religion forbids that, but I'm sure the Lord will forgive us when it's not our idea."

"He shall," Crouch said with authority. As if in explanation, he added, "I pray for all lost souls." He glanced sideways at Jenx. "Also, I saved enough tissue samples to satisfy any insurance company that the man is dead."

Marilee thanked him. "But I can't help wondering, since Dan wasn't who you thought he was, maybe the other victim wasn't, either?"

Crouch explained stiffly that he'd followed standard procedure in both cases, relying on the *presumed* next of kin to identify remains.

"But what do you think now?" Marilee persisted.

Crouch patted his mouth with a paper napkin. "I think it's in God's hands."

Before anyone could pray, I said, "If Edward Naylor is Gordon Santy, then he faked his own death. Isn't it likely that Ellianna Santy faked hers, too?"

Everyone stared at me. Jenx excused herself to make some calls.

What she found out: Edward Naylor had a legitimate New Brunswick address, driver's license, and license to practice law. Though not as handsome as his impostor, the real Edward Naylor was the former mayor of Fredericton. Passing for an upstanding citizen must have been Gordon Santy's idea of a game. We knew the score: the Santys were winning.

Jenx connected with the Fredericton police, who in turn linked her to the Royal Canadian Mounted Police, the national law enforcement agency to our north. They're not all on horseback. Who knew? The RCMP reported that Gordon and Ellianna Santy got themselves "into a bit of a jam" while running a gallery in Toronto. Both were indicted for art fraud but managed to vanish before their trial. That was two years ago. The RCMP believed that the Santys had been selling art on the Internet and probably still were.

Jenx was reporting this to Marilee and me when our cowboy realtor mayor arrived. He doffed his Stetson.

"Time to put on your crime-fighting hat, Chief. You need to crack this case and make Magnet Springs the safe haven we say it is."

Jenx said she'd love to, but there was a problem: The county prosecutor had assigned the case to the MSP.

"Say that in plain talk," Gil ordered.

"It's up to the state police now."

So that his visit wasn't a total waste, Gil introduced himself to Marilee and gave her his business card. His social gaffe made me groan.

"Is that your stomach growling, Whiskey?" said Gil. "You ought to try eating more regular. I hear you been drinking your dinner at the bar at Mother Tucker's. Now that's just sad."

I had to marvel at his original dialect, concocted from bad films and '50s TV.

"In case you're not aware, Gil, Mrs. Gallagher's husband is the man who died in Noonan's studio."

"Whoa! I thought that was some Canuck named Santy! My apologies, ma'am."

Marilee nodded graciously and excused herself to powder her nose. I half-expected Gil to ask for his card back. Instead, he focused on Jenx.

"If the state police are stepping all over you, I reckon you'd better nip at their heels. Find out what's up before the papers do. This kind of publicity's pure poison."

I said sweetly, "I thought scandals *made* money, Mr. Mayor. By the way, have you sold Murder House yet?"

Gil guffawed. "I like you, Whiskey, no matter how you conduct your life. Say, I hear the West Michigan Realtors Board has got some questions for you."

He winked and walked out.

Jenx said she had some questions for Noonan, and she'd like me to come along. We agreed to meet at the Goh Cup after Jenx settled Marilee Gallagher at the Broken Arrow Motel.

"I don't know what I can add." Noonan gazed at us over her herbal frappé, a foamy iced beverage created by Peg Goh. I might have ordered one myself if it had come in a palatable color.

"When we talked to you before, we thought Dan Gallagher was Gordon Santy," Jenx explained.

"I told you his name was Dan."

"Right. What I'm wondering was—did he seem jumpy to you?"

"He talked fast and tapped his fingers on my reception desk."

Jenx said, "Would it surprise you to learn he was coked up?"

Noonan looked distressed. "I can usually detect things like that."

"Frappé too sweet?" Peg Goh asked, noticing Noonan's frown as she cleared a nearby table.

Jenx explained that we were reviewing Tuesday afternoon's events in light of new evidence.

"Is this about the man from Canada who died on your table?" whispered Peg, not about to upset any leaf-peepers.

"Except he's not from Canada," I said and brought her up to speed.

Peg slipped into the empty fourth chair at our table.

"I've been meaning to talk to you," she told Jenx. "After you brought in that photo of the dead man, I remembered something."

We all leaned forward.

"I didn't work the lunch shift Tuesday because I had a dentist's appointment just down the street. When I passed Town & Gown, a young couple was coming out. They were laughing real hard—too hard for people who'd been shopping at a store as nice as Martha's. I mean, they sounded drunk or something. That's why I stared at them. I didn't get as good a view of the man as I did of the woman. But he had to be the guy who died on Noonan's table. The woman called him Dan. I remember that because it's my brother's name, too."

ELEVEN

JENX JUMPED IN HER seat. "Cell phone's vibrating."

After taking the call, she said, "What goes around comes around. That was my old pal Balboa from the police academy. She works with the boys from East Lansing and keeps me posted. As we speak, she's emailing me Holly Lomax's mug shots. Will you look at them, Peg? See if Holly's our Town & Gown gal."

At the station, Peg studied the image on Jenx's computer screen.

"That's her, all right. But she had bigger hair when I saw her."

"Like *Pretty Woman*?" I explained about the Julia Roberts movie, the magazine picture, and the desk clerk's comments. Peg saw the connection, but she predicted that eighty-year-old Town & Gown proprietor Martha Glenn wouldn't.

"Martha won't remember seeing her or Dan Gallagher. She can't remember what day it is. I don't know how she stays in business."

Jenx said, "I'll interview her again, but I don't expect much."

"You're officially off the case," I reminded her.

"And you're officially a realtor."

"But if you want Abra's help, I'm at the other end of the leash."

For some reason, everyone found that amusing. Peg said, "Speaking of Abra and her leash, has Judge Verbelow called you yet?"

"About what?" I said, alarmed.

"About a date, probably," said Jenx.

Peg asked, "Haven't you noticed how he looks at you?"

"He's giving off very strong vibes," agreed Noonan. "And you're both lonely."

"I am not!" I sputtered. "I have a very full life!"

A piercing scream interrupted me. We rose as one and dashed to the lobby. Brady was bending over a prostrate Marilee Gallagher, Officer Roscoe was licking her ghost-white face, and Chester was running in circles. Abra was absent.

Chester cried, "She did it again!"

My heart sank when I noticed that the unconscious Marilee did not have a handbag.

"Which way did she go?" I said, resigned to the inevitable.

Brady inserted two fingers in his mouth and whistled shrilly. Everyone froze. The station's front door flew open and in sailed Abra, a black leather shoulder bag swinging from her jaws.

Chester checked his sports watch. "One minute, fifty-five-and-forty-three-one-hundredths seconds. A new record!" He and Abra began leaping and rolling in a celebratory pack dance.

"I'll take that." Brady extracted the slimy purse strap from Abra's mouth. "Now that's what I call a good day's work."

I pointed to the widow on the linoleum. Jenx was administering smelling salts.

"Did Abra knock her down?" I said.

"No way!" said Chester. "She didn't even steal the purse."

"Technically, that's true," said Brady. "The citizen placed it on the counter, opened it, closed it, and passed out. Abra grabbed the bag *after* the owner had hit the tiles."

Chester said, "It's what we practiced all day. Abra thought it was another drill!"

Marilee Gallagher moaned as Jenx helped her sit up. She blinked at her surroundings, spotted her purse in Brady's hand, and promptly passed out again.

"There's something about that bag!" Jenx cried.

Abra yipped in agreement, and Brady popped open the clasp. We watched the color drain from his face.

"What is it?" demanded Jenx.

Brady closed the purse. "Uh—this is police business, Chief. Everybody else needs to leave."

"It's a finger!" Marilee wailed, sitting up again. "I found the purse behind the dresser in my motel room when I moved the TV to get better reception. I thought the purse might be a clue, so I brought it right over. I didn't open it till I got here."

A severed finger? That made me scream—for about two minutes. So I didn't hear what anybody else said in immediate response to Marilee's announcement. I was able to stop screaming when Jenx gripped my shoulders and shook me like a can of whipped topping. She pointed out that nobody, not even an eight-year-old child, was reacting as badly as I was. How humbling—or should I say humiliating. When Jenx swore us all to secrecy, I mutely nodded my assent.

"We don't know what this means," she insisted, "so don't go around speculating."

I had no desire to do that. Brady and Roscoe escorted Marilee back to the Broken Arrow. Peg scurried off to the Goh Cup, and Noonan headed home. That left Chester, Abra, Jenx, and me. Plus the finger. I tried to act normal.

"You need dinner about now, don't you?" I asked Chester.

He reminded me that Cassina was back. "You're off the hook—till she leaves on her world tour."

"Cassina's got another world tour?" asked Jenx. "Tell her Brady and I will check the house while she's gone. Are you going with her, buddy?"

Chester said, "Cassina wants Whiskey to watch me, only Whiskey's not sure."

"Why not?" Jenx demanded.

"Because I'm a realtor, not a child-care provider!" I pointed to the purse on Jenx's desk. "What will you do with that? Since the case isn't yours anymore."

"I'll think it over."

"For God's sake, you've got somebody's finger!"

"Well, it's too late to give it back. Want to see?"

Jenx pushed the purse in my direction. Reflexively, I leapt to my feet, knocking the chair into Abra, who had been cleaning herself. She snapped at me.

Definitely time to clear the room. I gave Chester ten bucks to go buy himself and Abra a treat, and I told him to take his time.

"You can't withhold evidence," I warned Jenx.

"No, but I can keep it on ice for a while. I want to see what I can find out. The boys from East Lansing will get the finger soon enough."

"How could the state police have missed the purse when they searched the motel room?"

"Maybe they were too lazy to move the furniture."

"Or maybe somebody put it there later?"

Jenx thought that was unlikely since the room had been sealed.

"'Sealed'? You mean with that lame piece of yellow tape Brady put up?"

"That's called police procedure, Whiskey. And so is this." With the care of a surgeon, she donned surgical gloves and laid the purse on its side.

Don't let the finger roll out, I prayed.

"Ever heard of Rare Art For Sale?" said Jenx.

"Hasn't everyone?"

"I mean the company. Their business card is in this bag. Read but don't touch."

She pushed the card across the desk to me. It bore no individual's name or title. No address or phone, either—just the company name, a fancy logo, a web site and an email address.

"Could this be the Santys?" I said.

"You're thinking about what the Mounties said—that they might be selling art online. If so, it's one more connection to Holly Lomax, who's very likely the dead woman we've been calling Mrs. Santy."

"How do we find out?"

"Check that web site while I call Balboa."

"Wait," I said. "If I help you with this, does that make me your accessory?"

Jenx grinned. "I'm not into accessories. Or haven't you noticed?"

I typed www.rareartforsale.com. What came up was one of those "This page cannot be displayed" messages. The web site was either currently unavailable or experiencing technical difficulties, or else my browser settings were screwed.

The email address was dealer@rareartforsale.com. I knew enough about the Internet to appreciate that emails leave footprints. Just for fun, Chester once showed me how to create an anonymous web-based email account.

At the time I said, "Why would I want to do that?"

He said, "Maybe someday you'll want to play in a Chat Room."

This wasn't about that, but I was ready to send my first email from WooWoo@coolmail.com. WooWoo was Leo's pet name for me.

Jenx had said to keep the message short. "Ask 'What's your price structure?' and hit 'send.'"

To my astonishment, I got an instant reply: "What are you looking for?"

"What have you got?" is what I wanted to write, but that seemed too obvious. So I typed "Paintings" instead.

"Real cute" came the reply. I tried again: "Watercolors."

"Artist?" he or she wrote back.

I almost said, "Yes, please," but opted for a name instead: "Matheney."

"Starting at $45k" was the answer. I stared at the screen a minute, then typed: "How do we do this?"

Reply: "You're beyond cute, you're hilarious. Try online with credit cards. Which Matheney do you want?"

Before I could answer, dealer@rareartforsale.com wrote: "Cumulus, Cirrus, or Nimbostratus?"

"Ask Brady, the scholar." Jenx was back, reading the screen. "He'll be here any minute, and he knows about art."

"How'd it go with Balboa?"

"The state boys found human hair in the bathroom at Shadow Play. Long brown hair, so it didn't belong to Mrs. Santy or Mrs. R. And they found hair dye."

"What color?"

"Who has more fun?"

"Living people," I said. "Our blonde got whacked."

"There's more." Jenx's eyes danced. "Balboa's cousin works for the Chicago P.D. Being a cop is a family tradition. She said the police kept a key fact about Matheney's death out of the news."

"Don't tell me. . . ."

"Yup. The corpse was missing a finger. Third one, left hand."

"He must have been murdered," I said.

"It looked like a heart attack. The finger removal came later." She held up the purse. "We've got Cloud Man's finger in the bag! But it's missing his Celtic ring. Supposedly, he never took it off, but the cops haven't found it."

"Matheney's Cloud Ring?" asked Brady, loping into Jenx's office, Roscoe at his side. "Man, it was huge! And butt-ugly. I saw it myself when he was at the West Shore Gallery. It was his trademark. Oprah asked him about it when he was on her show. You could tell she thought it was butt-ugly, too."

We brought Brady up to speed on Balboa's report and my current adventures on the Internet. He sat down to study the messages from dealer@rareartforsale.com.

Chester appeared in the doorway, munching a T-bone Teaser, the oversized sandwich sold at Bake-The-Steak. Abra was eating one, too.

"What's new with the finger?" said Chester.

"You didn't tell anyone about it, did you?" I asked.

He made a face. "That would be unethical."

"That can't be right," Brady said from his seat at the computer. "If you could even find a Matheney for sale right now, it'd cost four or five times this much. At least."

"Do we have Matheney's finger?" said Chester.

"Not on purpose," I said.

"What are you writing?" Jenx peered over Brady's shoulder.

"Test question. Let's see if they pass."

We moved toward the monitor to watch. Roscoe sniffed the non-regulation treat in Abra's mouth. With atypical generosity, she let him have half.

"Bingo!" Brady cried.

The reply from dealer@rareartforsale.com read: "Cumulonimbus not yet available."

"What does that mean?" said Jenx.

Brady scratched his chin. "Rumor had it Matheney was starting a Cumulonimbus series. There were no public showings, though."

He typed a question about provenance, which he explained to us means proof of origin.

"When you buy or sell fine art, you need documentation. It's like the pedigree you get with your dog."

The mere allusion to breeding was enough to set Abra off. She made a "come-hither" canine sound and displayed her hind end for Officer Roscoe's viewing pleasure.

"She's not in heat, is she?" Brady said. I recalled how she'd flirted with Roscoe the night they were at Shadow Play.

"Uh—," I began, realizing that I hadn't got around to spaying her.

"No," answered Chester with authority. "But it's imminent."

"I can't believe a kid your age knows words like that," Jenx said.

"I'm not six."

"Well, well . . ." mused Brady at the computer. "Our dealer's doing a little dance. He says buyers get papers of provenance when they take possession."

"And how do they do that?" Jenx asked.

"The old-fashioned way: credit cards and overnight express. All they need is a credit limit of at least seventy grand."

"Cassina charged a Mercedes once. With American Express," offered Chester. When we stared at him, he added, "You have to pay that card off every month."

"What did you tell the dealer?" I asked Brady.

"I said I'd get back to him. But he won't respond again. We asked too many questions. 'WooWoo'? Where'd you get that handle?"

I shrugged. Suddenly Brady jumped from his seat bellowing, "No, Abra, no!"

I looked where he was looking. Abra was prying open the purse on Jenx's desk.

"Who trained her to do that?" I cried.

"We had a good day," answered Brady. He grabbed what was left of Chester's sandwich and tossed it to Abra.

Chester said, "She'd rather have the finger!"

Roscoe was barking, Brady was yelling, and the room was spinning. When I came to, I was on the linoleum, not far from Marilee's spot. But Roscoe wasn't there to lick my face. Brady and Chester were gone, too. So was Abra.

"What the hell happened?" I asked Jenx.

She said that Abra had grabbed the purse and escaped. But the best tracking team in Magnet Springs was on her trail. I pointed out that it was the only tracking team. And it consisted of an art-history student and a child.

"And Officer Roscoe," Jenx reminded me.

"Officer Roscoe's in love."

Jenx bristled. "He's a neutered professional."

The door swung open. Brady and Chester shook their heads at us.

"Roscoe's still on the case," said Brady. "But Abra's too fast. No way I was going to crawl after her through those brambles on Schuyler Street."

"What do we do now?" I asked.

"Wait for Roscoe."

"And if he can't find her?"

Brady patted my shoulder. "Roscoe always gets his man."

"This is no man, Brady. This is an Afghan hound."

Chester suggested we go home. "Maybe she's waiting for us."

Jenx whispered in my ear, "Take no chances: double up on poop patrol."

When we pulled into the driveway at Vestige, it was nearly dark.

Furious as I was with her, I had hoped to see Abra dancing in my headlights. Instead, I spotted what looked like a large envelope duct-taped to my garage door. Chester didn't wait for the vehicle to come to a complete stop. He leapt out and ripped open the envelope.

"What is it?" I reached for what he was holding.

"Not so fast! You'll smudge any prints that are on it," he said.

I noticed then that Chester wore surgical gloves.

"Where did those come from?"

"I asked Brady for a pair before we left. Just in case."

He waved the note at me.

"This is bad news, Whiskey. Somebody kidnapped our dog."

TWELVE

I DON'T KNOW WHICH impressed me more—that Chester loved Abra enough to claim joint custody, or that someone would go to the trouble of kidnapping her.

"Technically, she hasn't been kidnapped," I told Chester after he'd held the note up so that I could read it.

"*Dognapped*, then," he said.

"No. This says she went willingly."

"Abra would never do that!" Chester cried.

But I knew better. I just wondered what they'd used as bait.

"Technically, this isn't a ransom note because they're not demanding money," I explained.

"They've got Abra, and they want something from us! That's ransom!"

Any minute now, Chester would start jumping up and down.

"Read it again!" he shouted.

Aloud I read, "'We have your dog. No force was used. She came willingly—'"

Chester made a rude noise.

"'—and is unhurt. For now. We assume you want to keep her that way.'"

Chester said, "Call Jenx! Or, better yet, get back in the car and drive to police headquarters. They need this note as evidence!"

"Evidence of what? We already know Abra's missing. This doesn't tell us anything. It doesn't even mention the purse or—you know."

"These people want something!" Chester insisted. "Why else would they duct-tape a note to your door? Why else wouldn't Abra come home?"

I could think of several reasons Abra wouldn't come home. Leo wasn't here anymore, for starters. Although I fed and cared for her, our primary bond was gone. And then there were her criminal tendencies. The only difference this time was that she hadn't had to find a purse worth stealing; the cops had conveniently provided one. They had even helped her polish her skills.

Chester said, "You've got to report this so Brady can put Officer Roscoe on the case!"

I reminded Chester that Officer Roscoe had punched out for the night and was probably snoring under Brady's desk by now. I, too, was troubled by the note, but if someone wanted something in exchange for Abra, they'd have to be more specific.

Frustrated, Chester started hopping from one foot to the other. "For the love of Abra, call Jenx now!"

Even though his mother was back at The Castle, I knew I couldn't just send Chester home. He was part of this now. I led the way into my kitchen. Already the house seemed ominously quiet without Abra, or the threat of her.

I assumed that Jenx would have switched the phone to Magnet Springs' overnight dispatcher system—an answering service for three local communities that can't afford police patrols 24/7, but the acting chief herself picked up my call.

"Still sitting here thinking," she explained. News of the note intrigued her.

"How about I cruise over there and have a look-see?"

"It's not like it's a ransom note," I said.

"It's like a ransom note!" Chester shouted. He had picked up the phone in the guest room.

"It's a threatening note," Jenx concluded. "Whoever wrote it is toying with us, and I'm nobody's toy."

"Me neither!" said Chester.

"I'll be there in ten, buddy," the Chief promised. I knew she wasn't talking to me.

Chester paced the great room, looking like a miniature expectant father: useless and partly to blame. His latex gloves enhanced the image.

"I feel responsible," he muttered. "All day long, I was rewarding her for grabbing handbags. She got a mixed message."

"It's not your fault. Abra knows what she's doing."

Chester looked at me. "Do you think she'll be okay?"

I nodded with a conviction I didn't quite feel. But I meant what I said: "Abra's a survivor."

His eyes brightened. "That's what Cassina says about *me*. Did you know I barely weighed four pounds when I was born?"

"Amazing. Where was that, anyway?" I didn't know much Cassina history except that she already had the kid when she built The Castle next door.

"Huntington, West Virginia. Backstage at the Marshall University Student Union Auditorium. Cassina was touring campuses to promote her first CD, *Wicked Kisses*. She didn't even know she was pregnant."

Maybe I looked skeptical because Chester added, "She thought she had gas. Cassina lived on junk food in those days. Not anymore, though."

I nodded. "Now she drinks shark-fin tea."

"Tahitian shark-fin tea," he amended.

That reminded me of Rupert, the person Cassina had cursed. I wanted to ask Chester about him, but just then Jenx arrived, blessedly without siren or flasher. Chester held up his gloved hands.

"Good thinking!" Jenx said. "What about Whiskey?"

"I knew she'd contaminate the evidence, so I didn't let her touch it. Think you can lift some prints?"

"I can try. The MSP has better equipment, but I don't want to call them yet."

"What about their case?" I said. "Could be a connection. Or maybe someone just wants to mess with me. Most of Magnet Springs knows I could afford to buy Abra back. What they don't know is . . . would I?"

"We all know you would," Jenx said.

"Why should I?" I demanded. "She makes me crazy! She disrupts my whole life!"

"She's Leo's legacy," said Jenx. "He adored that dog, and you adored Leo. Everybody knows that."

"I adore Abra, too," Chester said.

"Yeah? Well, you're a kid, I said. And kids love dogs. Especially big dogs. Or is it girl dogs? Maybe it's big girl dogs, which is what Abra is."

Jenx said, "We'll get her back, Whiskey. Officers Swancott and Roscoe will give this their all."

"Can I join the posse?" said Chester.

"What 'posse'?" I said.

"The volunteers who chase the bad guy!"

"In John Wayne movies, maybe."

"Well, I want to join one. To save Abra."

"Sounds good to me," said Jenx. "I hereby deputize you. Of course, you can't carry a weapon, and we no longer work on horseback."

Chester beamed. "When do I start?"

"I need your help right now. How about answering a real hard question?"

"Shoot." Chester assumed a fighting stance.

"You said you didn't tell anybody at Bake-The-Steak about the finger. Is that right?"

"Right. I didn't tell anybody."

"Are you sure you never mentioned it?"

"Positive."

Jenx looked hard at him. Suddenly, Chester's eyes widened, his jaw sagged, and then his entire face collapsed. He was sobbing.

"What's wrong?" I said, wanting to throw my arms around him but not quite knowing how.

"I didn't tell anybody anything! I swear I didn't!"

"Of course you didn't!" I said, casting a nasty glance at Jenx.

"But while we were waiting in line at Bake-The-Steak, Abra and I did discuss the finger."

"What?"

Chester sniffled, "I talk to Abra all the time. Sometimes in dog language. Sometimes in English. I needed to ask her whose finger she thought was in the purse, but I didn't know how to say it in dog language."

"What did she tell you?"

"She didn't know!"

"Good work, Deputy," Jenx said, wiping Chester's nose. "Dream deep tonight. See if you can remember anything else that might help us."

"You mean, like who might have overheard us at Bake-The-Steak?"

Jenx nodded. "Did you recognize anybody?"

Chester reminded her that he was a kid in private school. He didn't hang out with tourists or Main Street merchants, and they're the folks who frequent Bake-The-Steak. Jenx ordered her deputy to bed so that the posse could ride early the next morning. She also commanded him to show up with a belly full of breakfast.

Chester looked grim. "I don't think I can do that, ma'am. Whiskey's cupboards are bare."

I promised him a high-carb breakfast, come hell or high water, and sent him to sleep in the guest room. To Jenx, I said, "Are you sure it's wise to involve him? Chester's very emotional. Ever met his mother?"

"Many times. We watch her place when she's on tour. She autographs CDs for me and Brady and brings us back cool souvenirs. When she went to Japan, I got a tea set."

"What did Brady get?"

"A dagger. We traded."

Jenx urged me to reconsider the babysitting gig. "Cassina pays well."

I reminded her that I didn't need work as a nanny. I was trying to build a real estate empire. She sniffed and told me to concentrate on who might have a grudge against me or Abra.

I couldn't think of anyone who had it in for me except maybe a couple business rivals. As for Abra, the women whose purses she stole had wanted her euthanized, but the court resolved that matter.

"She might have offended Nesbitt," I mused, "but he didn't seem like a stalker."

"Who's Nesbitt?"

"An Afghan hound Abra dated in Chicago. Never mind." This was getting silly. Then I remembered something distinctly not silly. Something downright disturbing.

Jenx said. "You just got a weird look on your face."

"I just remembered a nasty experience."

"What?"

"I guess you'd call it a death threat."

THIRTEEN

WHAT I REMEMBERED WAS Abra's first and only Kennel Club show in Chicago, about six months after Leo got her.

I told Jenx that some guy wanted to buy Abra on the spot. He offered Leo a lot of money, way too much money for a dog with her show history. Not to mention her personality. The man was persistent and then obnoxious. What started as inappropriate behavior at a dog show quickly became alarming. Leo called security and had the man removed.

Jenx said, "What about the death threat?"

"I'm getting to that. The guy started calling us at home, at all hours. He insisted on buying Abra. Leo had our number changed, and the calls stopped. Then the letters started. Letters to Abra."

"Huh?"

"The guy from the dog show sent Abra *love letters*. I saw a couple of them. He wanted to make love to her."

Jenx groaned, "Sick puppy."

"When Abra didn't write back, he turned mean. Sent her long letters describing the ways he hoped she'd die."

"Such as?"

"Leo wouldn't let me read those. He said they involved torture."

"Who was this scumbag?"

"He called himself 'Sparky.'"

"Barf."

"Leo hired a private investigator to track down the guy from the dog show. His real name was Darrin Keogh, I remember that. Could he have come to Magnet Springs and stolen Abra?"

Jenx thought it unlikely. "What happened to Sparky when Leo's PI found him?"

"I don't know. Leo said he wouldn't bother us again. And as far as I know, he never did."

Jenx asked for the PI's name. I had never known it; I had let Leo handle the matter. She wondered whether I could identify Darrin Keogh today. I had seen him only once, at the dog show, when he was harassing Leo. And since I had been in the stands, I hadn't seen him up close. All I could recall was an agitated fair-skinned, light-haired guy who was probably under thirty. Jenx closed her notebook with a snap.

"I'll run a check on the name. If I find anything, I'll get in touch with Balboa's cousin in Chicago."

Upstairs a phone rang.

"Want to get that?" asked Jenx.

"That's my business line. They'll get my voicemail."

Jenx's hand was on the kitchen doorknob, but she made no move to leave.

"Listen, Whiskey, if you've been waiting for an excuse to sort through Leo's stuff, maybe this is it. Check his pockets for business cards. See if you can find anything about Sparky."

When I looked away, she added, "Leo's been gone six months."

"Five and a half!"

"So let the healing begin."

She was right, of course. I'd been postponing the inevitable. Maybe in the back of my mind I'd imagined someday selling Vestige and conveying all of Leo's things to the new owners. Or maybe I figured I'd eventually call a charity to clear his closet and den while I was at work. Either way, I'd never have to moon over my late husband's personal stuff.

But the time to get started was now. I bolstered my nerve with a cup of strong tea and a reminder that I love to snoop. Poking through the pockets of My Gone-Forever One-True-Love didn't feel like snooping, however. It felt like mourning. It hurt like hell. Leo's smell was in my head again for the first time since last spring: sensual and spicy. How is it that a scent can bring back everything but the life?

After checking just three suits, I was weak and teary and on the verge of giving up.

"Whiskey? I have a phone message for you." Chester, wearing his pajamas, cracked open the bedroom door. What I could see of his face looked scared. Maybe I'd been crying more loudly than I thought.

"I was walking by your office when the phone rang, so I answered it," he said. "Even though Abra's not here, I wanted to be helpful."

In his fingers was a yellow sticky note. I studied his childish scrawl.

"Wells Verbelow wants to have brunch with me? *Tomorrow*?"

"Don't let our breakfast date stand in your way. I'm sure Brady will have donuts for me at the station."

"I never blow off a date, Chester."

"This time you should. Wells Verbelow is a judge. Maybe he can help us find Abra."

"Except that nobody's even supposed to know about Abra," I reminded him.

"Oh yeah. Well, you should have brunch with him, anyway. You need to start dating again. And he thinks you're stunning."

"He told you that?"

Chester shuffled his slippered feet. "He might have thought he was talking to Tina, your office manager. He was impressed that I was working so late on a Saturday."

I stifled a laugh. Tina Breen's nasal, high-pitched voice probably didn't sound all that different from Chester's over the phone. And Tina was widely known as one of Magnet Springs' chattiest personalities. Good for the real estate biz, not so great for my personal life. I constantly struggle to separate the two. That's why I encourage Tina to do much of her work from home, where she can keep an eye on her two toddlers and her nose out of office gossip. Tina had gabbed with Wells Verbelow about me before. I knew this because she often said, "I'll bet he'd love to invest in real estate. You should give him a call."

I drew a deep breath and dialed the Honorable Judge Verbelow's home phone number. He recognized my voice at once.

"Whiskey! What a pleasure. Tina wasn't sure when you'd get my message. She said you've been extremely busy. That's why she was working late."

"Well, it's leaf-peeping season. That always brings new business."

He lowered his voice. "So sorry to hear about the murder at Shadow Play. That was yours, wasn't it?"

"Mine?"

"Your rental client who was killed. I heard you managed the property."

"Past tense is accurate," I said and changed the subject. "What can I help you with, Your Honor?"

"Nothing urgent. Frankly, I expected to reach your voicemail tonight. Did Tina tell you what I said?"

"No . . . Tina didn't."

"I've been wanting to ask you out, Whiskey. I realize you might still think it's too soon. But would you consider having brunch with me someday?"

I frowned. "Did you say *someday* or *Sunday*?"

"I said *someday*, but I meant *some Sunday*. The sooner the better."

"Then how about tomorrow?" I couldn't believe I'd said it. Then again, getting to the point was my style.

"Splendid!" the Judge exclaimed. "I hear they do a fine brunch at the Sugar Grove Inn. Have you been there?"

"Not since—. No, not lately." Sunday brunch at the Sugar Grove Inn had been a routine for Leo and me.

"I could pick you up at eleven," he said.

I swallowed a shard of guilt. Would brunch with another man at the Sugar Grove Inn betray Leo? Then I grasped the preposterous logistics: Leo and I had played up and down the west coast of Michigan. If I ruled out every place we'd been together, I'd go nowhere. Which is precisely where I'd been for five and a half months.

I asked the Judge if he knew where I lived.

"Next door to Cassina's Castle. And, Whiskey, please stop calling me 'Your Honor.'"

That would be difficult, given my memories of Abra's trial, but I said I'd work on it. We chatted a bit more about nothing much. I was aware of an unfamiliar tingle near my heart. Not my ribs this time. And not the lust I'd felt for the fake Edward Naylor. More like a reminder that I was still alive, after all.

I dashed up the stairs and executed a leap in the hall outside my bedroom. Fifteen years had passed since I led my high-school volleyball team, but I was still in good shape. And I like getting physical.

I also like sleeping in on Sundays, but my conversation with the Judge had infused me with rare energy. I woke an hour before my alarm was set to go off, ready for a run. When Leo was alive, I ran every morning before going to the office, but this would be my first run in five and a half months. I had several legitimate excuses for laying off so long. I'd been in Leo's accident, too; for the first couple months afterward I was healing. Then there were the troubles with Abra—her serial purse-snatchings and the hearings and the court-mandated counseling. Next came sultry August; excuses for not running are not required. That brings us to September, which brings leaf-peepers. And what do leaf-peepers bring? If we're lucky, lots of business.

This was the morning to start turning my life around. Before seven, I had splashed cold water on my face, slipped into my long-neglected running shorts and shoes, and started my warm-up stretches. But I got a little zealous with my right hamstring. It didn't rip, but it sure did scream. I screamed, too. Fortunately, I didn't wake Chester. As soon as I could, I limped back into the house to ice my strain. And curse myself for not having fixed the icemaker.

From my jock days, I recalled that freshly injured soft tissue should be worked a little. After a few minutes, I tried moving the leg. Not bad, but not up to a pounding run. That's when I remembered Blitzen, my touring bike, hanging in the garage. Blitzen was Leo's gift on my last birthday. Leo's last birthday gift to me. It's a serious machine, too ambitiously equipped for my dilettante ways. Nobody in Magnet Springs needs a temperature-compensated handlebar altimeter, but I appreciate the anatomically correct, gel-padded saddle. I vowed then and there to use that bike as God intended: for firming my thighs.

FOURTEEN

I COULDN'T HELP BUT think of the Judge as I pedaled down my curving driveway into the bright new day. The truth was that I'd never thought of him as anything but a jurist until the previous night. Wells Verbelow may not have had the estrogen-accelerating gorgeousness of George Clooney or the fake Edward Naylor, but he was attractive: slim and straight of spine with thick brown hair going gray, a firm jaw, and deep-set brown eyes. Although he wore a sober face at work, I had seen his eyes crinkle at the corners. They did the day Abra's trial concluded and I thanked him for his leniency in sending her to counseling instead of jail.

"Ms. Mattimoe," he replied, "the court does not sentence animals to prison. If we did, given Miss Abracadabra's history, I doubt that we could keep her there."

Giggles from the gallery. I expected him to strike his gavel and bellow, "Order in the court!" That didn't happen. Instead, he leaned forward in his throne—I mean chair—and said, "The court understands that you, Abra's owner, are a responsible citizen. Frankly, her threat to public safety is probably negligible. We are concerned about her impact on community pride. On the tourist industry, to be candid. Are you confident that you can control her?"

I looked at him directly. "Not at all, your honor." More giggles.

He nodded. "Then the court advises you to consult a therapist. On behalf of your dog."

Still more laughter. Abra's trial—dubbed "The Abra Show" by the weekly *Magnet*—was our town's midsummer highlight. A spate of soggy weather had turned tourists away from the shore, but we had an antidote. Go see that crazy long-haired dog on trial for stealing purses! The courtroom was packed. I wish I could have scalped tickets. Strangers asked if they could photograph the defendant. Women wanted to pose Abra with their purse in her mouth.

About Wells Verbelow: he was in his late forties with two grown kids who lived elsewhere. His first and only wife had died four years earlier from breast cancer. He was short, although the assessment is relative. After all, I'm six-foot-one. The Judge was probably five-foot-eight. Not that I had ever hesitated to date non-tall men. My soul mate, the late great Leo Mattimoe, was a full three inches shorter than I am, and I never cared. More important, neither did he.

Thinking about the Judge—and trying not to think of him as The Judge—I settled into my first bike ride since last spring. Bicycling is boring to runners, but when you can't run and you want to move, it works. After a few minutes, my heart rate picked up. The wind was in my hair, the golden autumn sun was on my skin, and I was starting to appreciate the colors all the tourists come to see, when something snagged my attention. Just inside the stand of trees lining the other side of the road was a flash of yellow, low and in motion, like a loping blonde Afghan hound moving in the opposite direction. I braked and called Abra's name. The image did not reappear. I parked Blitzen off the road and walked toward the woods. When my thigh protested, I stopped. No sound, not even a snapping twig. I called a few more times. Nothing.

I turned Blitzen around and started back toward Vestige. *If* I had seen Abra, she might be heading home. I pedaled cautiously, calling for her. The road was nearly deserted at that hour on a Sunday; only three cars had passed me so far. When I heard number four coming behind me, its pace seemed oddly slow. We were on a paved county road with decent shoulders and a posted speed limit of 50 mph. Number four was approaching at half that rate.

I swung onto the gravel shoulder, expecting my nubby tires to grip the loose stones. But as Blitzen skittered sideways, I felt her tires slide, not bite. In my hurry to hit the highway, I must have overfilled them. Leo had warned me against that; he'd even bought a pricey digital gauge so that I'd get the pressure right. I'd never used it.

A sleek midnight-blue Beamer with privacy glass hovered near me as I wobbled. Then the driver accelerated, and the car peeled away. I read the Indiana vanity plate: ARTZAKE. Meaning "art for art's sake?" I wondered. Or a man named Art Zake? Or maybe an exotic mushroom?

I concentrated on easing Blitzen back onto the pavement. By the time I got up to speed, the Beamer had turned around. I stared with dumb horror as it moved toward me, much faster than before. And the driver was now operating British style, heading down the left side of the road. *My* side.

I don't know what I was thinking, or if I was thinking, when my peripheral vision registered the golden flash again, much closer this time. I jerked my head and handlebars in that direction, and the whole world slipped sideways. The Beamer's tires squealed.

Gravel against bare skin burns. But not as bad as a Beamer doing sixty.

Both car and apparition were gone by the time I picked myself up. Did Abra save my life? Or did I have a major case of visual distortion? All I knew was that my tires were too hard, and someone in a BMW from Indiana had almost killed me.

I promised myself that I would find that tire gauge.

Like a worried sailor's wife on a widow's walk, Chester was pacing up and down my driveway, watching for me. I'd remembered to leave him what I thought was a parental-type note: "Back soon. Brush your teeth." It had failed to reassure him. As I turned up the drive, he waved my note like a semaphore.

"Did you forget the posse? We ride at nine!"

I assured him I hadn't forgotten. Chester frowned as I disembarked stiffly. "Did you fall off your bike?"

"I think she threw me."

He followed me into the garage, where I located the digital gauge and, better late than never, adjusted my tires' inflation.

"Something happened to you," he said accusingly.

Omitting the part about the Beamer, I told him I might have seen Abra. He whooped and tossed my note in the air. "I knew we'd find her!"

I didn't have the heart to point out that just because Abra found me didn't mean she wanted to be found. If I'd really even seen her.

At the station, Brady Swancott listened to my ARTZAKE story in silence. He promised to run a check on the plate and added, "Any chance you need a brain scan?"

"I didn't fall that hard."

"But you thought you saw Abra?" He looked concerned.

"That was before I fell."

"Right."

Before delivering Chester to the police station, I had had barely enough time to brush the gravel from my hair, and not enough time to close the garage, apparently. I arrived home to find my garage open and another pseudo-ransom note duct-taped to Blitzen's gel-padded seat. Ripping it free with my bare hands, I read, "Still hoping to see your dog again? Then stay off your bike and keep your big mouth shut."

The phone in my kitchen started ringing. At least I'd locked the door into the house. Or had I? I took a deep breath and turned the knob. Not locked. The door swung open. I grabbed the phone.

"ARTZAKE?" Jenx said by way of greeting.

"*Gesundheit.* Hey—were you planning to run surveillance in my neighborhood?"

"Maybe."

"How about the inside of my house?"

"Any reason I should?"

"Only that there might be a bad guy in here."

"And how might that have happened?"

"It's hard to believe, but I forgot to lock up. And someone left another note."

When I read it to her, Jenx roared, "Why have an alarm system when you don't even lock the damn door?"

"This time I didn't even close the damn door. But that's not the point. I think I saw Abra!"

Jenx wasn't impressed. "Brady thinks you need a brain scan."

I asked her how soon she could get here since I had to get ready for brunch with the Judge.

Jenx said, "He's going to ask about Abra. Are you prepared to lie?"

"I'm hoping the subject won't come up."

"You know it will. Forget you saw that finger, Whiskey."

"I wish!"

Jenx agreed to make sure my house was secure.

"Until I get there, take your car keys and wait outside. And while you're waiting, do a shit check."

"I beg your pardon?"

"See if Abra's been back."

I found several piles I should have picked up days ago. Or, rather, Abra's keeper should have. But nothing fresh. Jenx arrived, readied her service revolver, and entered my house. Just like a cop in a movie. After a few minutes, I checked my watch. If I didn't get on with washing my hair I'd be late for brunch, so I went indoors.

I had nearly finished blow-drying my unruly hair when Jenx kicked open my bathroom door.

I screamed, "What the hell's the matter with you?!"

"Did you hear an All-Clear?" she demanded. "No you did not. First, you think there's an intruder in your house. Then you decide to wash your hair. Of course, you don't bother to notify me. Or lock the bathroom door. . . . Do local law enforcement a favor and set the alarm for a change when you leave on your date."

"It's not a date," I said.

The Acting Chief of Police said, "While you're not on a date, I'll get the latest on Sparky."

The Judge arrived punctually as judges probably tend to do. Out of his robe—that is, in civilian casual clothes—Wells Verbelow wasn't intimidating. It helped that he wasn't sitting on a high throne behind a huge desk. His car gave me pause, however. I froze in my tracks at the sight of the midnight-blue Beamer.

"Something wrong?" he asked.

"Not if your car is registered in Michigan."

"It is." He looked at me oddly. I smiled and said, "Go, Blue!"

I had managed to make myself about as attractive as usual. My hair was tousled but shiny; I wore little make-up and less jewelry. I favor tailored suits in subdued colors. With my schedule, shopping for clothes is a necessary evil rather than a pastime. I trust Martha Glenn and her staff at Town & Gown to put together my professional wardrobe. Noonan is the only friend who comments on my taste in clothes. She's fond of saying, "You should wear your true colors, Whiskey." According to the Seven Suns of Solace, those would be sea green and coral.

The Judge didn't mind that I wore beige. In fact, he complimented me on my ensemble. Our brunch went well enough, considering it involved my revisiting an old haunt with a new man. After a couple hours, it felt almost natural to call him Wells rather than Your Honor.

I assumed that he'd suggested the Sugar Grove Inn as much for its privacy as for its menu. The former stagecoach stop is a half-hour drive from Magnet Springs. Wells was recognized the moment he stepped out of his car. As the only judge in rural Lanagan County, he's familiar to any resident who's ever been in court. And, as owner of the area's largest real estate company, I'm hardly anonymous. Three former clients found their way to our table. I had the uneasy feeling that word of our "date" would arrive back in Magnet Springs before we did.

Over English trifle with poached pears and raspberries, Wells said casually, "Any trouble lately containing Abra?"

My spoon clattered against my bowl.

"Oh, I wouldn't say I've had trouble." *More like total failure*, I thought. "Why do you ask?"

Wells smiled. "I feel awkward telling you this, but I had a call this morning from Emma Hartzell. My bailiff?"

He allowed me a moment to summon up the memory of a scowling woman straining to keep order in a courtroom-turned-tourist attraction. Mrs. Hartzell had not appreciated the circus that Abra brought to town.

Wells continued. "Emma lives out your way—on Dunhill Road. She swore she saw Abra in her backyard around sunrise. But by the time she got outside, the dog was gone."

"Did the dog do any damage?"

"Emma said she left only the usual doggie souvenir."

I began to choke. Wells offered me water.

"Perhaps I should dispose of that for her," I rasped.

Wells looked amused. "I'm sure Emma managed. So you think it might have been Abra?"

It might have been Cloud Man's finger.

Coolly I said, "I suppose it's possible, although I was pretty sure she was home this morning."

"I didn't notice her," Wells said.

"She likes to curl up in Leo's den. Sometimes *days* go by without my seeing her—except, of course, when I feed and walk her."

I offered the Judge my warmest, most innocent smile, the one usually reserved for traffic cops and IRS auditors.

"Not to worry," Wells replied. "It's a simple enough matter to settle when you get home."

That might have ended the matter if the next guest had never arrived at our table.

"Whiskey!" Tina Breen squealed. "What a surprise to see you two together! I've been meaning to call you. Last night I saw Abra running down Main Street!"

FIFTEEN

THE JUDGE SAID, "WHAT time was that?"

"Oh, gosh, around seven. I was coming out of Whiz Kids with my boys—the oldest just turned three, you know—and this long-haired yellow dog flies past us down the sidewalk. I don't think the boys had ever seen an animal like that. I said, 'Don't be scared! That's Whiskey's doggie, Abra!' She had something in her mouth, but I couldn't tell what it was."

I smiled lamely at the Judge.

Tina added, "She was followed by that harpist's son. That odd little boy with the funny name."

"Chester," I offered.

"Yes! By the time I calmed Winston and Neville down, Abra was gone. I would have phoned you last night, Whiskey, but the in-laws came over and—"

"Tina, we need to go!" a male voice boomed.

Two noisy balls of energy ricocheted around our small dining room chased by Tina's frazzled husband Tim. We exchanged hasty pleasantries, and then they were gone. And then I had to meet the Judge's eyes. They were kind.

"I know Abra is a challenge, Whiskey. Is there any way I can help?"

Can you keep a severed finger to yourself?

I said, "She's not a bad dog. She just has some bad habits."

"What happened last night?"

Lying to a judge is hard. It's even harder when he's holding your hand.

"Well, Chester took Abra with him to Bake-The-Steak, and she got away. I thought maybe she came home this morning."

"Why?"

"I thought I saw her while I was out riding my bike. She was in my peripheral vision running along the edge of the woods." *When someone in a car like yours tried to kill me.*

After the waitress had refilled our coffee cups, Wells said, "Whiskey, I want you to think of me as your friend. The way we met is history. I'll never judge Abra—or you—again."

"But what if—what if she got in trouble again? Hypothetically, I mean."

"She won't. You're making sure of that."

I swallowed. "But, just for the sake of argument, what if?"

"Then I'd withdraw from the case. Let another judge hear it. We won't worry about that." He grinned. "Abra's stayed out of trouble for three whole months. That's nearly two years in dog time. And she's accrued some public-service credits. I hear she's working with Officers Swancott and Roscoe."

True. They gave her a refresher course in purse-snatching.

"Perhaps you didn't know this about me, Whiskey, but I love dogs. I've never been without one."

"Has your dog ever been arrested?"

"I've never had one as clever as yours. Most canines live to please humans. Abra has a mind of her own."

"She lived to please Leo," I said. "Now she feels lost, I think."

"That only makes her more human."

Scary thought. I insisted we split the check. On the drive back to Magnet Springs, Wells said, "Your office manager is extremely stressed."

"What makes you say that?"

"She can't even remember working last night."

By four o'clock I had made brief appearances at two Mattimoe Realty open houses and was en route to a third—Odette's listing and our Featured Home: a stunning, contemporary mini-castle overlooking Lake Michigan, with five thousand square feet of living space plus an indoor pool and wine cellar. Since such a property requires a special buyer, Odette and I had tried to dissuade the owner from holding an open house, but the heiress-cum-interior-designer wanted the world to see what she was offering. I worried that we'd attract a legion of leaf-peepers, none qualified to do more than gawk. On my way over, I called Odette.

"Not now, darling," she hissed. "I've got two hotties in the next room. They're falling in love!"

In Odette's parlance "hotties" are rich prospects who look ready to buy. When I entered the cavernous great room, she was shaking hands with an expensively turned-out couple in their twenties. Odette cast a shining smile on me. I knew that expression and loved it a lot. It meant we were about to make major money.

"Were those the hotties?" I asked after they'd left.

"Two of them. There are more upstairs."

"Will we get an offer?"

"The hotties who just left will call me tomorrow. We discussed some numbers, and they're very interested."

"Who's upstairs?" I asked.

"Another couple with a trust fund or two. And someone you know."

"Who?"

I followed Odette's gaze to the curving staircase. A familiar figure was descending.

Under my breath I said, "Rico Anuncio doesn't have this kind of money. Is he window-shopping?"

Odette replied, "Let him tell you himself. I'm taking a break."

"Good to see you, Whiskey," said Rico Anuncio, not sounding as if he meant it. He proffered a satiny hand.

I'm direct, even brutal, when it makes financial sense to be.

"Rico, I thought you liked living above your store. I had no idea you wanted a coastal property."

He smiled. "I love downtown. But I'm coming into some money soon and thought I'd see what it could buy."

Rico Anuncio made me uneasy. It was probably because his persona seemed calculated. His name, for starters. I suppose his ancestors could have come from extreme northern Spain, but Rico had a Nordic look. Then there was the in-your-face sexuality. I was acutely aware of his cropped shirt with the scoop neckline. His taut hairless chest and washboard abs. As well as the nipple rings under the fabric. And I couldn't ignore his low-slung ultra-tight pants, which revealed a pierced navel and the outline of something else.

"Congratulations," I said. "Business must be good."

"Very. And I'm going to inherit some money. There was a death in the family."

"I'm sorry." I'd heard that line often enough to make it sound sincere.

Rico tucked a strand of sun-streaked hair behind a diamond-studded ear. "How are you, Whiskey? You haven't looked good since Leo died."

I thought I looked good enough. Before I could reply, the "hottie" couple from upstairs approached, seeking Odette. I excused myself to find her, no easy task in a large house whose floor plan I hadn't memorized. Fortunately, I ran into her in the curved hallway leading to the indoor pool.

"Hottie alert!"

"You can't mean Rico," she said.

"He pissed me off. Told me I haven't looked good since Leo died."

"You haven't. Though you do look better today. Must be brunch with the Judge." Odette winked.

"How did you know about that?"

"Oh, Whiskey, please! Let me go sell this place."

As she floated away, I caught the glint of a gilded antique wall mirror. Though it seemed out of place in this ultra-modern estate, I studied my face in it. A little plain, a little pale—but not bad. I'd never worried about not being beautiful, so how I looked since Leo died hadn't really registered. I had too many other concerns. Like running a business. And running after an Affie.

Odette had everything here under control. Rather than interrupt her meeting or risk encountering Rico again, I headed for the indoor pool. Odette had told me there was an exit from there to a terrace in the dunes, and a stairway from the dunes down to the street. I cringed at the owner's taste in floating pool toys: a life-size coupling couple, made of resin and tinted blood red, shivered on the surface.

From the terrace, I savored the view. It captured what we love about our West Coast: rolling dunes, dusky pines and shimmering sapphire water under a cloudless sky. It occurred to me that Warren Matheney would not have been moved to paint today.

"Not the kind of weather our favorite watercolorist could appreciate," said a voice behind me. I whirled around to find Rico lounging on an upholstered chaise lounge.

"Sorry if I scared you." But I knew he wasn't. "You missed Matheney's show, didn't you? And now he'll never grace another canvas with his heavenly vision. Luckily, I obtained a piece before he passed."

"Nimbostratus, Cirrus, or Cumulus?"

Rico looked surprised. "You're in the loop, after all! I hit the jackpot: Cumulus."

"Congrats. His earliest period."

Rico smiled. "Also his most valuable."

"What about the Cumulonimbus? Aren't those even rarer?"

"Matheney never offered any Cumulonimbus paintings for sale."

"None?"

"He *claimed* he was painting Cumulonimbus, but I heard he was working on something else."

"What?"

Rico's face darkened. "Dogs. Nobody saw any of those, either."

"Maybe they look like clouds," I suggested.

We turned toward the sound of heavy shoes pounding up the stone stairway.

"Mm-mm, steel toes," Rico crooned. "Love the macho footwear, Jenx!"

"Thanks, sweetie. Love the bulge."

"Everyone does." Rico produced his business card from I-couldn't-imagine-where. "Tell Odette I'm a hottie, too. She really should call me."

After he left, I told Jenx that he'd bragged about owning a Cumulus.

"Same period as the painting missing from Shadow Play," I reminded her. "How could he afford that?"

116

"Well, he had Cloud Man's show at his gallery. Maybe it was a hostess gift."

"What are you doing here?" I said.

"I was on patrol and saw your car out front. I figured you'd want to know the latest: our corpses have gone missing."

"What?"

"Gordon Santy, alias Edward Naylor, never took the flight he booked from Detroit. Neither did his cargo."

I said, "How could that happen? Weren't the remains in the care of a local funeral home?"

Jenx shrugged. "Balboa says 'The MSP is checking.' We also found your friend Sparky."

SIXTEEN

I STIFFENED. "DARRIN KEOGH is not my friend."

"That makes sense since he owns the car you say almost killed you."

"ARTZAKE is Darrin Keogh? I thought he lived in Chicago."

"Nope. ARTZAKE—make that For Art's Sake—is his company. It's in Angola, Indiana."

"Are you sure this is the same Darrin Keogh?"

"Odds are. Want to see his driver's license?"

I wasn't sure I did. This was the creep who had wanted to have sex with my dog, who was now missing. I made myself look at the print-out Jenx unfolded.

"That could be him. Got any mug shots?"

Jenx said, "He's clean."

"Clean?"

"Keogh may be a pervert, but he's got no record."

"How is that possible?"

"He never got caught! The sad truth about sex offenders is that most of them don't. Their victims don't come forward."

"Well, if Sparky molests dogs, I can guess why that is."

"Uh-oh," Jenx said, taking a step backward. "You're getting that look again."

"That sad, unattractive look I've had since Leo died? Rico told me all about it."

"No. That 'I'm-going-to-do-whatever-it-takes-to-fix-this' look you get before doing something foolish. But I'm glad to hear you say the words 'Leo died.' Finally, you're facing your loss and accepting your pain."

"And you're doing Seven Suns of Solace tele-counseling with Noonan! I'd know that lingo anywhere!"

Jenx deflected the accusation with a raised hand. "Hen's doing the tele-counseling, not me. She thought one of us should explore our feelings."

That night I had a dream that grabbed my heart so hard I woke up gasping. And that's remarkable because I never dream.

I'm running along a shadowy road that snakes through a thick forest. Every time I round a bend, I catch a glimpse of Abra far ahead, but then she disappears around the next curve. Even though I keep calling to her, she never slows down or looks back. That part's like real life.

Suddenly, I hear the roar of an engine behind me. I turn just in time to jump out of the way of a long, black car.

"Abra! Watch out!" I cry as soon as I can catch my breath.

The words are barely out of my mouth before I hear a crash followed by the piercing cries of a wounded dog. When I round the next bend, I glimpse Abra dragging herself into the woods. To my horror, there's a pool of blood on the road but no tire tracks. The damned car didn't even try to stop. I follow Abra's bloody trail, but it disappears in the dark forest. I realize I am lost.

Through the trees I see a patch of light, as if there's a sunny clearing beyond. I stumble into it and find Leo sitting on the ground holding Abra like a baby. I know he's been waiting for me. I rush toward him but stop when I see the blood on Abra's body.

"Is she dead, too?" I whisper.

Leo smiles. Abra turns her head toward me.

"She doesn't look dead," I say.

"Do I look dead?" Leo says.

"No." He seems so alive, so near, I feel my heart will burst.

"But I am dead, Whiskey. And there's nothing you can do about it."

"Why? Why do you have to be dead?"

He smiles but doesn't reply. Abra begins to lick his face, just like she used to. He laughs just like he used to.

"Why did you die? Why did you leave me?" I feel the tears coursing down my cheeks.

Leo keeps laughing as Abra licks his face.

I say, "What am I supposed to do now? I wasn't ready to lose you. And, believe it or not, I didn't want to lose Abra. She's the only living part of you I had left!"

Leo shakes his head.

"But I'm all alone now!"

He smiles tenderly. "I didn't leave you all alone."

Abra smiles at me, too.

"How profound is that," Noonan sighed as she massaged my ankles the next morning. I'd had to tell her the dream; I couldn't stop thinking about it. And she had sensed that something was up.

"You're so ready for the Seven Suns of Solace, Whiskey."

"No way!" I rolled away from her so hard that I almost wheeled right off the table.

"Then why does Leo say what he says in your dream?"

"Because . . . it's a dream! Who knows what that stuff means? If it means anything. . . ."

"It means everything about who you are and what you can be. You hold the key to knowing your heart and owning your future, if only you'd learn to look inward."

"You're trying to sell me," I said. "I'm a salesperson, Noonan, and I know when I'm getting sold."

"Seven Suns of Solace tele-counseling sells itself. It's a spiritual service, and people partake of it when they're ready. I'm merely the medium."

"Technically, the telephone's the medium," I pointed out.

She said, "I'm the human medium. We do it by phone so that I'm available 24/7, as my clients' souls evolve. Spiritual growth is not bound by office hours."

"Well, unfortunately, my business is," I said, checking my watch. "I've got to go."

"I only did one side," Noonan protested.

"We'll even me out later. I feel fifty percent better than when I got here, and that's good enough for a Monday."

It didn't last, though. I knew as soon as I walked through the front door of Mattimoe Realty that this particular Monday would turn out worse than most.

My usually cool receptionist appeared on the verge of tears. Every phone line was lighted, and the lobby held more people than it did chairs. But that wasn't the problem.

The problem introduced herself as soon as I reached my office. Jane VanDam, a Laura Bush look-alike, was waiting for me, her business card raised like a weapon. I couldn't have been less pleased to meet her if she were employed by the IRS.

"*Miz* Mattimoe," she began, "I oversee P.S.P. for the West Michigan Realtors Board."

"P.S.P.?" I hoped it was nothing like ESP. Between Noonan and Odette, we seemed to have enough of that already.

"Professional Standards and Practices," she explained coolly. "We've had complaints from some of your clients, and I'll need to examine your files."

"With all due respect," I said in my most cordial tone, "aren't you here because of a call from one of my competitors? It's no secret that Gil Gruen and I have a healthy rivalry, which he may have carried a little too far."

Jane VanDam removed a manila folder from her briefcase and scanned its contents. "Mr. Gruen's name appears nowhere on this list of complaints."

"*List* of complaints? How many are there?"

"Three clients have filed, each citing at least one instance of negligence."

"*Negligence*? Who filed? What are the complaints? And why wasn't I notified before the Realtors Board sent you over here?"

"You *were* notified, Miz Mattimoe. First by telephone. Then in writing, by registered mail."

"This is the first I've heard of the matter," I said, keeping my voice calm. "I need to know who in this office you've talked to."

Jane VanDam checked her notes again. "On three separate occasions, I spoke with your office manager, Tina Breen. She returned the calls I left on your voicemail."

I thought *I* returned the calls left on my voicemail. Apparently, Tina had been editing my messages. I excused myself and speed-dialed Tina's home office. She answered on the fourth ring. Before she spoke, I heard Winston and/or Neville shrieking in the background.

"Tina Breen, Mattimoe Realty Office Manager. How may I help you?" Her phone voice was remarkably Chester-like.

"Tina, this is Whiskey. I'm sitting here in my office across from Jane VanDam, P.S.P. manager for the West Michigan Realtors Board."

I heard her sharp intake of breath.

"Did you forget to give me some important messages and registered mail?"

"I can explain. If the messages concern office business that I would usually handle, then I handle them."

"But apparently you didn't handle them. That's why Mrs. VanDam is here." I softened my tone. "Anything from the Realtors Board is *my* business, Tina, and I need to know about it. Immediately."

She was starting to cry, and that made her boys cry, too. It sounded like a nursery school meltdown on her end of the line.

"Here's the thing, Whiskey. You've been so distracted since Leo died, we've all been covering for you."

"We'll discuss this later," I said through my teeth. "Please bring the phone log and those letters. *Now.*"

"But I've got the boys at home."

"Then bring the boys," I hissed and clicked off.

Jane VanDam was staring at me. "I just made the connection: You were married to Leo Mattimoe. I knew him years ago, when he was married to his first wife, Georgia. I remember their little daughter. What was her name?"

"Avery."

"Ah, yes. I heard she went to live with her mother when Georgia moved to Belize with that builder. I bet you'd love to have Avery around now."

"Why?" I wanted to say, "Why on earth?"

"She's Leo's only daughter. A living reminder of your dear dead husband. It would be the next best thing to bringing him back, I imagine."

I imagined not. Avery blamed me for her parents' divorce when even Mrs. VanDam knew that Georgia had fallen in love with a contractor before I came on the scene.

"Could we talk about why you're here?" I said. "I need to know who filed the complaints."

Mrs. VanDam reopened her folder. "The clients charging you with negligence are Mr. and Mrs. Robert Reitbauer of Chicago—"

No surprise there, I thought grimly.

"—Martha Glenn of Magnet Springs—"

I saw Martha at least twice a month when I patronized Town & Gown, located in one of my buildings. She had never complained although, as Peg observed, she was confused.

"—and Rico Anuncio, also of Magnet Springs."

"What's his beef?" I demanded. "I've never sold him real estate, and I don't own or manage the building where he lives and has his gallery."

She checked her notes. "He claims you've violated your contract. You've been negligent in your role as buyer's broker."

SEVENTEEN

THE CHARGE WAS PREPOSTEROUS. I'd never made a contract with Rico Anuncio.

Laura Bush's doppelganger disagreed. "He claims that he contracted with Mattimoe Realty to locate a property for purchase, and you have failed to represent his best interests. He says that you have repeatedly refused to follow instructions."

I asked Mrs. VanDam to let me read Rico's claim for myself. He alleged that we were "deliberately withholding suitable properties, including those listed by other realtors and those for sale by owner."

"Piffle!" I fumed, wondering even as I said it where I'd heard such a wimpy expletive. Probably from Laura Bush.

"*Piffle* what?" Odette was in my office doorway. She had struck her usual irreverent pose, arms crossed over her chest, hip and head cocked.

I introduced her to Jane VanDam and then presented Rico's complaint.

Odette sniffed. "What can Rico expect? He is most uncooperative."

Apparently, we needed to talk. I invited Mrs. VanDam to sample some coffee and pastry in our conference room. She went willingly. I wheeled on Odette. She was checking her scarlet fingernails from her perch on the edge of my desk.

"You signed a buyer's agreement with Rico? What were you thinking?"

"Handsome commission. What does anyone think about in this business?"

"I should have been informed!"

Odette shrugged. "Tina processed the paperwork. You should have got a copy."

Tina again. As if on cue, our wayward office manager was at my door, darlings in tow. I don't like children in the workplace, especially my workplace.

"You told me to bring them," Tina said, reading my mood.

"Yes, well—can you put them somewhere?"

She gave them each a juice box and dispatched them, loudly sucking, to another room. As I read the phone log and registered letters, I could hear Tina sniffling and Odette filing her nails.

"What I don't understand," I began, "is why you've both kept me out of the loop about my own business."

Odette replied, "We've tried to keep you in the loop, but you don't hear us since Leo died."

"Are you saying that I've been negligent?"

"I'm saying you've been distracted and disorganized and a real pain in the ass. Right, Tina?"

"Well, I don't think I'd put it—"

"Has Whiskey been a pain in the ass or not?" Odette demanded.

"She's been a pain in the ass," Tina sighed.

Everyone should have a pain—or be one—now and then. If only to appreciate the pain-free times when they roll around again. That's what I told Odette and Tina, but they merely stared at me. So I suggested we review the complaints.

Rico was a disgruntled buyer who felt we were holding out on him.

The Reitbauers claimed that I had failed to secure their home as per the terms of our property management contract. I expected as much from Mrs. R.

Martha Glenn's complaint concerned a damaged waterline, which she said had ruined her entire backroom stock. But Tina insisted that we had not received a single phone call or letter from anyone at Town & Gown, and Martha had never mentioned a problem to me.

I vowed to personally contact all three clients and find a way to make things right. As we concluded our meeting, Jane VanDam reappeared with Tina's sticky sons. She was smiling.

"They remind me of my grandchildren in North Dakota."

I assured her that I would promptly resolve every problem.

"You do that, dear." She no longer seemed interested. To Tina she said, "If you need a sitter, I'm available on very short notice."

Clients who are angry enough to complain to the Realtors Board sometimes sue. Whether they have a case or not—whether they win or not—is another matter. I found no comfort in Odette's and Tina's insistence that they had been covering for me. Within the past twenty-four hours, I had learned that I hadn't looked good and hadn't done good work since Leo died.

First, I phoned the Reitbauers at their Chicago home. The maid informed me that neither Mr. nor Mrs. was available, but I could leave a voicemail message for either or both. I opted for both. Having faced disgruntled clients before, I knew the kind of conciliatory song and dance required. The key is a genuine willingness to solve the problem. I expressed my concern, apologized for any inconvenience they had experienced, and asked them to call me toll-free any time to discuss what I could do to correct the matter. I made a note to myself to follow up the phone call with a letter.

Next I headed for Martha's Town & Gown. En route, I bought a dozen pink and white roses laced with baby's breath. Pink and white were the colors of the dress shop, and I knew that roses were Martha's favorite flower. She gasped when I came through the door.

"Dear me! It's not my birthday! Is it?"

I told her that didn't matter. What mattered was that we figure out what I could do to solve her problem.

"My problem?" She seemed clueless. So I reviewed her complaint. Martha blinked at me vaguely, her watery blue eyes framed by a fuzzy halo of snow-white hair.

"Why would I make trouble, dear? I'm very fond of you. And I adored Leo." Her voice trailed off. "What were we talking about?"

"We were talking about your problems with this property. Apparently, you had some water damage to your stock? I want to fix everything to your complete satisfaction."

A few more blinks and then the light flickered on.

"Oh! Yes! The pipe that broke! I remember now. I wondered what you were going to do about that."

Martha couldn't put her hands on any receipts, but she said she'd ask her assistant manager. On the spot, I wrote a check refunding her September rent, and I promised to cover repair and replacement costs. It would probably come straight out of my pocket since I doubted that she'd be able to provide the information my insurance company required.

"I need to know something, Martha. Did your assistant manager file the complaint against me with the Realtors Board?"

"Oh no, dear. That was me. I complained."

"Why didn't you call me first? We're old friends. And I shop here regularly."

"Well, I would have, but that young man from the Chamber was in here when the pipe burst, and he told me I should go right to the top. 'Martha, you need to complain to the Realtors Board about negligence like this.' That's what he said. And, well, I was so upset about the mess that I did what he told me. I'm sorry if that was wrong, but he seemed so sure of himself."

"Young man from the Chamber? Who do you mean?"

"Oh, you know—the artistic one." Martha was losing interest in our conversation as she arranged the roses in a crystal vase.

Magnet Springs being Magnet Springs, half our local business owners were artsy. Then it hit me.

"Do you mean Rico Anuncio?"

Martha didn't answer. She was fussing with a pink bud that didn't want to stand exactly where she'd placed it.

When I repeated myself, she glanced up.

"Oh! I didn't see you there. Did you need help with something, dear?"

Rico Anuncio didn't seem surprised when I strode into the West Shore Gallery.

"Having a nice day, Whiskey?"

"It'll be nicer once I figure out what's bothering you."

"What could be bothering me? I'm a happy man, about to be happier yet."

I recounted my conversations with Jane VanDam and Martha Glenn.

"What's your problem with me?" I demanded.

"I am a man of means, Whiskey, and I expect to be treated as such. You and Odette have been holding out on me."

"You were at the Open House for our Featured Home, weren't you?"

He snorted. "It was an Open House. Odette didn't offer it to me; I arrived with the uninvited masses! The only properties she's shown me are four-room cottages five miles from the beach, every single one of them listed by Mattimoe Realty."

I took a deep breath. "What exactly would you like us to show you, Rico?"

"The very best of the Coast, offered for sale by every agency and owner."

I promised we would do that starting today. Then I forced myself to apologize even though it made my ribs hurt.

Rico said, "Someone was asking about you."

"Who?"

"A guy came in here Saturday. I think he said his name was Keogh. He wanted to know if you still had that Afghan hound."

I no longer cared about the damned finger. Just about Abra and Chester and the sanctity of my own home. As I rounded the bend before Vestige, an oncoming stretch limo honked at me. I checked my rear-view mirror. Was that Chester's arm waving from the passenger window?

Sinister scenarios played in my brain:

(1) Chester honking for help as he was kidnapped by Darrin Keogh.

(2) Chester rushing Abra to the vet after she'd been injured by Darrin Keogh.

(3) Chester banished to boarding school because I'd refused to keep him during Cassina's World Tour.

My car phone rang. It was Chester.

"My father wants to see me! He sent this limo! I'm catching a plane to L.A.!"

Without thinking, I said, "I didn't know you had a father."

"Stop the car!" Chester bellowed. Over the phone I heard brakes squeal.

"I didn't mean to upset you," I said.

"You didn't. Abra's in the middle of the road!"

"Dead?"

"No. She's a mess, though. I bet she'll need a week at the doggie spa."

I heard the limo door open and Chester call her name. Then I heard the driver mutter something in a foreign language. Probably something about the mess Abra was tracking into his limo.

Back on the line, Chester said, "We're turning around, Whiskey. I'm bringing Abra home!"

"What about your father?"

"Rupert's waited eight years to meet me. I guess he can wait a little longer." Chester lowered his voice so the driver couldn't hear. "Should I check the purse for the finger, or do you want to do it when we get home?"

EIGHTEEN

I wasn't sure whether Abra was happy to see me, but I was relieved beyond words to have that piece of Leo back in my life. Burrs and all. Chester's toothless smile touched my heart, too. I wished I had a steak on hand so that they could share it, cheek to jowl.

Jenx arrived within four minutes of our 9-1-1 call. Chester timed it on his techno-wonder watch and proclaimed a new record in rapid response. As Jenx snapped on a pair of surgical gloves, I looked away. Then I heard the rustle of paper.

"No finger in here. But there's a message for you, Whiskey."

"A message for me?"

"Before I let you read it, you've got to promise not to overreact."

"How can I know what's overreacting until I see it?"

"Fair enough." Jenx passed me a folded piece of notebook paper. I opened it, read it, and screamed.

"*That* was overreacting," she said.

Maybe. But the unsigned note was a list of sexual fantasies involving my dog. The last line said, "I could have my way with her, but I'm letting her go. If she leads me to what's mine, I'll leave her alone. Stay out of it."

"This has got to be from that wacko Darrin Keogh!" I said. "It's his sick-puppy routine, only now he wants a dead man's finger!"

"More likely his ring," said Jenx.

"Either you call the MSP, or I will!"

"I already did. They're sending a cruiser." Jenx checked her Timex. "My response time is much better."

"Did you tell them about the finger?"

"Not yet. But I told them about the missing dog and the threatening messages."

Chester said, "You've got to tell them about the finger!"

"I will. And I'll insist that we work together. Balboa says those boys need our help as much as we need theirs."

Chester looked worried. "Will you get in trouble for withholding evidence?"

Jenx ruffled his hair, which was already standing on end. "I don't think so, Deputy. Withholding evidence depends on intent. My intent is and always has been to solve this crime."

Abra yipped and initiated a spirited *pas de deux* with Chester.

"That dog needs a bath," Jenx said, fanning the air.

"And a shave and a bodyguard. So do I." When Jenx looked at me, I said, "I need the bodyguard."

We heard a siren.

"Finally, the state boys," announced Chester. He frowned at his watch. "Their response time is unacceptable!"

Abra, Chester, and I hung back while Jenx went to greet the officer. He was one of those wrestler-types with wrap-around reflective sunglasses that stay on all shift. I asked Chester what he thought Abra had done with the finger.

He cocked his head at her, and she returned the look.

"She's too excited to talk about it, Whiskey."

"You know that by looking at her?"

"Body language is eighty-five percent of canine communication."

Apparently, Jenx's body language wasn't serving her so well. I watched as she thrust the purse and note toward the officer, who jumped back as if stung. I half-expected him to reach for his sidearm. He recovered quickly, folding burly arms across his chest as he listened to Jenx's story. A few minutes later, she was striding toward us, fists clenched.

"You okay?" I asked. "The last time your face was that red, the Holy Spirit joined us."

"Boy Officer insists I 'come in' with him and answer questions."

"Before he talks to *me*?"

"It's not about you, Whiskey. It's about whether or not I've impeded a police investigation."

"But I'm in danger here! Well—I could be. Abra could be, for sure."

"Call Brady and ask him to look out for you till I get back. I have to follow the kid in my car."

Boy Officer was in his cruiser already, talking on the radio. He never glanced our way.

"Will she lose her job?" Chester said, hugging Abra, who had nodded off.

"Not Jenx. She's a player."

"What does that mean?"

"She's . . . like Abra. Nobody beats her at her own game."

Abra gave a sleepy woof of agreement, her head resting on Chester's bare knees. I thought about poison ivy and wondered if it was already too late.

"Chester, you should wash with Fels Naptha right now!" Not that I was sure what that was or where to get any. I seemed to be channeling my mother.

"Okay . . . but can I take Abra to a safe house?"

He explained that Rupert's private plane was standing by to fly him to L.A.

"Rupert said I could bring a friend. And we'll all be better off if Abra's with me."

A tempting offer, but I pointed out the tangles and twigs in her coat. Chester swore he'd get her a makeover and keep working the program while they were gone.

"What program?" I asked.

"Dogs-Train-You-dot-com, remember? The secret to our success."

I wasn't sure we'd had any. And I couldn't in good conscience inflict Abra on a stranger, even a man who'd never bothered to know his son.

Chester said, "No problem. Cassina says he's having his first 'bout of guilt,' so I should make the most of it. Besides, he has a beach house in Malibu. Abra will feel right at home."

For Rupert's sake, I hoped not.

"Do you even know if your father likes dogs? He could be allergic."

Chester shook his head. "Cassina says he picks up strays all the time."

She could be speaking metaphorically, but I let that go. Maybe it would be safer for everyone if Abra were gone. It would certainly be simpler.

"What does your father do for a living?"

"He was a musician in my mom's band. Now he's a Hollywood producer. Cassina says he had a near-death experience and saw God. That's why he wants to meet me."

I told Chester to call me if he had any problems. I expected to hear from him soon.

Brady assured me that he and Officer Roscoe would swing by later, so I decided to work at home. With Abra gone, my alarm system activated, and police protection on the way, I felt safe from Sparky.

I told my receptionist to forward only those calls that qualified as urgent or lucrative. The first time the phone rang, I figured it was too soon to be Chester.

"How dare you?" a familiar voice demanded.

"Pardon?"

"How dare you try to sweet-talk my husband out of seeking restitution? Thanks to you, our beautiful beach home was like totally trashed, and our priceless Matheney got stolen!"

At least the savage murder didn't bother Mrs. R.

"My husband is a very busy, very important man. He will not play the fool," she declared. "So don't phone us again. You'll hear from our attorneys."

"That's unnecessary. I'm willing to do whatever it takes—"

"We're taking you to court. For negligence. Remember the clause in our contract about screening tenants? The people you rented to weren't even the people you said they were. They were like . . . Canadian criminals!"

They were precisely Canadian criminals, but I didn't say so.

"You approved Mrs. Santy as tenant," I reminded her.

"Do you have that in writing? No, you don't! And our contract says you have to."

She was right about that. In the interest of saving time, I had accepted her verbal approval over the phone.

"That's not all, Mrs. Mattimoe. *Your* fingerprints were all over *our* house!"

"Because you asked me to remove valuables to your bedroom safe."

"Then why did you leave our most valuable possession to be stolen?"

"Because it wasn't on your list to be locked up!"

"Oh, but it was, Mrs. Mattimoe. You put the wrong fucking picture in the safe!"

I mentally replayed reading the list and stashing the goods. I had locked up a small watercolor that was *not* the Matheney before I even knew what a Matheney was. But I had locked up the right watercolor, the one stipulated in Mrs. R.'s instructions.

She said, "The Magnet Springs police will testify that your dog had our Matheney. It's in their report. And your dog is a known felon!"

"My dog retrieved your Matheney!"

"For *you*, Mrs. Mattimoe! And when that didn't work, you went back in and got it again."

"That's ridiculous!"

"We'll see what a jury says."

I paced my office until my heart rate slowed. When the phone rang again, I wasn't sure I wanted to answer.

"I owe you an apology, Mrs. Mattimoe."

"Who is this?"

"Robert Reitbauer. I believe you just spoke with my wife."

"Oh. Yes."

"I apologize on her behalf. Kimba has been . . . well, overly emotional since the problems at Shadow Play."

Ah, yes—*Kimba*. I had forgotten Mrs. R.'s first name.

"I let her oversee our real estate interests. I suppose you could call it her little hobby."

And my little livelihood.

"Kimba is used to getting what she wants, and she wants to take you to court. I'll do my best to convince her otherwise and to keep our attorneys at bay. But you'll have to let the matter go, Mrs. Mattimoe. Stop calling and aggravating her."

I assured him I would.

Mr. Reitbauer added, "I believe you had good intentions."

Not exactly a professional commendation. I summoned enough grace to thank him, anyway. We had barely disconnected when Odette buzzed.

"I took that call first, Whiskey, and I'm sure of one thing: the caller was not Mr. Reitbauer."

"I hope your telephone telepathy is wrong this time. We don't need a lawsuit."

"You don't need your stepdaughter, either, but she's here."

That was a shocker. "Avery's in the lobby? What does she want?"

Odette lowered her voice. "I haven't asked, but from the looks of her, a maternity wardrobe would be nice."

NINETEEN

AVERY MATTIMOE WAS NEVER my friend. She was in her mid-teens when her father married me. By then, she and her mother Georgia had already moved to Belize with a hunky builder named Garth. Once upon a time, Garth and Leo had been partners. That was how Garth met Georgia, and the two fell in love. Yet Avery convinced herself that the divorce was my fault. Maybe she just liked Garth better than she liked me. She sure didn't want to share Leo. The distance between Central America and Middle America made visitation difficult. Avery spent the first couple Christmases and summer vacations with us. From then on she begged Leo to meet her for visits in more exotic locations. I hadn't seen her in three years—except at Leo's funeral. And that was a painful blur.

My late beloved was going to be a grandpa in absentia. I couldn't imagine Avery pregnant. She was about as maternal as—well, as I was. Maybe less.

Though I already knew the answer, I asked Odette to ask Avery whether she would rather meet me for lunch at the Goh Cup or drive out to Vestige.

Odette said, "She wants to come 'home.'"

I was sure she had put it just that way. Odette asked me to hold a moment. Back on the line, she said, "I'm watching her squeeze her big belly into her little Honda CRX. Cute car, but you'll need to buy her a minivan."

"I'm sure it's on her list."

I scrambled to find something, anything, edible in the house. Without Chester around to nag me, I hadn't gone to the store. So I called Walter St. Mary at Mother Tucker's and implored him to send over a couple of wonderful lunches for Leo's daughter and me. Inspired, he said he'd deliver them himself.

"I remember what a sweet tooth Avery used to have," he said. "And how she loved her cherries: cherry pop, cherry pie, cherry ice cream, cherry tarts."

I winced.

Walter added, "Jonny saw her in the Goh Cup this morning. He said that must be one big baby she's carrying."

I watched my estranged and enlarged stepdaughter pry herself from her car. Once standing, she stuck her tongue out. That didn't mean she knew I was watching. Avery sticks her tongue out many times a day. What started as a childhood gesture of insolence evolved into a grotesque nervous tic. Maybe, once upon a time, Leo or Georgia told her it was cute. Not anymore.

"I didn't come here for a lecture," she said the instant I opened the door.

"Fine by me. So how the hell are you?"

"Fat, bored, and flat broke. Pregnant, too, in case you can't tell."

Just for the fun of it, I waited a beat for her to ask me how I was. It didn't happen. I let her come in anyway. She lumbered over to the picture window and stared out.

"I can't believe my dad left this place to you."

Willing my blood pressure to stay in the non-stroking range, I replied, "I put as much of my own money into this property as Leo did. We owned it together."

"Most of his estate went to you!"

"We co-owned everything. Debts and all."

She stuck her tongue out. "That's what tenants are for, right? To pay the mortgage? Nobody's paying my bills."

In a controlled voice, I said, "What about your trust fund?"

Avery snorted. "What about it? It's like a joke!"

"Well, tell that 'joke' to everyone who doesn't have a trust fund—which is almost everyone."

"It won't pay enough to live on till I'm thirty! Even then, I'll probably have to work."

"I believe that was Leo's intent."

She narrowed her eyes at me. "But he didn't know I'd be a mother, did he?"

"I think he assumed you might breed eventually."

Groaning, she lowered herself into the largest chair in the room. Her lack of resemblance to Leo had always helped me maintain an emotional distance. She had never seemed genuinely linked to her father or our life. Now that he was gone, and she was here, I felt a wave of overwhelming resentment.

"You don't understand family obligation, do you, Whiskey?"

That made *me* want to stick my tongue out. "Gosh. I think I understand it as well as the next Daughter-Sister-Wife-Stepmother."

Avery blinked. "I guess that's what Dad saw in you. You're almost funny. You've even got funny hair."

My unruly curls had never amused anyone, least of all me and my hair stylist.

"I remember how you made Dad laugh, how he used to play with the hair on your neck when he sat by you. That made me crazy."

"Why?"

"Because it meant he loved you without even thinking about it."

Leo had done that. It was such an old, subtle habit that I hadn't thought about it in ages. That didn't mean I didn't miss it, though. Suddenly, I missed it so acutely that I had to bolt for the kitchen.

"What would you like to drink?" I called back to her.

It didn't matter since she was having what I was having, the only drink in the house: tap water. I would have offered it on the rocks if the icemaker were working.

A few minutes later we sat on the terrace overlooking Lake Michigan, sipping lukewarm water in strained silence and waiting for Walter to arrive with our food. Finally I worked up the nerve to ask when she was due.

Avery flicked her eyes away. "I'm in my third trimester."

"So . . . you're, what, seven months? Eight?"

I was no expert on pregnancy, but Avery seemed enormous. No way she'd be able to drive her CRX to term. Even in her slender days, she'd been a big-boned gal like her mom. I guessed she weighed two hundred pounds.

"Must be one big baby!" I quipped, echoing Walter and Jonny.

"It's two big babies."

"Two?" I stared at her stupidly.

"I'm having twins, Whiskey. Fraternal twins."

"Fraternal?" For an instant I thought she meant the father was Sigma Beta Chi.

"*Not* identical. I'm carrying a boy and a girl."

Stalling for inspiration, I downed my entire glass of water. Then I said, "Is that so? Well, well. Do they have a name?"

"If you mean a last name, I'm giving them mine. Their father is out of this. I'm doing it all on my own. And I need a place to have my babies."

"You mean like a hospital?"

"No, I mean like here. A place to live. Till the twins get older and I get my life back."

"Avery, I hate to tell you this, but your life with twins is never going to be like your life before twins."

"I know that! But if I have help, it won't be bad."

"What kind of help are you talking about?"

"A nanny. And a personal assistant."

"Excuse me?"

"There's plenty of room for live-in help at Vestige. My dad would have wanted me here. With his grandchildren."

She stuck her tongue out. I was tempted to do the same.

"We have no way of knowing that since your father is dead."

"Well, I know it! And I know I have a right to stay!" She burst into tears. A flood of snotty, smeary tears. Some women are pretty when they cry. Avery Mattimoe isn't one of them. As I handed her a box of tissues, a consoling notion struck me: the mother-to-be had a mother.

"Georgia must be thrilled about having grandchildren."

"Ha! She thinks I've ruined my life. I'm never talking to her again."

"Let's not be hasty. I'm sure she would love to help."

"There's no room for me in her life, let alone two babies. Did you know that her boyfriend is my age?"

"What happened to Garth?"

"History. When he got fat and lost his hair, my mom lost interest. She's into the club scene now. Since she had a face lift, tummy tuck, and boob job, she thinks she's twenty-five. She has more tattoos and piercings than I do."

I didn't care to picture that. Quietly I said, "Avery, you can't stay here."

"Why not?"

"Because your father is dead, and I'm not your mother, and we don't even like each other."

"I don't like most people! What's your point?"

"I'm not a child-care provider." I was growing very tired of explaining that.

"So hire someone! You can afford to."

"Avery, sweetheart!" Walter St. Mary appeared on the terrace with Mother Tucker's succor, so to speak.

Avery began sobbing anew. Walter reached out to comfort her. I reached out to take the food. That was when we heard the shot. Mother Tucker's vegetable lasagna, which Walter was still holding, exploded. He reeled back, I hit the ground, and Avery screamed. I might have screamed, too; I don't remember. What I do remember is seeing an immense pair of bright yellow wings drift up and out of sight beyond the dunes.

TWENTY

"The shooter used a long-range deer rifle, a 30.06, with ballistic-tip ammo. That much we're sure of," said Brady. He eyed me uncertainly. "You say he escaped in a hang glider."

"I saw it!"

Brady scratched Officer Roscoe behind the ears. "I'm sure you think you saw it, Whiskey. Yesterday you thought you saw Abra."

"I did see Abra, as it turned out! She came back, remember? Then she left again, this time for California."

Brady said, "Yesterday you needed a brain scan."

"Well, today I need police protection! Someone's trying to kill me, and we already know who it is!"

"You mean Darrin Keogh."

"A.K.A. Sparky the Sicko. When is Jenx going to get here? She knows what I'm talking about."

"The state police are questioning her about the Reitbauers' missing watercolor and the missing bodies bound for Canada and the missing girl from Grand Rapids and the missing finger with the missing ring. It could take a while."

"Are you sure Walter will be all right?" I asked.

"Minor flesh wound. But the lasagna is history."

"And Avery?"

"I checked with Peg Goh. She said Avery could stay with her, so I sent her over. That lady's the best at calming people down. Ironic, isn't it?"

"Why?"

"She's in the caffeine business."

I asked Brady whether the state police would bring Keogh in.

"They might want to question him, but there's something you need to know. With or without a hang glider, Darrin Keogh couldn't have shot at you."

"Why the hell not?"

"Because he was selling antiques and collectibles in Angola, Indiana."

"How can you know that?"

"I called the Angola Chief of Police. She personally vouches for Keogh. Said she stopped by his store at noon to discuss church business. They take turns delivering meals to shut-ins."

I groaned. Brady continued, "Nobody could get here from Angola, Indiana, in an hour. Glider or no glider."

"Maybe the man she saw wasn't Keogh! Or maybe he hired someone to shoot me!"

"The chief says she's known Keogh for years. He's practically a saint."

"He's a perv among pervs! He's . . . the perviest!"

"The chief says he sings in the choir, helps maintain the church cemetery, reads to the blind—"

"Oh, shut up." I buried my face in my hands. Roscoe began licking my fingers.

"Is he trained to do that? To comfort victims?"

"There's lasagna on your fingers."

When my telephone rang, I welcomed the distraction. But Chester's voice made my heart clench. No way he'd made it to California already. Plus, he was using his extra-high Tina Breen voice, which always meant trouble. I told him to take a breath and start over.

"Abra ran away again! We stopped at the Canine Coastal Salon on our way to the airport, like you said we should. When we came out, Abra froze, like she saw something in the distance. She was staring and growling and her hackles went up. And then she took off! I'm sorry, Whiskey!"

"Calm down. She probably saw a squirrel. She'll come back in an hour or two. Or tomorrow. Or the next day."

"No! She jumped into a car! Somebody at the other end of the parking lot opened their passenger door, and she jumped in. Then the car pulled away! I tried to order my driver to follow them, but he doesn't speak English. We lost her again, Whiskey!"

Calmly, I asked what kind of car it was. Chester said it was a Beamer. He was sure because half the kids at his school have them. This one was dark blue. I asked Chester if he'd seen the license plate. He hadn't.

He said he felt too depressed to go to California now. I told him that was why people go to California, to feel better. Or was it to feel nothing at all? I told him to go, and I promised to call the minute I knew something about Abra. I thought it best not to mention the shooting incident or the hang glider or the fraternal twins. Even in California, Chester wouldn't need one more thing to obsess about.

When I hung up, Brady was concluding a call on his cell phone.

"I owe you an apology, Whiskey. DNR reports an unauthorized hang glider on the dunes in the state park at the time of the shooting."

"Bright yellow wings?"

He nodded. I told him the latest Abra story, insisting that Sparky was here. Brady said he was sorry, but he had to believe a fellow officer of the law. Suddenly I knew what I had to do, and I told him. He hated the idea.

"If you go to Angola, we can't help you, Whiskey. That's not our jurisdiction."

"But you said Keogh is practically a saint! If that's true, we have no problem. If it's not, I'll bring back evidence."

Brady threatened to hang crime scene tape around my terrace if I left town. I dared him to. He said he supposed he should head over to the Coastal Canine Salon.

"Thank you!" I said. "So Officer Roscoe can sniff out clues!"

"I was thinking he needed a makeover."

I called Odette to tell her I might be away overnight, depending on what I found out in Angola. She had already heard about the hang glider.

"I can see why you don't want to sleep at Vestige, but why Indiana? You could stay at our house. It would be a nice change for you: we have food."

I thanked her but declined. Odette added that Rico Anuncio had just phoned with the best offer on this month's Featured Home.

"How is that possible?" I said.

"Same story he gave at the Open House: he recently came into money and expects to come into more. If he gets his dream home, he might not sue you."

"Sue *us*, you mean."

I asked Odette to stop at Vestige a little later in case Abra was trying to get in.

She said, "Why don't you install one of those doggie flaps so she can come and go as she pleases?"

"Abra already does that. That's the problem."

Odette said, "If Avery is scratching at the door, should I let her in?"

"No way."

I grabbed a map and my overnight bag, just in case. This would be my first road trip since recovering from the accident. I stared at Leo's photo on the mantel.

"I've got to confront the creep you kept away from us," I said aloud. I slid his picture, like a talisman, into my bag.

Although I had never been to Angola, Indiana, I was confident that I could find my way. In fact, I immediately spotted For Art's Sake on Maumee Street less than a block from the soldiers' monument in the center of town. My problem wasn't finding the place; my problem was finding it open. Since Indiana doesn't follow Michigan into daylight savings time, I'd gained an hour on the trip in. Still, I reached the door exactly seven minutes after closing. Locked up tight. I could see lights on inside, though, through the narrow frosted panels on both sides of the door. I knocked. Hard.

Who should open it but a dead woman known as Ellianna Santy. She looked very much alive but not the least bit happy to see me. She slammed the door in my face.

The store had to have a rear exit. I started running full-out down the sidewalk toward the corner of the building. Then my pesky quadriceps piped up. They wished to remind me that I'd just spent two hours in a car and hadn't bothered to stretch. Gasping in pain, I forced my legs to keep pumping. I rounded the back of the building in time to see a door fly open and two fair-haired figures rush out. One paused to play with the lock on the door while the other leapt into a midnight-blue Beamer. The driver gunned the engine, roared forward and narrowly missed me.

Darrin Keogh was still trying to lock his back door.

"Nothing works the way you think it should," he said quietly. I wondered whether he meant hardware or a life of crime.

When he turned to me, I expected to feel the force of evil. Whatever that is. But close up, Darrin Keogh seemed about as sinister as Chester.

"How about a beer, Mrs. Mattimoe? There's a nice little bar across the street. Seeing how you've come all this way, I'd say I owe you a drink."

"She's supposed to be dead!"

I had waited as long as I could before saying it. We were sitting across from each other in The Boot, which may or may not have been a nice little bar. It was definitely a dark little bar. I could barely make out Darrin Keogh's face, but he seemed to be pressing a finger to his lips. I lowered my voice and leaned closer. "She's wanted by the police!"

"Not if the police think she's dead."

"Two bodies are missing! And they're not the bodies we thought they were."

He shook his head. I couldn't tell if he was disagreeing with me or just reminding me to be quiet. "Tell me why you're here."

I peered at Darrin Keogh through the darkness. "Did you shoot at me with a deer rifle today? And then escape in a hang glider from the dunes?"

He laughed so hard he nearly spilled his Amstel Lite.

"Do I look like the deer-hunting, hang-gliding type?"

"You don't look like a dog molester, either, but you are!"

That came out louder than intended. I could feel, if not see, several heads swivel our way. The bar was suddenly silent.

"How about coming over to my house?" Keogh said. "It's two blocks from here, on Superior Street. You need to see something."

"I don't think so, thank you." I sounded like a Sunday School teacher declining Satan. But I knew Darrin Keogh was no devil. In the flesh, in the dark, he seemed like a dweeb.

"Give me a half-hour, counting the walk over," he said. When I hesitated, he raised his voice in the still-quiet bar. "Everybody here knows I'm taking you to my house. You couldn't be safer. Right, everybody?"

There was a murmur of amused consensus. One male voice rasped, "His mama will make sure of that."

A chorus of ragged laughter followed us out the door. In the slanting early-evening light, I studied Darrin Keogh. He was short, pale, and bookish with wire-rim glasses. His pants were two inches too short.

"I'm onto you, Sparky," I said menacingly.

"I'm *not* Sparky." He adjusted his glasses. "You're all wrong about this."

"Do you have my dog? Or does Mrs. Santy? Where are you hiding Abra?"

He shook his head and started up the sidewalk.

I caught up with him. "Why were you in Magnet Springs asking Rico Anuncio about me? Why do you want to hurt me and my dog?"

"You need to see some things."

TWENTY-ONE

As we passed the Angola Police Department, I quipped, "How convenient that you hang out with the Chief."

Keogh said, "We sing in the choir at First Methodist. And we both teach Sunday School. I baby-sit her kids."

"You're kidding."

"They call me Uncle Darrin."

I let him walk a few yards ahead of me. About five feet seven inches tall, Keogh was soft, with round shoulders and thinning sandy hair. All in all, not a scary man. More like an invisible one.

His home turned out to be the best maintained of three Victorians on a block of ranch houses. Neatly trimmed burning-bushes and clumps of bright chrysanthemums lined his front lawn.

"Sweet property," I murmured.

"Leo liked it."

"Leo was here?"

"Three times. Twice before you were married."

That's when the barking began. It sounded like three or four dogs. When Keogh opened the front door, I saw six. All of them beautiful. All of them Afghan hounds.

"Meet Souriya, Badria, Pashtoon, Ajmal, Wali, and Nadir. Of course, their kennel names are longer."

Keogh ordered them to sit. Incredibly, they all did.

"These are yours?" I asked, slow on the uptake.

"I used to breed them, but there's less demand these days. Probably a good thing. Such a magnificent and ancient bloodline requires a dedicated owner, as you well know."

No comment from this party. A large black Affie barked his assent.

"Wali should know," Keogh said. "He's the boss of us all."

"Darrin, is that you?" A querulous voice floated down the curving staircase.

"Yes, Mother. I'll be up in a moment."

Keogh smiled sheepishly. "Correction: She's the boss of us all, but we let Wali think he is."

"Wali should meet Abra," I murmured.

"He has. Wali is Abra's father. And Souriya is her mother. Can you see the family resemblance?"

Souriya, a demure blonde, was smaller and less exuberant than Abra, who had inherited her mother's coloring and her father's gusto.

"Leo bought Abra here?" I was trying to catch up.

"That's part of the story, but nowhere near the beginning. Please sit down. You'll need to be sitting when you hear this."

I would have preferred to lie down. That way I could have let the facts wash over me like the waves on Lake Michigan. Darrin Keogh was overwhelming me.

"When she was fourteen and I was twenty, I fell in love with Avery Mattimoe. I was a counselor at Camp Crystal, about thirty miles from here. Leo sent Avery there for the summer while he and his first wife finalized their divorce. Avery hated Camp Crystal. She was furious at Leo and frightened that her mother would make her move to Belize.

"That wasn't a great year for me, either. My father had just died, and my mother's health was frail. I saw my future written on these walls: I'd end up stuck in Angola taking care of her for the rest of her life."

"Did you say you were twenty and Avery was fourteen?" I tried to keep the "yuck" out of my voice.

Keogh said, "Age is just a number. Our relationship wasn't sexual. It was romantic."

"What was the attraction?"

He looked surprised. "Maybe you don't know Avery. She's a sensitive, gifted artist. I knew it the first day I saw her paint. She belonged in a first-tier art school, not some backwater in Belize."

According to Keogh, Leo misinterpreted their friendship. Something Avery said in a letter home caused Leo to yank her out of Camp Crystal three weeks before the season ended. Leo informed the camp management that Counselor Keogh had seduced a minor. He was promptly dismissed.

"My supervisor said I was lucky Leo didn't press charges. Avery felt awful, but it wasn't her fault. We wrote letters, sent emails, talked on the phone. Avery would have rather died than go to Belize. That's when I thought of Uncle Warren."

"Who?"

"My uncle—Warren Matheney, the water colorist."

"Cloud Man was your uncle?"

"My mom's younger brother. The one that got away—from Angola. Seven years ago, he was coming up fast. I thought he could help Avery."

"How?"

"He knew people in Chicago. Important people who taught art and bought art. I thought maybe he could introduce her, help her make connections. But Leo wouldn't listen. Until Avery tried to kill herself."

I hadn't known about that.

Keogh said, "I'm not sure how serious the attempt was, but it got Leo's attention. He agreed to meet my uncle. The four of us met right here in this room to discuss Avery's future."

My eyes followed his to a small framed cloudscape on the far wall. "Is that a —?"

"Cumulus. One of Uncle Warren's first. He gave it to my mother years ago. I should probably lock it up. But this is Angola, not Chicago."

And not Magnet Springs, I thought, crossing to the picture. It was remarkably like the one stolen from Shadow Play. Then again, how many ways can you paint cumulus clouds?

"Uncle Warren agreed to help Leo enroll Avery in a private fine-arts school outside Chicago. Then Leo tried to make up for the trouble he'd caused at camp. He bought the failing antiques shop where I was working and hired me to run it. I promised to buy him out as soon as I could find another backer."

"What went wrong? Avery ended up in Belize, anyway, and you kidnapped Abra."

"That's not what happened."

Keogh explained that Avery had been homesick and vulnerable at art school. He stayed away from her, partly out of respect for Leo and partly out of necessity since he was struggling to run his shop. Warren Matheney, a part-time faculty member and Avery's first friend in Chicago, abused his position. Sexual comments gave way to sexual advances. Avery confided in Keogh, who confronted his uncle. Nothing changed, however. If anything, Matheney seemed more determined to seduce her. One night he locked his office door and pressured her to pleasure him. The next day, she called her mother and begged for a ticket to Belize.

"Leo thought I had betrayed him—again. He demanded his loan money back. I didn't have any cash. If he'd known where I had to get it from, I doubt he would have taken it."

"Your uncle?"

Keogh nodded.

"And yet Leo bought Abra from you a few years later? I don't get it."

"Because of you, Mrs. Mattimoe."

"Me?"

"Leo called me two years ago. He said his 'charming wife' had seen her first Afghan hound and fallen in love. He wanted one for her."

I knew what Keogh was talking about. One afternoon I'd watched a tourist walking an Afghan hound in downtown Magnet Springs. Its grace and gloss had mesmerized me.

Keogh said, "Leo remembered meeting our dogs when he was here with Uncle Warren. He ordered one for you."

"You're leaving out so much. What about the dog show? The threatening letters? Mrs. Santy—?"

"Leo got the wrong dog."

"Pardon?"

"Leo reserved a different dog, not Abra. I wasn't here when he came to pick his up. My mother gave him the wrong pup."

"And Leo never found out?"

"Of course he did. I called him immediately. But he wouldn't return Abra. He insisted she was the one he wanted."

"What happened to the other one?"

Keogh looked uneasy. "She . . . went to Uncle Warren. He had reserved Abra and wasn't happy, to say the least, about the confusion. Once again, I had a problem."

"When you approached Leo at the dog show, were you trying to get Abra back?"

"For Uncle Warren. He told me to offer Leo a lot of money."

"And after that, why not let it go? Why the threatening phone calls and the sick letters?"

"That wasn't me, Mrs. Mattimoe. I never contacted Leo again."

"You're saying you didn't write the sick notes?"

"I could never do that." His expression was earnest.

"But you knew about them, didn't you? Who wrote them?"

He gazed sadly at the Cumulus watercolor. It didn't seem to soothe him.

"Darrin! Are you down there, Darrin? It's time for my dinner!"

Keogh rose. "I'm sorry, Mrs. Mattimoe. My mother keeps a strict schedule."

"But you haven't finished explaining!"

"I've told you all I can."

"What about Mrs. Santy? Why was she at your shop? Why is she pretending to be dead?"

The shrill voice came again. "Can't you hear me? I'm *hungry*! I want my dinner *now*!"

Two of the dogs whined in sympathy. Keogh said, "I promised you a half-hour, Mrs. Mattimoe, and that's what you got. Please leave now."

A cream-colored Afghan hound with a charming black mask followed us to the door.

"Which one is this?" I asked.

Keogh said her name was Pashtoon. Suddenly I understood.

"She's the one Leo reserved, isn't she? What happened to her eye?"

"She . . . had an accident when she was a puppy."

"An accident?"

"No, not an accident," he admitted. "My uncle was a mean man, Mrs. Mattimoe. I'm glad he's dead."

TWENTY-TWO

I SAT IN MY car a long time before turning the key. How much I didn't know about Leo. How much I would never know. And then there were the scattered pieces, like the ones Keogh had shared, which I had no way to understand or verify. Almost no way.

On my car phone I called Peg Goh. I needed to talk with my step-daughter.

"Avery's all right," Peg assured me. "But she's not here. She's with Noonan, getting tele-counseled, only they're doing it face-to-face."

"What are you talking about?"

"You know—the Seven Suns of . . . Something. I might try it, too. When you're local, you don't have to do it over the phone."

"You're kidding, right? You feel the same way about New Age that I do!"

"Not necessarily. I believe in personal growth."

I changed the subject. "Have you seen Jenx today?"

"After the state police grilled her, she came in," Peg said. "Ordered an extra-large espresso to go, so you know she was hurting. I think she's still at the station."

159

I asked her to have Avery call me, and then I dialed Jenx.

"She's alive and well in Angola, Indiana!" I announced.

"You found Abra?" asked Jenx.

"No! I found Mrs. Santy—for a minute. And now I'm coming home."

From the Indiana Toll Way, I recounted my adventures. Jenx listened without comment.

"Are you all right?" I could hear crackling, which might have been a mounting magnetic force.

"Rough day. I'm crumpling my notes. So you're saying Mrs. Santy is alive and well and driving Keogh's BMW?"

"Yes. How can Keogh afford a late-model Beamer? I never got inside his store, but his house is modest. Except for the six Afghan hounds. And the Cumulus."

I explained the Warren Matheney connection.

"All you know about Keogh is what he wants you to know," said Jenx. "Take some free advice from your local law enforcement: Doubt everybody. Especially the guy hanging out with the dead woman."

I reminded her that Angola's Police Chief had vouched for Keogh.

"Just that he was minding his store this morning," Jenx said.

"But he loves dogs and takes care of his sick mother."

"Did you see his mother?"

"No, but I heard her. She kept shouting at him."

"Uh-huh." Jenx did not sound convinced.

"The dogs are healthy. One had a bad eye, but that was Matheney's fault."

"Right."

When I protested, Jenx said, "You're the one who called him Sparky the Sicko, remember?"

"All right. But I saw Mrs. Santy! She slammed a door in my face."

"That sounds like Ellianna. I'll tell the MSP she's in Angola."

"How did your interview go?"

"They want to ask me more questions tomorrow."

"If they want to talk to me—"

"It's not about you, Whiskey."

Cruising across northern Indiana, I checked my voicemail. With vicarious lust, Tina reported that Judge Verbelow needed to talk to me about a "personal matter." Odette checked in to say that there was no sign of Abra at Vestige although Chester was hanging around.

"He said he was too worried to go to California," Odette said. "I told him California is where you go to forget you're worried."

I sincerely hoped Brady had not strung crime scene tape around my terrace after I left. God knows what Chester would make of that.

I was already west of South Bend when my car phone rang. Expecting to hear Avery's voice, I was pleasantly surprised to find Wells Verbelow on the line.

"Tina gave me your number. I hope you don't mind . . ."

Of course she did, and of course I didn't. He said he had something "urgent" to show me.

"Is there a problem?" I said.

He assured me that all was well and wondered what time I'd be back in Magnet Springs. My ETA was about 9:30, allowing for a burger stop. Growling innards reminded me that I hadn't eaten lunch or dinner. Consorting with criminals wreaks havoc with your digestion.

"How about coming straight to my house—if you can last that long? I'll cook something for you. Do you like lake perch?"

I hoped he hadn't heard about Abra's latest vanishing act. When I arrived Wells greeted me by laying a finger across his lips and leading me to the guest room. Sprawled across a chenille bedspread lay Abra.

"Dead?" I gasped. She opened one eye and thumped her tail twice. Then she fell back to sleep.

The Judge said, "Did you ever notice how, in profile, she looks like Sarah Jessica Parker?"

He was right. Wells explained that Abra leapt into his car at the Coastal Strip Mall, where Chester had taken her for a makeover. She looked good—despite the pink bows in her hair. The girly-dog look doesn't suit her.

"It was the strangest thing," Wells said. "My secretary had just stepped out of the car when Abra jumped in."

"Your secretary?" Tina had failed to mention a rival for the Judge's affection.

"Edith Davies. She'll retire at the end of the year. Her husband had a stroke, so I chauffeur her to appointments. She was getting her hair done."

I imagined a wizened woman with a headful of pink bows.

"Why are you smiling?" he said.

"Because you drive a midnight-blue Beamer!" At last, a revelation that made sense. Since Jenx had come clean with the MSP, I felt at liberty to share what I knew with Wells. Over a fine bottle of Chardonnay and some excellent fresh fish, I recounted my day—the visit from the West Michigan Realtors Board, the return of Avery, the shooting on my terrace, the drive to Angola, the brush with Mrs. Santy, and the tales of Darrin Keogh. Plus I told him all about Abra.

Wells listened without comment.

Downing the last of the wine, I said, "Be honest, Judge. What do you think?"

He gathered both my hands in his. "I think you have a lot of problems," he said. "But they're solvable."

"You think?"

"They require action, however."

"What kind of action?"

He advised me to hire a lawyer.

"Spoken like a member in good standing with the Michigan Bar! I already have a lawyer. He's a paper pusher. I need protection."

Wells began explaining how attorneys exist to protect people's rights, and I tuned out. It had been a long day. But I perked up when I heard him say something about a bodyguard.

"You mean like in that movie? Starring the other Whitney Houston?"

I imagined living 24/7 with Kevin Costner as he looked in 1990. Maybe my luck was changing.

"You still need a good attorney to protect you from potential lawsuits, including—though I hate to say it—problems with Leo's daughter. She may be planning to contest his will."

"Let's go back to the part about the bodyguard. Where do I get one?"

I had preferred Kevin Costner in *Bull Durham* and *Field of Dreams*, so I was wondering if I could request a ball-playing bodyguard. Wells interrupted that train of thought.

"I may have exactly what you need. Right out back."

That seemed unlikely, but I followed him. The instant we stepped outside, we were met by an unearthly howl.

"What the hell is that?" I shouted.

"That's enough!" Wells bellowed. I was pretty sure he didn't mean me.

The howl faded as if someone were spinning a volume dial down. I peered into a kennel next to the garage.

"What the hell is that?" I said again.

"Whiskey, meet Mooney," said the Judge.

I still didn't know what it was.

"Is it . . . yours?" I said cautiously.

"He's mine," the Judge said. "But *what* is he?"

I hate pop quizzes.

"Uh—a hound, maybe? A really big scent hound?"

"Good, but what else do you see in him?"

What I saw, quite honestly, was the ugliest dog on earth: a large, thickly built black and tan canine with a broad head, floppy ears, sunken eyes, and a square jaw oozing drool. His chest was deep, his legs muscular, his paws wide, and his tail improbably thick and long.

"I don't know. Rottweiler, maybe?"

"Excellent! Yes, I do believe Mooney's father was a Rottie!'"

Wells made it sound like the equivalent of a Yalie.

"And his mother?" I asked.

"A Bloodhound, of course. Mooney's mother was one of the best trackers ever trained by the Michigan State Police."

"Was Mooney an experiment? Or an accident?"

Wells chuckled. "If you judge him by looks alone, I suppose Mooney makes a good case for birth control."

"Oh, no. . . ," I protested weakly.

"It's all right, Whiskey. I know he's not handsome. Otherwise, he combines the best traits of both breeds."

I couldn't imagine what any of this had to do with Kevin Costner.

"Mooney's mother's handlers hadn't spayed her yet. With her talent and temperament, they wanted to breed her. But on assignment one day, she got in trouble. The handlers hadn't noticed she was in heat."

"You mean—?"

"She fraternized with the male officers: Retrievers and Rottweilers. I think there was also a beagle." Wells shuddered. "They may all have had their way with her—we'll never know—but only the Rottie left his mark."

"Does Mooney have siblings?" I asked, not sure I was ready for the answer.

"Two. They look like purebred Bloodhounds, but they can't track a scent."

"Too bad."

"Yes. But you should see them with a frisbee. They've got a professional act. They've been on *David Letterman* and *The Today Show*."

Wells opened the kennel door, and Mooney emerged. They demonstrated a series of commands and responses, all of which involved smelling, finding, jumping, and drooling. Mostly drooling. I was mesmerized by Mooney's continuous saliva output.

"What do you think?" said Wells.

"Does he always leak like that?"

"Drool, you mean? Well, yes, it's the Bloodhound in him. Part of the scenting mechanism. You get used to it."

I doubted that. And I still didn't see what Mooney the Drooling Mutt had to do with Kevin Costner.

"He's yours," Wells said.

"Oh, no. He's yours. I already have a problem. I mean, a dog."

Wells smiled. "He's yours to use—as a bodyguard—for as long as you need him. Mooney is legendary in these parts."

I didn't doubt it. He was repulsive enough to keep criminals at bay.

"Don't thank me, Whiskey. I lend this fine dog only to special people with special needs."

"I read somewhere that Bloodhounds aren't good guard dogs," I ventured.

"True," Wells said. "That's where the Rottweiler kicks in. This dog would die for you. First he sniffs 'em out, then he snuffs 'em out. If necessary."

I studied Mooney. "What does he weigh? About a hundred?"

"One hundred thirty, and it's all sinew."

And drool. Wells offered to send along a few days' worth of food, which amounted to a fifty-pound bag.

So it was that Mooney came to live at Vestige on loan. Since Abra was sleeping deeply, Wells suggested I let her stay with him. After all, she'd been on the lam since Saturday and needed her beauty rest. What better safe house than the home of the local jurist? I knew Chester would approve.

In the driveway Mooney and I bid Wells good night. The Judge took my hand.

"Whiskey, I didn't say much when you told me about your day, but now I'd like to ask a question: Why would Ellianna Santy, who wants people to think she's dead, open the door of Darrin Keogh's store?"

He made it sound like a riddle, so I played along. "Because I knocked?"

Wells shook his head. "Because she was expecting someone. Someone who looks like you. Didn't you say that you could see through the panels by the door?"

"A little."

"Be careful, Whiskey."

As I turned to open the passenger door for Mooney, my foot slipped. The yard light revealed a puddle in the Judge's driveway.

"That's not what you think it is," Wells said quickly.

"I'm thinking it's drool."

"Then it is what you think it is."

Suddenly I realized that I didn't know Mooney's vocabulary. If living with Chester and Abra had taught me anything, it was that you'd better know the language.

"How will I tell him what to do?" I asked.

"First thing in the morning, go online. Print out the Guard Dog Commands at Dogs-Train-You-dot-com. Mooney knows 'em all."

TWENTY-THREE

BACK AT VESTIGE, EVERYTHING seemed normal. Brady had not posted crime scene tape, and Avery had left a typically curt phone message. She'd be staying for a while with Peg "because she cares," the implication being that I didn't. What could she expect from her heartless shrew of a stepmother? I wondered if I could consider myself her *former* stepmother since her father was dead. Probably not. Probably being a stepmother was like being a Catholic: you'd always be one, whether you practiced or not.

Mooney paced around the house until I guessed the command for "go to bed." It was "Go to bed." He settled on the Berber rug by the front door. At least it was absorbent.

My bedside phone woke me out of a blissfully dreamless sleep. The room was still black, so I knew it was nowhere near time to get up. I blinked at my digital clock, which blinked back 3:14.

"What is it?" I mumbled into the phone.

I couldn't believe what I heard even though I wanted to. It was my husband.

"This is Leo Mattimoe. Thanks for calling. You've reached my cell phone, but I can't talk right now, so leave a message. Or feel free to call my wife and partner, Whiskey Mattimoe, at the following number. Anything I can do, she can do better."

I sat up in bed, gasping. The message repeated. I should have disconnected at once. But I couldn't, even though I realized that someone was playing a cruel joke on me. Someone had recorded Leo's voice-mail message. Someone who knew his cell-phone number and also that I had never cancelled the account.

It was one of my most shameful self-pitying secrets following Leo's death: I'd saved everything with his voice on it. Almost six months after I'd lost him, I could still conjure up his sound. All I had to do was stay up late enough, feel sad enough, and drink enough wine. Then I would lie on our bed in the dark and dial up his voice-mail messages, again and again and again.

An inhuman, spine-tingling moan erupted from downstairs. I shrieked and dropped the phone. Then I remembered Mooney. He was barking, baying, and snarling like one of the hounds of the Baskerville. If only I had downloaded the Dogs-Train-You-dot-com command sheet. How the hell was I going to shut him up?

Glass shattered at the back of the house. Damn that alarm system. Damn me for forgetting to activate it. I heard Mooney shift into killer mode as "the Rottweiler kicked in." He scrambled across my hardwood floors, roaring as he flew. Then came a couple thuds, another crash, more guttural yowls. I thought I caught a human voice—make that a human scream—amid the chaos, but I wasn't sure, and I wasn't about to go downstairs. I fumbled on the floor for the phone. Leo's voice was still droning.

"Sorry, darling," I whispered. "Gotta go."

I pressed the "end" button and held my breath till I heard a dial tone. Then I punched 9-1-1.

Within seconds I'd reached the off-hours county-wide emergency services dispatcher. She took my name and other information and promised to have an officer on the scene within ten minutes. Neither Jenx nor Brady was on duty that night, so a sheriff's deputy would respond.

"Stay where you are, and be as quiet as possible. Can you lock yourself in?"

I assured her I could. Crawling toward the open door, I wasn't sure why I needed to be quiet. The racket from downstairs was deafening. I thought I heard someone begging for mercy.

The dispatcher asked whether there was more than one intruder. I said I couldn't tell, but she should probably advise the responding officer that I had an attack dog.

"What kind?" she asked.

"He's a cross between a Rottweiler and a Bloodhound."

"Oh! Mooney's there!" she exclaimed. "I thought that sounded like him. Well, you're in good hands—or should I say 'paws.' That dog has a reputation."

I was about to ask for what when a bloodcurdling scream sliced the air.

"I heard that!" the dispatcher said. "Mooney's in top form. I'll send over two officers, just in case."

In case of what, I didn't want to speculate. The intruder screamed again, and it occurred to me that men don't scream although I supposed that meeting Mooney might have that effect.

With all the commotion, I wasn't sure how close the sirens were when I first heard them. My bedroom window faces north, toward Cassina's Castle, so I couldn't see the cruisers arrive. Suddenly I heard footsteps racing up the stairs toward my room.

"Sheriff's Department," a male voice boomed. "Mrs. Mattimoe? Are you all right in there?"

I unlocked the door to find a tall, macho man in his late twenties.

"Deputy Tanner, ma'am." And he was. Tanner than the average guy. Fitter, too. I introduced myself, suddenly wishing I had bothered to get dressed while Mooney was terrifying the intruder. At least the oversized T-shirt I had on was clean. And it showed off my recently shaved legs. And my still-perky breasts. I caught the officer's approving glance. He was almost all business, though.

"Good thing you had Mooney down there. He not only protected you, but he held the intruder till we arrived. She's in custody now."

"She?" I had been right about the scream.

"We need to know if you recognize her," he said. "She has no ID. And, of course, she can't talk."

"What do you mean, she can't talk? Before you got here, she was screaming nonstop."

"I'm sure she was, ma'am. But then Mooney did his paw thing."

I cocked my head at Deputy Tanner. "*Paw thing*?"

"The Judge didn't tell you? See, after Mooney knocks 'em down, he presses his front paws into their solar plexus to immobilize 'em. They can hardly breathe. Works like a stun gun, only better. It'll be an hour, easy, before she can talk."

I asked the nice officer if I could throw on some clothes before coming down. He said I could, but he looked disappointed.

Not half as disappointed as I must have looked when I laid eyes on my intruder. To be accurate, I felt a mix of emotions: Shock. Dismay. Horror. Sprawled on my leather sofa was a pale and gasping pregnant woman. My stepdaughter.

"Oh my God! Is she all right?" My voice cracked with panic. The thought of Mooney pressing his weight into the belly containing Leo's heirs made my knees weak.

"We think so. She's carrying the baby low, and Mooney aimed high—at her diaphragm."

"*Two* babies! Twins!" I cried, more upset now than I had been all night. "There are *two* babies in there! Did you hear me? Call an ambulance! She needs a doctor! What if she goes into labor or something?! She can't have those kids here!"

I managed to sound more frightened for myself than for her.

"So you know her?" Tanner asked.

"She's my husband's daughter. My late husband's daughter. He's dead. She's pregnant. And from Belize. I hardly know her." I paused for breath, always advisable. "Call an ambulance!"

"There's one on the way," the other deputy replied. Then he asked for Avery's full name and vital statistics. I told him what I knew, which wasn't much. I couldn't even remember her middle name.

Tanner said, "Any idea why she'd break in?"

"She hates me," I offered. Other than that, I was clueless. I stared at Avery, who was staring back, her eyes unusually wide as she struggled for breath. For years she had squinted at me in what I took to be a habitually suspicious or hateful manner. Tonight she looked terrified. It was almost endearing. Part of me wondered whether I should try to comfort her. Then I reminded myself that she had broken into my house.

"Where's Mooney?" I said, scanning the room.

"In the kitchen," the second deputy said.

"Should I do something? Does he need anything?"

"You might want to give him a dog biscuit or a pat on the head. Maybe tell him to lie down. Let him know he's off duty now."

I explained that I couldn't talk to Mooney because the words I needed were online. The second deputy looked confused until I explained about Dogs-Train-You-dot-com. Turned out he had used the same system with his own guard dog, so he gave me some canine phrases. Verbally armed, I headed for the kitchen.

I screamed the instant I opened the door. Mooney was on top of Chester, who lay flat on the floor in his pajamas, apparently being crushed. Or licked to death.

"I'm okay, Whiskey!" he managed between swipes of Mooney's enormous tongue. "He's not on my solar plexus. See!"

Indeed. Mooney was astride Chester. But that tongue looked big enough to suffocate Shaquille O'Neal.

I wanted to ask how he knew about Mooney and the solar plexus, but first things first.

"How did you get in here?" I demanded.

"The usual way," Chester said, pushing Mooney back with calm authority. "You left that window over your sink unlocked again."

"Too bad Avery didn't notice," I sighed.

"She's too fat to fit through it," he said. "What did she want, anyway? Something of Leo's?" He stroked Mooney lovingly.

I said, "How do you know this dog?"

"Everybody knows Mooney. Why did the Judge lend him to you? Were you expecting more trouble?"

More trouble than what? I didn't think Chester knew about the hang glider with the deer rifle. And at that moment I didn't have the strength to tell him. Besides, the two deputies had appeared in the doorway.

"Can we get your mom's autograph?" Tanner asked. "We have all her CDs, don't we, Butch?"

"You bet! *Random Rain* is my fave!"

"It's good, but not as good as *Wind in My Heartstrings*," Tanner insisted.

"Do I hear an ambulance?" I glared at them until they went to check.

Mooney was resting his immense drooling head on Chester's lap as a puddle formed around them on the floor.

"Maybe you shouldn't let him get quite that close," I said, remembering how nervous my mother used to be when she watched us kids play with big dogs.

"He's a nice Rott Hound," Chester cooed, and Mooney slapped him affectionately with his wet sponge of a tongue.

"*Rott Hound*?"

"It beats Bloodweiler, doesn't it?"

There were two sirens—one for the ambulance, the other for Jenx.

"You're supposed to be off duty!" I said when she walked in.

"Right." Jenx yawned. "I was coming back from Hamlin County— tell you later. You okay?"

I said I was afraid that Mooney might have hurt Avery's babies.

"No way! He knows what he's doing."

After Jenx had finished chatting with the sheriff's deputies, I asked, "Does this fall under their jurisdiction or yours?"

"It's complicated. Got coffee?"

In the kitchen, Mooney and Chester greeted Jenx like a long-lost friend.

"My favorite deputy! And my favorite deputy-dog!" she exclaimed, hugging them both and making it look easy.

"So you know Mooney, too." I was groping around my cupboards for coffee. The gesture seemed futile. I couldn't remember when I'd last bought any.

"We deputize Mooney whenever we need canine back-up."

"There's coffee in the freezer," Chester said helpfully. He was holding the carafe and a paper filter. I hoped he'd washed his hands.

Jenx yawned. "Almost 4:30! I could sure use some breakfast."

"Me, too!" said Chester. "Too bad we're at Whiskey's."

My cupboards were not completely bare. Chester found an old box of pop-tarts. How old I didn't care to speculate, for I was sure

Leo had bought them. Chester wouldn't let me check the expiration date.

"It's just an FDA formality," he said. "What do you think all those chemicals are for?"

Jenx and I were on our second cup of black coffee when we noticed that Chester and Mooney had collapsed against each other in a snoring boy-dog pile. I suggested moving the boy to a bed and the dog to the yard, but she shook her head.

"There's been a development," Jenx whispered. "Disturbing stuff. Let's talk in your office."

I sat at my desk while she paced, coffee mug in hand.

"I got a call from the Hamlin County coroner earlier tonight. Some kids found two bodies in a shallow grave. Caucasian male and female in their early thirties. Both dead less than a week. Female's skull was crushed. Both had had autopsies."

My mouth was too dry to say anything, so Jenx said it for me.

"Our missing bodies."

"How—?"

"Crouch uses a funeral home in Ritchie as his morgue. Does every autopsy there. The morning after he released the remains, they disappeared. Funeral director couldn't explain what happened."

"Someone stole the corpses?"

"Probably someone named Santy," Jenx said.

I thought about Marilee Gallagher. At least now she'd have her husband's remains.

"What about Holly Lomax?" I said. "Anybody report her missing?"

"Only her parole officer. Lomax was a lost soul. A hooker and druggie who fell down the well."

"What was her connection to the Santys?"

"Besides the fact that they probably killed her? I think she worked for them—and probably killed Dan Gallagher. Why, I don't know.

174

How, I don't know yet, either. We're still waiting for the rest of Crouch's tox screens to come back." Jenx finished her coffee. "Somehow it all connects to Warren Matheney's finger. And that missing butt-ugly Cloud Ring."

I told Jenx about the recorded phone message that jarred me awake. She asked who knew I hadn't cancelled Leo's cell phone.

"Anyone who's called that number since he died."

"Hey!" she said suddenly. "Where's that photo of Leo I always liked?"

I followed her gaze to the empty space on the mantel behind my desk. Then I remembered: the picture was in my purse. I had grabbed it for luck when I left for Angola.

"So it was there when Avery was here earlier? For the lunch with gunshots?"

"Yeah. What's your point?"

TWENTY-FOUR

"YOU DON'T KNOW THE story behind that picture, Whiskey?"

The way Jenx was giving me the fisheye I was pretty sure I didn't want to know it. Here I'd thought it was just a nice picture of my now-dead dear love.

But according to Jenx, ever since she hit town, Avery had been telling anyone who would listen that she wanted that photo of Leo because it belonged to her.

I said, "Leo gave me that picture last Christmas."

"Do you know who took it? Or where?"

I didn't. "Are you saying Avery took that photo?"

"That's what Avery says. Look at the background. Can you tell where it is?"

I fished the picture out of my purse.

"Looks like the beach," I said and passed it to Jenx.

"What beach?" She examined the photo under my desk lamp.

"Around here somewhere, probably."

"Look again." Jenx tapped the glass. Next to her finger, in the background, was an image that seemed both strange and familiar—

the way the Eiffel Tower might strike you if you finally noticed it in the background of an old family portrait.

"That's Christ the Redeemer!" I said.

Jenx nodded. "Giant Jesus on the Mountain with His arms stretched out. Where is that?"

"Rio."

"Rio where?"

"de Janeiro," I said hoarsely. "Brazil. You know—*The Girl from Ipanema*? That's the beach in the song."

"I didn't know you'd been there."

"I haven't. Leo and I talked about going. But we never made it."

"Looks like Leo did."

I stared at the photo. He smiled back—happy, tanned, relaxed. All the qualities that made this picture one of my favorites.

"So, Leo went to Brazil with Avery and didn't tell you," Jenx said.

"*If* Avery took the picture. You're sure she took the picture?"

"You'd rather he was with somebody else?"

"No! I'm sure it was Avery. If Avery says so."

"Avery says she took the picture, it's supposed to be hers, and she wants it back."

"Then why doesn't she ask me for it?"

"She did. Remember Leo's funeral? You told her to go to hell."

A sickening memory snaked across my mental view-finder.

"Shit," I said. "I did say that."

"I know. I was there. So was half of Magnet Springs."

I closed my eyes and willed the ugliness away. "Not a good scene."

"Awful," Jenx agreed. "Avery accused you of stealing her picture, and you called her a 'lying little manipulative bitch.' But you were in bad shape. It was three days after the accident."

"I'm sorry I said it—even though I was right. She is a bitch. But Leo loved his daughter."

"Leo loved *you*. Like crazy. Everybody knew that."

I studied the photo. "Christ the Redeemer in the background. I can't believe I never noticed it. Maybe I didn't want to."

"Don't be too hard on yourself. It's not like you're a trained observer."

"I'm a real estate professional! I notice things!"

Jenx shrugged.

I said, "You're thinking Avery shattered my patio door just to get this photo of her father? Why would she pull a stunt like that when she's pregnant?"

"Avery didn't break in. But she was right behind whoever did, probably some guy. Neither of them knew Mooney was here. When the guy saw the dog, he freaked and ran. In her present condition, Avery couldn't." Jenx unclipped a magnum flashlight from her hip. "Let's take a look outside. I'll bet we find two sets of footprints coming and one set running away."

We did. To my untrained eye, both sets looked like boot prints. The ones running away were smaller.

"I don't get why Avery thought she had to break in. I'd open the door for her anytime. Well, anytime I had to."

"Like I said, Avery went along with somebody. Somebody with a bigger agenda."

"Like a missing finger? Like a Cloud Ring?"

"Let's see if Avery can tell us."

I wasn't sure I wanted to talk with my hostile pregnant step-daughter so soon after her bungled burglary. But going back to bed wasn't an option. Mooney and Chester were awake and chasing each other through the house. The two deputies sat in my kitchen drinking what was left of the coffee and brainstorming excuses to interview Cassina. When I said I was leaving, they fell all over themselves with promises to escort Chester home.

At Coastal Medical Center, Avery was still in the ER. Jenx went to inquire about her condition while I sat in the waiting room watching early-morning TV with a handful of other miserable souls. Maybe it was the fluorescent lighting; maybe it was the ungodly hour. I couldn't tell those waiting for family from those waiting for a doctor. Everybody looked sick.

"She won't see you," Jenx announced. "She says you're not family."

"Except when we're discussing money. Will she see you?"

"After she lawyers up. We've got to get her a public defender. Unless you want to hire somebody."

I stuck my tongue out.

Jenx said, "She already made her one phone call—to guess who?"

"Her mother." My voice was flat with fatigue. "Can't wait to see Georgia's new boobs and tattoos."

"Nope. Avery called Antiques Boy in Angola. He's on his way."

I was suddenly wide awake. "She phoned Darrin Keogh?"

Jenx said, "Or should I call him Afghan-Breeder Boy? You know—the guy you were sure was a perv . . . till he bought you a beer and showed you his doggies."

My face got hot. "Darrin Keogh is nice. He even likes Avery. Wait till you meet him!"

Jenx ignored me. "We're taking Avery to the station as soon as she's released. She and the babies checked out fine. Did you know she's due this month? The ob-gyn says she could deliver any day now."

That news left me unable to do anything but go to work. When I opened the front door of Mattimoe Realty, Odette was already in her cubicle—on her third cup of coffee and her fourth phone call. Or so she whispered as I walked by. I'm in awe of her ability to pitch real estate before sunrise.

I was pouring a cup of coffee when she announced, "Our Featured Home seller accepted Rico's offer!"

"Congratulations," I said. "Now will he stop trying to ruin us?"

"One would expect so. If the sale goes through."

"Will it?"

Odette's thin shoulders rose and fell. "The seller is a tad leery of Rico's financing, and so am I. But he's making a $30,000 deposit. He says he has sixty percent in available funds; the other forty will come from a private lender."

"Undisclosed?"

"He implies that it's a close friend. Who knew he had any?"

"Is there a back-up offer?"

"Yes—but also with questionable financing. One of those super-rich, super-young couples you saw at the Open House. They're already over-leveraged. And their bid's ten percent below the asking price."

"What's Rico's?"

"Five percent below."

If I recalled correctly, the heiress who owned the mini-castle with wine cellar was asking one-point-two million, a fair price in the current market. Rico Anuncio had sixty percent of five percent less than that? I started tapping on my calculator.

"How could Rico have $684,000 on hand?"

"He says business is good."

"He runs an art gallery!"

"Well, he did host Cloud Man," Odette reminded me.

Rico had bragged about owning a Cumulus. Maybe Brady could estimate its worth.

Odette had other hopeful news to report. One of her pre-breakfast phone chats had been with Carol Felkey, who wanted to sell her home in Shadow Point.

"Since the murders, Carol says it's like living in Hell's Theme Park. The subdivision is clogged with gawkers. Total strangers ring their doorbell every day asking for gruesome details."

"I'll be delighted to list their home," I said. "But I dread dealing with ghouls."

Odette cocked her head, a strange light in her eyes. "I embrace the Ghoul Factor and make it work for me."

"Great. Then you can sit down with Carol and Ed."

"And with the Schlegels," she said. "They're a Christian couple who can't bear living two doors down from Satan's handiwork. One possible glitch, though: both the Felkeys and the Schlegels know *you* managed Murder House."

"You mean Shadow Play—"

"So they're understandably nervous about letting you near their properties."

"They think I'm jinxed?!"

"They've also heard about the pending lawsuits."

"There are no pending lawsuits! That I know of. Just some stupid written complaints stirred up by that wacko Rico."

I was so angry I was spitting. Odette stepped discreetly from the line of spray.

"My point is that I'll handle it," she said and slipped away.

TWENTY-FIVE

AROUND NINE I DECIDED to grab a latte and muffin at the Goh Cup. Brady and Officer Roscoe were coming down the sidewalk as I approached. I did a double take. Maybe it was the bright autumn sunshine, but Roscoe's coat had a pale golden sheen I'd never seen before. And Brady was sporting a spiky new hairstyle.

"You look great," I said. "Both of you."

"Thanks. Turns out the Coastal Canine Salon has specials for cop dogs, so Roscoe got a Swedish-Citrus conditioning rinse on the house. Makes him look younger, don't you think?"

"Blonder, for sure. What about you? Do they have specials for cop guys, too?"

He blushed. "Nah. Once I saw how good Roscoe looked, I told Bob the Barber to give me the works."

"Hey—I've got a grad-school art question for you. The other day you said Matheney's paintings are soaring in value."

"Yup. There was something about that in *USA Today*."

"An article on Cloud Man?"

"It was about what's hot in art—which contemporary artists command the biggest bucks. Matheney's near the top of the list. He was hot when he was alive, but he's a lot hotter dead."

I asked Brady to estimate what a Cumulus might be worth now.

"*USA Today* says they're going up. The best ones could sell now for a few hundred thou. Maybe more. Depends on what you got and when you sell it."

"And who you sell it to. Right? I mean, you'd have to find the right buyer."

"They're out there. And here's another thing." Brady surveyed the street. I noticed that Officer Roscoe did the same. "If the news ever gets out about Cloud Man's finger—."

"What?" I leaned closer.

"Well, think about Van Gogh's ear. . . ."

"Van Gogh cut off his own ear. You don't think Matheney . . . ?"

"No way! But sordid stories sell art."

And real estate. Odette was right about the neighborhood surrounding Murder House. I mean, Shadow Play. Someone out there would buy proximity to grisly history.

"Okay, Brady. You're saying anyone who owns a Cumulus could be confident of selling it for a huge profit? Finger or no finger?"

"For a fortune."

"Do you think the finger will ever make the news?"

"That's not up to us, Whiskey."

Officers Swancott and Roscoe regarded me sharply. Brady said, "Somebody, somewhere has Matheney's Cloud Ring, and it's priceless. If or when that thing surfaces, the art market will have convulsions."

Back at the office, I called Walter St. Mary to check on his recovery from the attack on my deck. His housekeeper informed me that he had already returned to work. Sure enough, he answered the phone when I dialed Mother Tucker's.

"Do you forgive me?" I said.

"Unless you hired the glider guy with the gun."

And that set me to thinking. I called Wells Verbelow to thank him for lending me Mooney. He already knew about the previous night's trauma, so I was spared more talk about Avery, at least for a while. Wells offered to bring me dinner—and Abra—at around eight. I wanted to accept the dinner and decline the dog, but that didn't seem sociable.

"Wells, do you think it's possible that someone was hired to hit me?"

"As in a mob hit, you mean?" I detected a grin in his voice.

"Don't regular criminals hire hit men, too?"

"Yes, but who would want to have you killed?"

"Who would want to burgle my house? Someone hates me, or at the very least needs me out of the way."

He suggested we discuss it over dinner. The rest of the day did its usual fly-by routine with me buried in paperwork at my desk. When I looked up in response to Odette's three raps, it was after five.

"You're still here," I said.

"And now I'm leaving. With you."

"Where are we going?"

"Shadow Point."

Maybe I didn't want to play. "Why would we go there?"

"To convince the Schlegels that you are neither unlucky nor incompetent."

"How will we manage that?"

"By letting me do the talking. You're a prop tonight, Whiskey. Please speak only when spoken to, and then not much. Got it?"

I got it. Odette let me drive. I parked in front of a one-and-a-half-story stone cottage two doors down from Shadow Play. Though this was a more modest home on a smaller lot, it was perfectly landscaped. Odette informed me that Dr. Schlegel was a retired professor of horticulture from Ohio State. His wife shared his passion for making green things grow. They also shared a passion for Jesus.

"Praise the Lord that Mrs. Mutombo understands our plight," Mrs. Schlegel exclaimed. A petite blue-haired lady infused with energy and inclined to make large gestures, she led us into a sitting room dominated by an oil painting of the Rapture.

"Hal and I can't bear to think about suffering." Mrs. Schlegel smiled brightly and went to fetch us sodas.

I studied the painting, which measured roughly three feet by six. In the background were row after row of empty graves. In the foreground, hordes of men and women, faces twisted in terror, screamed for help as the earth imploded and flames consumed them.

"Lovely," I told Odette.

"They have a similar painting upstairs, over their bed. And a couple more in the guest room. And the kitchen. They collect apocalyptic art."

Our hostess rustled back in with ginger ale fizzing in aluminum tumblers.

"Hal will join us just as soon as he washes up. He's been out in our prayer garden, repairing some damage."

"Squirrels?" I said helpfully. When Odette shot me a look, I remembered I was a prop.

"Oh, my, no. Not squirrels." Mrs. Schlegel leaned toward us, her eyes wide. "More likely the work of Lucifer."

"The Devil?" It just popped out. Odette coughed and glared at me. I took a long swig of soda and mentally vowed to keep quiet. This house would list at five hundred thou, and, Satan or no Satan, I wanted to sell it.

"Assuming the shape of an animal," a man's voice intoned. We turned to see Dr. Schlegel, still wearing his gardening clothes. His deeply lined, leathery face was grim.

"Claudette and I saw it the night of the murder—before we knew about the murder. We now believe it was the Lord's way of telling us that we were in the path of evil."

So help me, my neck hair stood straight up.

Mrs. Schlegel held out a plate of Toll House cookies. I took one just to see if I could.

The retired professor said, "The goat, you know, is one of Lucifer's preferred incarnations."

"You saw a . . . goat?" I inhaled part of my cookie.

"Not your average garden-variety goat," Mrs. Schlegel said. "This one was strictly Old Testament—designed to get your attention. This goat had very long hair."

"Blonde hair," Dr. Schlegel added.

Because I was choking, Mrs. Schlegel slapped me on the back. She said, "I know this sounds strange, but we're talking about Satan's handiwork. In profile, that goat looked just like Sarah Jessica Parker."

I was still coughing, so Odette slapped me, too. Sweetly she asked the Schlegels, "What did Satan's celebrity goat do?"

"It tore our prayer garden to pieces, like a creature possessed."

"Which, of course, it was," said Dr. Schlegel. "It turned over our Nativity birdbath and destroyed Claudette's prize-winning white azaleas."

"Flowers are God's love made visible," his wife added. "We can always plant more. Somewhere else."

To Odette and me she hissed, "Please help get us out of here!"

Although I was under strict instructions to say little, I assured the nice woman that Mattimoe Realty would do just that. In a timely, customer-friendly, thoroughly professional manner. Moreover, we would get the Schlegels the best price possible—regardless of Satan.

While Odette did a walk-through with the couple, I stayed behind with the Rapture. I considered Abra's possible contributions to their prayer garden and wondered how soon I could start digging. It couldn't be Matheney's finger. We'd seen that days after the Shadow Play murder. Unless someone had dug it up and put it in Holly Lomax's purse in time for Marilee Gallagher to find it hidden in her motel room.

Assuming that Abra hadn't been digging for the pure joy of destruction, which she often did, whatever was buried in the garden was probably something not seen since the murder. Such as the missing Cumulus. Or the Reitbauers' ivory candlestick holders. Or Mrs. Santy's Piaget watch. No. Those items were most likely in the possession of the still-living Santys, wherever they now were. Maybe in Angola, Indiana—if Darrin Keogh wasn't the nice guy I wanted him to be.

What was my Satanic dog doing in the Schlegels' prayer garden the night Holly Lomax got her head smashed in? Abra was supposed to be home at Vestige learning obedience online with Chester. Did he know she had gotten out? If so, why hadn't he told me? Did Abra take something of value from the crime scene, something we couldn't yet name? Or did she simply pull another stupid anti-social stunt, one which had almost gone unreported? The Shadow Point subdivision is about a mile from Vestige, and Abra is fast. It would have been possible for her to get there and back—and do whatever—in an hour.

But what? And why?

After the Schlegels signed the papers necessary to list their home, Odette let me say good night. Mrs. Schlegel was closing the door behind us when she remembered something.

"I suppose I should mention that the mayor was here a few days ago. He's in real estate, too, you know."

"So I've heard." Odette stifled a yawn.

"He wondered whether we were thinking of selling. Or could we refer him to any neighbors who were."

Odette squeezed my arm. She probably wanted to clap a hand over my mouth.

"What did you tell him?"

"I said we weren't ready to discuss that with strangers, and neither were our neighbors. Truth is, I don't like his politics. He's a liberal."

We nodded.

"Did he say anything else?" asked Odette.

"Well, he said that some real estate companies in town aren't ethical."

"Oh? Which companies are those?" Odette's grip on my arm was so tight that my fingers tingled.

"He didn't say, exactly. . . ." Mrs. Schlegel's voice trailed off, and she looked uncertain. "Anyway, you two gals *seem* like Christians— not liberals—so I'm sure Hal and I are in good hands. By the way, we're sorry for your loss, Mrs. Mattimoe. We knew your late husband. Such a nice man."

Outside Odette said, "I know what you're thinking, Whiskey, and we're not going to."

"Not going to what?"

"Dig up the Schlegels' garden looking for that finger. Or the ring that belongs on it. Or whatever else Abra might have stolen lately."

"She hasn't stolen anything! Lately. She's reformed."

Odette raised a pencil-thin eyebrow.

I said, "She ran off with the purse from the police station, but that was a misunderstanding. The cops were drilling her all day long! As for the finger—well, we've seen that too recently for it to be under the Schlegels' birdbath."

"I suggest we phone Jenx, tell her about the 'goat' and let her look into it. You're in real estate, remember? Let's make money."

She offered to call Jenx. After dropping her off, I turned the wheel toward home. Anxieties about Abra and Avery threatened to over-shadow the prospect of a pleasant dinner with a thoughtful man. Both females seemed to be conspiring against me. Or was my fatigue inducing paranoia? I decided to discard my worries and let myself relax. Rounding the bend before Vestige, I spotted three emergency vehicles in my driveway, their flashers blinking blood red.

TWENTY-SIX

As I drew closer, I could see flames licking my garage roof and arcs of blue water aimed at extinguishing them.

That was when I flashed on Chester and Mooney chasing each other around the house that morning. Had the deputies escorted Chester home? And what had become of the Judge's Rott Hound?

I screeched to a halt on the street in front of my house and dashed up the driveway. Jenx intercepted me.

"Easy, Whiskey." She raised both palms to stop me. "It's under control."

"My house is on fire!" I panted.

"Just your garage and breezeway. Your kitchen'll probably be okay. You don't use that room, anyhow."

"Is Chester safe?"

"He's fine. And so's Mooney. They called in the alarm."

Jenx brought me up to speed. After obtaining Cassina's autograph for the deputies, Chester had talked them into letting him back into Vestige. Today was an at-home study day, and he preferred to use my house because Mooney was there.

"You forgot about that dog," Jenx scolded me. "Chester said you didn't even leave him food and water."

"I'd just been burgled. I'm usually a much better host."

"Anyway, Chester was here, drilling Mooney on defense maneuvers from that web site."

"Dogs-Train-You-dot-com," I supplied.

"And they heard an explosion. When Chester looked out the window, he saw your propane tank had blown. Your backyard was on fire, with flames racing toward the garage. He reached for the phone, but Mooney had it in his mouth already. That's one well-trained canine."

After calling 9-1-1, Chester and Mooney had bolted for Cassina's Castle, where the diva ordered Mother Tucker's filet mignons for everyone.

"You just missed Walter; he delivered," said Jenx. "And he said to tell you you're a dead woman unless you get out of here. What's that about?"

"His lasagna took a bullet for me on the patio, remember? I'm surprised he still delivers in this neighborhood."

"After tonight, he might not. Walter thinks the hang glider came back and shot your propane tank."

Headlights swept across the front of my house. I turned to see a dark BMW park by my car. Wells Verbelow flung open his door.

"Here come da Judge!" Jenx said. "And Abra."

I groaned as a blonde Satanic creature bounded toward us. Then I realized that the Judge had her on a retractable leash. Maybe someone would escort her next door to share Chester's pre-chewed steak.

"Fire bomb?" Wells asked after hugging me. Abra was already wrapping her razor-wire lead around my legs.

"We're thinking deer rifle fired at the propane tank," said Jenx.

"Lucky you didn't have it filled recently," Wells said. "Everything might have been vaporized."

"What do you mean?"

Jenx made a "pffffft" noise.

An appropriately heavy silence ensued.

"The hang glider again?" asked Wells.

"Maybe," said Jenx. "But he was probably in a car this time. It was too dark to fly."

I needed a chair, but there were none in the vicinity, so I staggered a little.

Wells said, "Somebody's trying to kill you, Whiskey. You and Abra are coming home with me and Mooney. Right now."

If I can get that far. Suddenly the smoke and flames and stink of burning plastic overpowered me. I blacked out. When I awoke, I seemed to be inside a fairy tale—on an immense feather bed draped in netting.

"Hello—?" I said.

A familiar face popped up along the edge of the bed. Then a second one, and then a third.

"You need full-time protection," Chester declared. On each side of him, a large canine head bobbed in agreement. One dripped copiously on the satin bedspread.

"Is this the witness protection program?" I murmured, still groggy.

"No, this is Cassina's Cloud Room, in our guest wing. Jenx and the Judge carried you here after you fainted. Your house was closer, but it's on fire."

I let my head sink back against the pillow. And what a pillow it was. Inside the satin case was so much soft down that it felt like a cloud. A fake cumulus cloud. I must have mumbled something.

"What about the Cumulus?" said Chester. He slid under the netting and perched on the edge of the bed. "Did you say it's a fake?"

"Oh my god!" I cried, my head clearing. "Where's Jenx?"

I sat up so fast that I sent Chester over the side.

"Downstairs. With Cassina and the Judge. They're eating the extra filet mignons Walter delivered."

"Get Jenx in here! Now!"

Chester picked himself up off the floor and straightened his glasses. "They'll save you some."

"It's not about the food!" Getting out of this bed was a lot harder than it should have been. My arms tangled in the netting as I tried to yank it back. "What's this for?" I said, flailing away at the fabric.

"Set dressing," said Chester. "Like at her concerts. Cassina wants everything to look romantic."

I wanted to point out that getting tangled up in bedding isn't romantic, but I had bigger issues. "Bring Jenx up here. Alone."

He and Abra traipsed off, leaving a moist Mooney to study me from the other side of the veil.

"I don't think I've thanked you properly. You're a hell of a Rott Hound."

Mooney gurgled in reply. Jenx appeared holding what looked like a half-eaten turkey drumstick.

"I thought you were having filet mignon," I said.

"We did. Then Cassina's cook whipped this up." She took a juicy bite from the bone. "We'll save you some."

"Close the door," I hissed. "I just had a brainstorm."

"You hit your head when you fainted, but there can't be much damage. What's with the mosquito netting?"

"It's supposed to be romantic," I said, sliding down the side of the mattress and under the veil, as Chester had done. Then I was on my knees, but at least I was free. Jenx hoisted me to my feet.

"I figured it out," I cried. "It's about fake clouds!"

Jenx studied the room, uncertain. "Well, it's a look."

"I mean, what's going on! The hang glider, the burglary, the dog-napping, the finger. And the murders! Somebody's forging art—somebody we know."

Jenx stopped chewing. "Rico?"

"Maybe."

She looked unsure. "We know the Santys deal in stolen or forged art. The Mounties told us that. What's the connection to Rico?"

"What's the thread that runs through everything?" I demanded. "Warren Matheney! He has a show at the West Shore Gallery and then he's dead and then Rico's rich. The Santys show up and pretend to die. We find Matheney's missing finger in a dead woman's purse. A Cumulus painting—Matheney's most valuable—goes missing. So does his Celtic Cloud Ring. Abra disappears, too. When she comes back, people start trying to kill me! "

Jenx said, "You left out Matheney's nephew and the not-dead lady at his store."

"And the fact that Keogh is a friend of my stepdaughter—who broke into my house last night with a second set of boot prints." Then I remembered the Schlegels. "Did you get Odette's message?"

Jenx said, "I'll check my voice mail after dessert."

I saved her the trouble, explaining that Abra had buried something two doors down from Shadow Play the night of the murder.

"You'll want to dig that up," I told her.

First Jenx wanted to question Chester, who arrived with a plate of cookies. He admitted falling asleep while dog-sitting at Vestige that night.

"I'm sorry, Whiskey," he said. "But we'd had a hard day of training. I dozed off in front of the TV. I knew Abra must have let herself out because when I woke up, she was doing that cat thing."

"What 'cat thing'?" said Jenx.

Obligingly, Abra demonstrated by licking her paws.

Chester said, "She only does that when her feet are dirty."

"But how did she get out if you didn't let her out?" I asked.

"The same way I get in: through the window over your kitchen sink." Mooney groaned admiringly. Stretched out at Chester's feet, Abra gave the Rott Hound a seductive, sideways glance. Her *Sarah Jessica Parker* look.

"Any idea how long she was gone?" asked Jenx.

"I was watching the Pet Psychic, and I woke up to the Crocodile Hunter."

"That means Abra was gone two hours or less. All right, Whiskey, I'll get a warrant for the Schlegels' back yard."

"Their prayer garden, under the Nativity birdbath," I said. "And you should know *they* think it was Satan."

We looked at Abra, who had begun rubbing herself against a softly moaning Mooney.

"They were right," Jenx said. "How long has she been in heat?"

TWENTY-SEVEN

Judge Verbelow agreed at once to prepare the warrant Jenx would need to dig up the Schlegels' prayer garden. Abra's alleged activities near the murder scene seemed like further proof of my deficiencies as a dog owner.

"Abra may be a material witness to a murder," the Judge said. "Do you know what that means, Whiskey?"

"That I broke the leash law again?" I tried to keep the hopefulness out of my voice when I asked if she'd be incarcerated.

"She's too much for you too handle, isn't she?" Wells said.

I wanted to protest, but something in his brown eyes stopped me. The man, after all, is a judge.

"Yes," I confessed.

"That's why I'm on the case!" Chester piped up. "By the time I'm done, all Whiskey will need is a handy wallet-sized print-out of the commands from Dogs-Train-You-dot-com."

Wells smiled. "It works for Mooney. Of course, he trained at the K-9 Institute in Detroit."

"And did graduate work at the Track & Attack Academy in Marquette," Chester added.

"Mooney told you that?" I asked.

"I read the tag on his collar."

Jenx urged the Judge to issue the warrant so that she could execute it at daybreak. He prepared to leave.

"What do you need from me, Whiskey?"

"I just want to go home."

"Not an option," Jenx interjected. She was peering out the guest room window. "Fire's out, but nobody's sleeping there tonight."

"You're welcome to stay here."

A voice as feathery as the bed I had sat upon floated through the open doorway. We all turned toward Cassina in her trademark gauzy white gown. I wondered if the woman owned a single piece of clothing with pigment. Her magnificent mane of hair flowed around her shoulders like a scarlet curtain.

"You're our guest," she said. "Besides, my son seems to like you."

"I can't stay—" I began.

"Your dog can stay, too, if that will make things easier."

"It won't," I assured her.

"How about Mooney? Can he stay?" Chester asked, jumping up and down.

"Is he the wet one?" Cassina eyed the Rott Hound.

"I'll wipe up after him," Chester promised. "Or he can wear his drool bucket."

Chester produced a kid's beach pail on a plastic collar. Deftly, he slipped it over Mooney's head. The dog promptly made a deposit. *Kerplunk.*

"How about that," said Wells. "Now he'll be welcome everywhere."

Cassina didn't look so sure.

That's how I ended up spending the night in Cassina's Cloud Room with two big dogs asleep at my side. Notice I said nothing about getting any sleep myself. I tossed and turned. Or tried to. It's not easy to change positions when sharing your mattress with four-legged beings, one of whom didn't wear his drool bucket. Yes, there was a wet spot. I won't even mention the snoring.

As for Abra being in heat—Mooney, thankfully, was neutered. All I could do for the next few days was what I'd never been able to do: contain Abra. And hope that no males had already visited.

Just before four o'clock I managed to slide over the side of the bed and under the layers of netting without waking my roommates. Maybe I should have taken Mooney along as bodyguard. His credentials were impressive, and the drool bucket did help, but I had no time to retrieve my laptop from the office, and without going online, I couldn't talk to him.

I left a note reminding Chester to keep Abra indoors. Then I wandered on tiptoe through Cassina's Castle, seeking a door to the outside world. When I finally found one, I listened breathlessly for an alarm system to activate. None did. I flung the door wide and fled, sprinting like the high-school athlete I used to be.

Dashing across Cassina's broad lawn toward Vestige, I could smell the now-dead fire: charred wood and melted rubber. My heart fluttered as I realized that one of Leo's last gifts to me must have perished in the flames. Then I skidded on a muddy patch near the ash pile that had been my garage and landed on my ass. That's when I saw it— propped against my front steps, gleaming in the light from my still-functioning security lamp. Damn if Blitzen didn't look as fine as the last time I'd fallen off her. Some firefighter had made a heroic rescue.

Briefly I considered letting myself into the house for a change of clothes. But, no doubt courtesy of Brady Swancott, a yellow crime scene tape stretched across the door. I keep a change of clothes in my car. Huddled in the shadows between the vehicle and a hedgerow, I slipped into clean underwear, a Magnet Springs High sweatshirt, and a pair of jeans. On impulse I strode up to the house, grabbed the bike, which is made of some lightweight alloy, and tossed it into the back of my Lexus. What the hell. Blitzen was valuable, and crime was on the rise in Magnet Springs.

The sun was still new in the sky when I rolled into Angola, Indiana. For Art's Sake wasn't open yet, but I cruised around the block once just to check it out. No midnight-blue Beamer was parked anywhere in the vicinity. So I drove on over to Keogh's house on Superior Street.

With few exceptions, I've always had the gift of good timing. My mother gets a little credit in that department since she gave birth to me at a high point in women's history. I went to school after Title Nine, which allowed me to excel in sports, develop lots of self-confidence, and learn that I could always take care of myself. I got into real estate just as the market was taking off. Then I met and married Leo Mattimoe. We had only five years together, but we made them count.

My excellent timing landed me in front of Darrin Keogh's Victorian home just as he was concluding an early walk with his dogs. All six Afghan hounds trotted regally on leashes. Walking six Abras would pull a person apart at the joints. Involuntarily, I looked at Pashtoon, the dog that was supposed to have been Leo's. The dog that Cloud Man had injured, or so Keogh claimed. She looked queenly in the morning light, her masked face held high as the sun made her golden coat blaze. I was facing them from the opposite side of the street, parked between a minivan and a pickup truck four doors down. Suddenly Pashtoon froze in her tracks. Cocking her head exactly as Abra does, she trained her one good eye on me. I slid down behind the wheel, praying that Keogh wouldn't follow her gaze. My heart thudded. What was I doing here, anyway, playing amateur sleuth when I had a business to run and a garage to rebuild?

Breathlessly I counted to thirty before daring to peek over the dashboard again. When I let myself look, the sidewalk was empty, and so were Keogh's yard and porch. I checked my mirrors. Nothing. The entire street was still.

Then tires squealed behind me. In my sideview mirror I saw a midnight-blue Beamer careening around the corner. It screeched to a stop in front of Keogh's house. Although I couldn't see who was driving, I knew the license plate. My revving heart shifted into overdrive. Almost instantly, Keogh's front door flew open, and he dashed out. Maybe he wanted to leave before his sick mother had time to detain him. If he had a sick mother.

The Beamer peeled away from the curb. I waited one beat and then followed, my trembling hands clamped on the wheel. We were heading north out of town at a rate significantly higher than the local law allowed. For better or for worse, no cops appeared. Traffic at that hour was extremely light. In minutes we were in the country, still northbound. Concerned that someone in the Beamer might identify me, I kept a healthy distance between us and prayed that no one would check their mirrors.

We had traveled five miles on a two-lane road when the Beamer turned west. I slowed and took the turn, too. Our new way was narrow, still paved but less than two lanes. In minutes the surface degenerated into gravel. I gave the Beamer more headway, knowing I'd be doomed if anyone looked back. After a few minutes, the road got rougher. Clouds of dust obscured my view. I couldn't see the Beamer, so I assumed the Beamer couldn't see me. I slowed, hoping not to miss anything. Like a rear bumper or the grill of an oncoming truck. I lowered my window and listened; I thought I heard a car ahead of me, maintaining more or less the same speed. The road wound and undulated; I could make out a dense woods and slowed again for safety's sake. When I nearly missed a turn—and narrowly missed a tree—I stomped on the brake. Gradually the dust settled, and so did my pulse rate.

Trees arched over the road, the morning sun leaking like liquid gold between their interlaced boughs. Birds sang. Leaves drifted down. It was a lovely fall morning, and I was lost in Indiana.

Then I heard an engine. A new dust cloud appeared down the road, shrouding the oncoming vehicle. I tried to pull off, but there was nowhere to go. The cloud rolled noisily toward me. Whatever was inside was approaching fast, and I knew they couldn't see me. Survival instincts took hold: I squeezed my eyes shut and leaned into the horn.

Brakes shrieked. The cloud cleared. It did not contain a Beamer. But I didn't know that yet. I didn't open my eyes till I heard the voice at my window. The voice said, "You all right?" I screamed in response. Then I opened my eyes and instantly felt better. The man was no one I knew, and his vehicle was a pick-up truck that looked older than I was.

"I'm fine!" I declared. "I'm wonderful! How are you?"

He ignored the question. "You lost?"

"Not really." I smiled warmly. He didn't smile back. He was scowling at my Lexus.

"Where you headed?"

"Uh—well—uh—" That was a tough one. I took a deep breath and decided to try the truth: "Actually, I was following someone, and we got separated."

"I don't suppose you mean the BMW I just passed back there?"

"Yes! Did you happen to see where it went?"

"Didn't have to," the man said. "Cars like that are only going one place."

I thought he meant Hell, but he said, "Archer Road. That fancy new development's over there."

"What development?"

"That resort development—on Lake James." He spat a wad of tobacco clear across the road. "Damned real-estate vultures. They're wrecking this state. I ain't selling my farm, no matter how much they offer me."

I nodded sympathetically. "About that BMW—"

"Turn right at the next road. It'll take you clear out there. 'Lost Fog' or something, they call it. Used to be Fred Swenson's farm, now it's all condos. Oughta call it Lost Farm. Only nobody gives a damn."

I thanked him, and he waved me on. The road didn't seem wide enough for his old truck and my SUV. Inching past, I cringed, expecting the grate of metal on metal.

"Keep going!" he roared. "You're all right!"

In my rearview mirror I saw him spit again. Who could blame him? Proceeding slowly enough not to kick up much dust—and noting that a resort area needs better access—I turned at Archer Road. This was a scenic region of low hills, patchy woods, and rocky streams. No wonder my fellow vultures had seized it. Ahead a tasteful sign announced that I had arrived at "Lost Mists—The Resort Overlooking Lake James." Beyond, three high-rise condos, one still under construction, framed a shimmering expanse of blue water. That was all I could see from my side of the guardhouse. Next task: getting past security.

"Good morning," I said cheerily to the uniformed man at the gate.

He returned my smile, expecting more information. I handed him my business card.

"I'm here to see Management. On behalf of the Chicago investors." My voice rose just a tad at the end, as if to remind him that I had an appointment. He studied the card a little longer than necessary. That didn't alarm me, but his reaching for the phone did.

"I called ahead on my car phone," I said. "They're in a meeting and won't appreciate another interruption."

He replaced the receiver. "First building on your left. Park in the back." He raised the gate for me to enter.

I noticed at once that each condo had its own garage, and most of them were closed. Finding the Beamer might be harder than expected. I circled the development twice without success. My next idea was to park by the unfinished building and investigate on foot. I pulled on a baggy cotton jacket, a broad-rimmed hat, and oversized sunglasses. Then I surveyed the scene. The air was crisp and invigorating, the fall colors stunning. I really should spend more time outdoors.

Something snagged my peripheral vision. I whipped my head around in time to see Darrin Keogh, one parking lot over, sail past on a bicycle. He didn't see me. Where was the Beamer? And where was Keogh off to in such a hurry? He pedaled away from me along the lakeshore toward what looked like a distant park. Then I remembered that I had a bike, too. I popped the hatchback and hauled mine out. Now that her tires were properly inflated, Blitzen could handle anything. I climbed on, hoping Keogh wasn't out just for the exercise. It was a lovely day, and I needed a workout, but first I needed answers.

In a minute I realized that I could pass Keogh without half trying, so I downshifted and willed myself to enjoy the scenery. The working world was gainfully employed, as I should have been. I realized that I had no cell phone with me. Odette and the rest of my staff must be wondering where I was. And for Pete's sake, who was running For Art's Sake while Keogh was out having fun? Ahead of me he faded into the shadows of a woodsy glen. I slowed to consider what might await me. If he knew he was being followed, would he ditch me? Or attack me? Or invite me home to meet his mom?

By now he was invisible while I was still bathed in sunlight. *Lame disguise, don't fail me now.* Blitzen and I glided into the cool of the trees; when my eyes adjusted, I caught a glimpse of Keogh rounding the bend ahead. The trail had degraded from a paved path to a dirt one that was still relatively smooth. I shivered as the temperature dipped ten degrees.

The path became increasingly uneven and winding. Lake James could have been miles away; for all I knew, I was deep in a forest. Birds sang in the richly hued leaves overhead. The woods smelled of must and decay. Occasionally, I spotted Keogh ahead, dappled in sunlight. He was pedaling hard on a bike whose gear ratio couldn't compete with Blitzen's. Then, on a straightaway, I saw him starting up a steep incline. He was laboring, so I let myself fall back another fifty yards. What if he chose this spot to stop suddenly and look around?

But he made it over the top of the hill, so I put some oomph into my efforts. Approaching the crest, I tensed. What if he were resting there? I doubted my disguise would work under close scrutiny. I decided I'd pretend to be scouting the area on behalf of a client who planned to retire in Indiana. I'm a real estate professional. I know how to shade the truth.

But I didn't have to. Darrin Keogh's bike lay on the trail before me. He stood a short distance away on a rocky outcropping. But he was too busy pleading for his life to notice my arrival. The man I had known and lusted after as Edward Naylor held him at gunpoint. Keogh inched backward toward the edge of ledge, whimpering pathetically. Gordon Santy aimed his rifle with the confidence of a trained assassin.

Keogh said, "Let's talk about this. You need me, Gordon!"

For the first time, I heard Santy laugh. It wasn't a happy sound. "You've made enough Matheneys. Thank you very much, but your services are no longer required."

Keogh took another step backward and stumbled. Santy laughed again.

"Get up. You're making this way too easy!"

Keogh took a long moment before he moved. I assumed he was wondering what difference it would make. If he stood up, he'd get shot. If he stayed down, he'd get shot.

"I said, get up! Now!" Santy released the safety.

Either Keogh had bigger balls than I'd imagined, or he just wanted to be done with it. He rolled forward onto his knees and pushed himself upright. As he did so, he glanced my way. In the fraction of a second when our eyes met, I realized that my hat had slid off. Attached by a string, it now rested on the back of my neck exposing my infamous unfunny hair. My curls are my calling card, and Darrin Keogh read it out loud.

"Whiskey Mattimoe!" he gasped.

Santy reacted as if Keogh had picked that moment to order a cocktail. He followed his gaze.

"Well, well. It's the dog lady with the hots for me."

I've been called worse, but that hurt. The Canadian swung his rifle in my direction. "Drop the bike *now* and get over here!"

"He'll kill us both!" Keogh cried. "And Avery, too. I told her about the forgeries! He'll never let her live!"

Santy said, "You told *who*?"

"*Whom*," Keogh corrected him. "Whiskey's stepdaughter. You saw her the other day."

"*Former* stepdaughter," I said quickly. "Now that her dad's dead, I don't think it counts."

"The fat chick who got in the way of my shot?" Santy asked.

"She's pregnant," I explained. "Though she was never thin."

Santy was once again advancing on the antiques dealer. "You told her *what*?"

"Everything—about the paintings and the blackmail. You name it, she knows about it."

"You little fuck. I don't care *whom* you told. You're dead. And so is she."

Then Blitzen and I were bearing down on him, tearing across the rocky ground toward the ledge as if planning to hang-glide over the side. Those big yellow wings would have come in handy. Keogh saw us coming. His watery eyes widened, but this time he said nothing. In the last instant that we accelerated toward Santy's unsuspecting back, Keogh leapt deftly aside. I squeezed my handle grips tight, and we slammed our target. Santy's shoulders and head flew back; his spine flexed into an inverted C. The gun fired. He lifted into the air with me and Blitzen. The last thing I recall—besides his surprisingly girlish scream and the eerie sense that my wheels were no longer in contact with Earth—was the altimeter on my handlebars. The digital readout said 329. *Feet or meters?* I wondered.

TWENTY-EIGHT

I DON'T CARE WHAT actors say on TV. When you wake up in a hospital room, you know that's where you are. There's no confusing it with anyplace else. I asked where I was, though, because I had no memory of getting there. The nice nurse said I was at Cameron Memorial Hospital in Angola, Indiana.

I moaned, more from frustration than pain, although my head hurt and so did my right side. The nurse explained that I had a concussion, a fractured ulna (elbow), and two broken ribs.

"Only two this time?" I asked weakly.

She nodded. "But your X-rays say they're two of the same ribs you broke before."

"I'm matchsticks. At least I broke a new arm."

She assured me that I'd be fine, that they were keeping me for observation. Then she adjusted some tube running into me somewhere, and I was gone again. The next time I opened my eyes, Darrin Keogh was staring at me. He didn't look much better than I felt.

"What the hell happened?" I said.

"You saved me. And probably Avery, too."

"I mean, what the hell happened to *me*?"

He recapped my impetuous Bicycle-as-Battering Ram maneuver.

"So Blitzen and I took Gordon Santy over the edge of a cliff. . . ."

"More like the edge of a ravine. You fell sixty feet."

"My altimeter said 329."

"Meters above sea level. We were at one of the highest points in the state."

"How come I'm not dead?"

"Your bike saved you. That and the tree you fell into."

"What about Santy?"

Keogh shook his head. "He didn't have a bike. Or a tree. He hit a rock."

I had killed a man. I must have passed out again. When I woke, Darrin Keogh was still there looking anxious.

"Thanks for saving me, Whiskey. I'm not a bad guy."

My brain buzzed, reconnecting a couple synapses.

"Santy said you made Matheneys. You're a forger?"

"Let's say I'm good at following directions."

"What does that mean?"

Keogh poured me water and started explaining. "A few years ago, my uncle hired me to finish his paintings. He couldn't sustain an interest, didn't have the focus anymore. I think he was doing a lot of drugs. All I knew for sure was he had a problem, and I could help. And I needed money. My antiques business was going under."

"You can paint?"

He shrugged. "Clouds aren't that hard."

"How does finishing paintings turn into forging them?"

"I don't consider what I did a forgery," Keogh said. "My uncle hired me to do it."

"You signed his name to works that weren't his but were sold as his. I'm thinking that's forgery."

Keogh wiped a bead of sweat from his brow.

"Please listen. Before long Uncle Warren couldn't paint at all anymore, but he had commissions to fulfill. He said he was in a lot of trouble. He begged me to do the paintings, and he promised he'd pay me more than I'd ever dreamed of earning. So . . . I took over. At first, he gave me a lot of feedback. After a few months, he didn't say much at all. But the orders kept coming."

"So," I concluded, "you're the real Cloud Man."

"No way! Warren Matheney was Cloud Man. Whether he could paint anymore or not, it was his *mystique* that sold the pictures. His appearances on TV and at galleries. I was . . . the hired help."

"Then why did Gordon Santy want to kill you?"

"He was afraid I'd talk."

"To who?"

"To *whom*," Keogh said automatically. "I'm . . . not sure I should say. I think I might need a lawyer."

"You think?"

"I never meant to do anything wrong!"

"Nothing worse, that is, than forging art?"

I was doing my best imitation bad cop. But it's hard to look menacing in a hospital bed.

"I never met Santy till after Uncle Warren died, but I recognized his voice. He'd been the one who phoned me with 'commissions'—only then he used a different name."

"Do you remember it?"

"Robert Reitbauer."

"The cement tycoon? Why would Robert Reitbauer call you to order art?"

"Because his wife hung out with my uncle."

I tried to picture the adolescent-acting Mrs. R. in the company of a world-famous artist, but the image wouldn't come. It was hard enough picturing her married to a mogul.

Keogh mumbled, "Kimba's my sister."

I gestured frantically at my water glass. I needed a drink, and I'd take what I could get.

"So, Mrs. R.—*Kimba*—is your sister, and the man pretending to be her husband on the phone is Gordon Santy?"

"That's right."

"How the hell—?"

"The real Robert Reitbauer is in a nursing home. He'd had a few strokes before Kimba married him. Then he had a massive one. The guy's a vegetable."

I recalled Odette's insistence that the live voice of Mr. Reitbauer didn't match the recorded version on their home answering machine, but that the live voice had seemed familiar. It should have seemed familiar to me, too, but I had missed the link.

"Why did Gordon Santy pretend to be Robert Reitbauer?"

"Because, in the beginning, the real Robert Reitbauer asked him to. He hired Santy to be Kimba's escort. He knew my sister needed more of a social life than he was able to give her. But he didn't know Santy would actually pretend to be him. Santy took advantage of the situation. He started selling forged art to Reitbauer's business contacts. My sister helped him pull it off."

"What was their hold over Matheney? Why would he agree to play?"

Keogh lowered his voice. "Like I told you, my uncle had problems. He did drugs. But that wasn't all he was into. He liked strange sex."

"How strange?"

"He liked to hurt his partner, and he wasn't particular about the partner he had."

210

Keogh's stories about Avery as a young art student and Pashtoon as a puppy came back to me. Then I replayed knocking on the door of Keogh's store. Wells had said that Mrs. Santy probably expected someone tall like me, which is why I'd passed muster through the frosted panes.

"You and Mrs. Santy were expecting Kimba the day I came to your store!"

Keogh nodded. "It was Kimba's idea to hide the Santys. She leased the condo at Lost Mists in her name so they could stay there. She makes me share my Beamer."

"What do you know about the murders?"

Keogh paled. "I don't know anything!"

"You think your uncle died of natural causes?"

"Yes."

"Then how'd he lose his finger? The one with his famous Celtic Cloud Ring? Dan Gallagher's widow found it in her motel room—minus the ring—and then my dog ran off with it. Actually, we think my dog had the finger first, while the ring was still on it. She probably buried it, and then someone dug it up—"

My story had a surprising effect: Keogh puked on the floor, narrowly missing his shoes. I didn't mind because we were in a hospital. Someone else would clean it up.

Now I knew how Keogh could afford the Beamer and who had picked him up this morning. What I wondered was why he'd bicycled into the woods. I delayed asking till the nurse's aide had mopped the floor.

Keogh said, "Last night, Gordon Santy came to my mother's house and stole the Cumulus off our wall. Right in front of me. He just laughed when I tried to stop him. Said he now had everything he needed. This morning Kimba called from the condo to say Gordon was going to stash it at the ice house."

211

"Where's that?"

"In the woods, near the spot where you found us. There's an old ice house built out of stone. It used to be part of a farm. I delivered my last few paintings there."

"Why not to the condo?"

Keogh sniffed. "Have you been inside? The security stinks."

"But why would you confront Santy?"

"You think I couldn't take him?"

I raised an eyebrow. Keogh said, "Kimba told me to get the painting back. It's part of our inheritance. Santy had gone too far. Like I said, I follow directions."

"Why didn't you bring a weapon?"

"I don't own a weapon. I have a naturally calming effect."

That I believed. Afghan hounds aren't known for their tranquility, yet his were as docile as rabbits.

"When was the last time you calmed Avery?" I said.

"Those aren't my twins!" he protested.

I hadn't thought they were. Keogh struck me as asexual.

"What about the burglary attempt at my house? Was that you?"

"That was a complete misjudgment, which we both regret. Especially me—since I got away, and Avery didn't."

"What were you looking for?"

"Avery was working with a healer who told her that the Second Sun of Solace is to claim what's rightfully yours.

Noonan.

"You mean the photo of Leo in Rio?"

"Avery said you thought the picture was taken in Michigan."

"I did. Just out of curiosity, what's the First Sun of Solace?"

"I think Avery said it's admitting what you want."

"She's never had a problem there. What did you want?"

212

Keogh hesitated. "Let's say I had both a good motive and a bad motive."

"I'm listening."

"I wanted to help Avery, and I thought maybe I could . . ."

His voice trailed off, but I knew the answer.

"You thought you could get Abra to leave with you! You didn't know she was away that night, and Mooney was with me. So, you *are* the dog-napper!"

"I breed Afghan hounds. I don't steal them. Grabbing Abra was Kimba's job. She was the one driving around Magnet Springs in the Beamer. But she's no good with animals. Abra got away from her twice."

"Abra's a handful," I conceded.

"I was going to *borrow* her," Keogh insisted. "The Santys put a lot of pressure on me to find out where she buried Warren's ring. I thought I could get her to lead me to it. Then I was going to bring her back to you. In perfect condition."

He looked ill again, and suddenly I understood.

"If you didn't come through, the Santys were going to harm your dogs."

"Gordon said he'd put out Pashtoon's remaining eye. He wrote the note you found about torturing Abra. I thought I could make her trust me, and then we could end this thing. Once and for all. I just wanted to finish my business and walk away."

I leaned as far toward him as the tubes would allow. "Did you get back the family Cumulus? The one Santy stole last night?"

"Thanks to you and your bicycle. It was in the ice house."

"What about the Cumulus at Shadow Play? What happened to that one?"

He smiled with pride. "I painted that one. It was so good, Kimba fooled the insurance company."

"And you don't think that's wrong? Not to mention that the Santys killed someone named Holly Lomax that night and pretended she was Mrs. Santy. Mr. Santy had already killed Dan Gallagher and made us think it was him."

Keogh stared at me, slack-jawed. Either he was truly in the dark or he was an excellent actor.

I said, "You didn't know that?"

"I didn't know any of that," he insisted. "I just did what I was told and didn't ask questions."

"Ignorance isn't the same as innocence. Your sister's wicked, but you're no saint. If the cops don't get you, I'd be afraid that your sister will."

TWENTY-NINE

WHO SHOULD WALK INTO my hospital room just then but my very own mother, Irene Houston. With the dreaded chicken soup. Once upon a time, someone—probably my late, sainted father—gave her the misguided impression that she could cook. Ever since then my mother has descended upon those in need with what she considers her curative broth. The stuff is vile. It even smells vile, thanks to the generous portions of slimy okra she includes. Edging toward the door, Darrin Keogh wrinkled his nose at the covered dish.

"What's in that?"

My mother winked at him. "Secret ingredients. But we can put you on the list."

"What list?"

"The recipe list. After I die, Whitney is going to mail out copies to everyone who asked."

"I'm her executrix," I explained.

Recipe distribution wouldn't be onerous. No one had ever requested a copy. "Mom, how did you get here?"

"Your nice beau brought me. You should have told me you were dating the Judge. I had to hear it from my card club."

I was a beat or two behind.

My mother continued. "Chief Jenkins came to see me when she got the report of your accident. Then she told Judge Verbelow about it, and he called to offer me a ride. I'd never been in a Beamer before!"

I tried to imagine Wells stuck in his car with my mother, her non-stop talk, and her stinky soup. The hundred or so miles must have been torture.

"Where is the Judge?" I asked.

"Parking the Beamer! He dropped me off. Would you like your soup now? There's got to be a microwave around here."

"I have to leave," Keogh announced. "Get well soon, Whiskey." And he was gone.

My mother said, "He seems nervous. What's with him?"

Then Wells appeared in the doorway.

"Whiskey! You don't look half bad, considering."

"What's this about killing a man with your bicycle?" said my mother, stirring her soup. "Chief Jenkins said it was self-defense, but how does something like that happen?"

I wish I could say that my heart soared when I saw Wells Verbelow, but it didn't. I was pleased to see him, especially since another person in the room helps dilute the tension with my mother. But I wasn't thrilled or elated. I didn't remotely feel what I used to feel when Leo arrived on the scene. Or, for that matter, during the early part of my ill-fated marriage to Jeb Halloran. To put it bluntly, I didn't feel passion. Wells is a good man, a prominent man, and a reasonably attractive man. But he doesn't stoke my furnace. Gazing at him from my hospital bed, I wondered what the hell was wrong with me. Maybe my "equipment" was failing.

Wells tactfully cleared the room of both my mother and her soup by summoning an aide who could find a microwave. As soon as the employee sniffed the brew, she looked at me in alarm. I mouthed the words *thank you*, but what I meant was *throw it away*.

"The local police arrested Ellianna Santy at Kimba Reitbauer's condo," Wells said. "Darrin Keogh called 9-1-1 for you and then turned her in."

"What about his sister?"

I told Wells about Kimba Keogh Reitbauer and her brother's visit to my hospital room. His face darkened.

"The police want to talk to both Mrs. Reitbauer and her brother. The FBI has a few questions, too, about art forgery. And I have an update on Avery."

I held my breath. "Did she deliver?"

"No. But she confessed to breaking into your house. Since she didn't steal anything, it's up to you whether you want to press charges."

"Did she name her accomplice?"

"No, and that's a problem. Jenx and the MSP think the other party might have been involved with the Santys."

I sighed deeply, letting myself sink into my pillow. The stench of Irene Houston's Chicken Soup was almost gone from the room. Wells touched my hand.

"Was I out of line, Whiskey?"

"What do you mean?"

"Bringing your mother here. I thought it was the right thing to do."

I waved away his concern. "There's no way you could have known about the soup."

"I meant that I thought it was my role to come as soon as I heard. And to bring your mother. My role as someone who cares about you, who's involved in your life. What I'm seeing in your eyes, though, tells me you don't feel that way."

I squeezed my lids shut. "I'm sorry, Wells. Maybe I'm just too tired."

"I don't think so, but it's all right. Honesty counts for something."

I opened my eyes. "You're a judge. What counts more than honesty?"

He smiled. "Reality."

Neither of us spoke for a moment. Then Wells changed the topic. "Jenx executed her warrant for the Schlegels' prayer garden. She'll want to give you the details herself. But the short version is . . . they found a ring."

"*A* ring or *the* ring?"

"It matches the description of Warren Matheney's Celtic Cloud Ring. Man, that thing's ugly."

I said, "Any idea how Abra got hold of it?"

"The Chicago police think Holly Lomax was with Matheney when he died. She probably stole whatever she could from his apartment. When she couldn't get the ring off, she removed the finger. We know she worked for the Santys, and we know she was a prostitute. The Chicago police say she visited Cloud Man on numerous occasions."

I thought about Matheney's dark side and then tried not to.

Wells continued, "Either she planned to sell the Santys the ring, or she planned to sell it to someone else. In either case, Jenx thinks Lomax had it in her purse the night she was murdered. Maybe she realized the Santys weren't going to pay her for it or let her leave without a fight. So she tossed the purse. Abra picked it up—and we know the rest."

"Do we?" I sat up as straight as I could. "How did the purse and the finger, minus the ring, end up in Holly's motel room?"

"The buried ring was in a purse, yes, but not *that* purse. Jenx thinks Lomax managed to get the ring off the finger before she went to Shadow Play. She hid the finger in a different purse, probably with the intention of discarding it later."

"Only she didn't have a 'later,'" I said.

"Jenx thinks the Santys saw Abra run off with Lomax's purse, and they figured the ring was in it. Either that or they forced Lomax to tell them. The Santys knew Abra's 'criminal history' and thought she would lead them to it."

"Here's what confuses me," I said. "How could anyone sell Matheney's Celtic Cloud Ring without causing an uproar? Everyone knows it belongs to his estate."

"You don't sell something like that on the open market," Wells said.

I remembered Brady's account of Matheney's posthumous popularity and the ascendant value of his art.

"So there are collectors, and then there are *collectors*," I ventured.

"Soup's on!"

I turned to see my mother standing in the doorway with the nurse's aide. Both were smiling broadly, holding steaming bowls. I inhaled cautiously. "What happened to the smell?"

"Hm?" My mother set a spoon and bowl on my tray as the aide served Wells.

"This smells *good*," I said, confused. "What happened to the okra?" I looked to the aide for an explanation.

"We had us a little accident. When I was stirring the soup before I put it in the microwave, I accidentally spilled it all."

My instinct was to high-five the woman, but my arm was in a sling. We winked at each other instead.

My mother said, "The nice gals working in the kitchen let me have some of their soup. It's different from mine, but you'll like it."

The aide grinned. "I am so clumsy. But this worked out all right. Your mama got herself a brand new recipe."

I tasted it. Possibly the best soup I'd ever eaten. Wells agreed.

"We'll be adding names to my recipe list, for sure," my mother declared, rubbing her hands in anticipation. "Remember, Whitney, nobody gets a copy till I'm dead."

The doctor in charge of my case insisted that I spend the night in Angola. I gave Wells my keys, and he promised to make sure that my car was moved from Lost Mists to Cameron Memorial. I was confident I would be able to get myself home. I had driven broken before.

Wells assured me that he'd keep Abra at his house until I was stronger. I wished he'd keep her forever. As he and my mother were leaving, I remembered to ask about Blitzen.

"Can she be saved?"

Wells said, "I hear she looks bad but is probably repairable. You knew that the police impounded her?"

"Why?"

"She killed a man, Whiskey."

The Angola police interviewed me the following morning. Although I didn't get to meet Darrin Keogh's loyal friend and choir-buddy, the Chief, the officer who came to my hospital room was respectful. He declared that no charges would be filed concerning the death of Gordon Santy, alias Edward Naylor. It's always nice to know that there's no warrant pending against you.

Avery was waiting for me when I got home. I was in too much pain to ask how she'd gotten in or what had happened to her too-small car. At least she'd had the decency to remove the crime scene tape.

Obviously miserable, she was even more bloated than the last time I'd seen her. I hadn't realized someone could be that pregnant.

Ignoring my injuries, she greeted me with "We need to talk."

I considered taking a double dose of my prescribed pain medication but doubted it would ease this ache.

"I know you don't like me, you've never liked me, and you plan to never like me," she began.

I held up my good arm to stop her.

"For clarification: doesn't that also sum up your feelings toward me?"

"What does that matter? You married my father. I'm not supposed to like you."

"But automatically I'm supposed to like you?"

"Yeah." I saw no doubt in her eyes. "Dad would have liked any kids you had, but you didn't have any."

I shook my head, and it hurt. But what hurt more was the realization that Avery was right. Leo would have loved any child of mine. He was like that.

"When did he take you to Rio?" I asked, plunging ahead.

"Last winter. We didn't go to Mexico, like you thought."

"Why not?"

"Because I begged him to take me to Rio." She stuck her tongue out, probably unconsciously. I fought a powerful urge to smack her.

"Why didn't he tell me that?"

"He didn't want to hurt you. He said you were planning your first trip there to celebrate your anniversary, and he didn't think he should go before that. But I was studying Portuguese in school and wanted to go to Brazil more than anything. I knew Mom would never take me, and it would be forever before I could afford to go by myself. Dad wanted to make me happy."

Avery added, "He spent half the time collecting tourist brochures for you. You never got them?"

I never did.

"Maybe he forgot to unpack them," she suggested. "Maybe he was saving them to surprise you."

It wasn't like Avery to try to make me feel better. She sighed. "I guess we both lost something. You were supposed to have a nice trip. I was supposed to have a grandfather for my kids."

A stab of pain doubled me over. With my good hand, I gripped the edge of the kitchen counter, groaning. I could barely draw a breath.

"You sound awful," Avery said reproachfully. "What's wrong with you? And what did you do to our garage?"

After my next moan, I was dizzy. I must have staggered, for Avery cried, "Why are you doing this to me? Sit down before you fall down!"

Too late.

I'm doing this way too often. That was my first thought on regaining consciousness. For someone who had managed not to faint from age sixteen to thirty-three, I was suddenly exceeding the national average. At least I'd been fortunate enough to land on my good side, so I didn't feel shooting pains upon waking. Avery looked ghastly, however, when her wide, white face floated into view.

"Don't ever do that to me again! I'm pregnant, for crying out loud. You could have scared me right into labor!"

I thanked God for sparing us that trauma. Then we faced an intriguing dilemma: a woman on the floor who couldn't get up and a woman standing who couldn't (or wouldn't) help her up. After a few minutes, we started laughing.

"It would have been even funnier with you on the floor!" I giggled. "You're so big and fat, you'd never get up. And I've only got one good arm to pull with. You'd have to lie there like road kill!"

Avery stopped laughing and stomped out of the room. Eventually, I got up by myself.

After the drive from Angola and the encounter with Avery, returning to work was easy. Pleasant, even. Everyone in the office knew about my adventure with Blitzen. They just didn't know what to say about it. Their employer had killed a client. There's no stock comment for that one.

Odette rapped three times and flung open my door.

"You never told us about your secret life as a Super Hero!"

"I didn't think I had to. Don't you have psychic powers?"

"*Telephone* telepathy. And you didn't call. What the hell happened?"

I told her she'd been right about the phone version of Mr. Reitbauer not being the real Mr. Reitbauer.

Odette looked reflective. "Perhaps we can find more lucrative ways to apply my powers."

"I thought it was bad karma to use psychic gifts for profit."

"It's good karma to get rich, Whiskey. Killing clients is bad karma."

I reminded her that the Santys were *former* clients—and murderous felons. Then I filled in the rest of the story. She had no comment. I wondered if she'd even been listening.

Dreamily, Odette poured herself coffee from the pot on my credenza and added cream from my mini-fridge. After settling herself across from me, she said, "Rico Anuncio is involved in this."

I was about to say that I thought so, too, when my phone buzzed.

"Call for Odette on line three," said my receptionist. "Rico Anuncio. And he's upset."

Rico Anuncio wasn't upset; he was hysterical. Odette switched on the speaker phone so that I could listen. Fortunately, her slow, rhythmic speech pattern soon calmed him to the point of coherence.

"That money was supposed to be mine!" he exclaimed. "Warren showed me his will when he was here for the show. He was leaving half his estate to me!"

"What's the problem?" said Odette.

"The estate is frozen! The Chicago police just sent me a fax. They said he may have been murdered, and that changes everything!"

"Did you murder him?" Odette asked calmly.

"Of course not! I *loved* him! I lived with him—and put up with him—for seven and a half years! I still loved him when we broke up, but I had to leave. The thing with the dogs made me crazy."

"Tell me about the dogs," Odette said. Rico did—in more detail than either of us wanted.

"I'm not what you'd call an animal lover," he concluded. "But I'm no sadist. I didn't care what Warren did to me; I could take it. I could even take knowing he was doing it to other people because they were consenting adults." He paused. "Okay, there may have been a few minors. But he forced himself on animals. And *they* couldn't walk out the door."

THIRTY

"DID YOU KNOW THE Santys or Kimba Reitbauer or Darrin Keogh?"

Odette read what I had jotted on a sticky note and passed to her. Rico guessed that I was there. "Why don't you ask your own questions, Whiskey?"

So I did, from then on. Although Rico insisted that he was not involved in Matheney's sordid world, he was aware of it.

"Darrin was in and out of Warren's life, mainly begging for money. Of course I knew who he was when he asked about you at my gallery. I didn't want you to know I knew him."

"And Kimba?"

"I saw her at a couple of Warren's parties. Before she married money, she used to whore around. She was part of a 'twins' act: 'Kimba and Holly.'"

"Holly Lomax?"

"She didn't use a last name."

I asked if he thought Holly was her real first name.

"Probably. Kimba went by Kimba. People thought that was an alias. Her mother had trailer-trash taste in names."

"What did the Santys have to do with Matheney?" I said.

"In the beginning, they gave parties. Gordon and Ellianna got Warren all the drugs and lovers he could handle. Skanky people. Pretty, but oh-so-nasty."

"Then why did you pretend not to know Gordon Santy when he posed as Edward Naylor in the bar at Mother Tucker's? Walter told us."

"When I was planning Cloud Man's show at my gallery, Santy acted as Warren's business manager. He insisted I include two *faux* Matheneys. He didn't say they were *faux*, but I knew. When I refused, he threatened to—blackmail me."

"About what?"

"A personal matter. Nothing important. To keep the counterfeits out of the show, I had to make a deal with Santy. Promise I'd do him a favor later. Something small, he said. Last week he gave me the script for that little scene at Mother Tucker's. I didn't understand it, but I didn't ask questions. By the way, Whiskey, how does it feel to kill a man?"

"I prefer to think I saved a man."

"Ah, yes. Thanks to you, Keogh's a fugitive now."

"He's not a completely bad guy," I said.

"He's kind to animals. That much is true."

"And he takes care of his sick mother."

"His mother lives in a condo in Coconut Grove!"

"No, she's an invalid in that old house in Angola. He waits on her hand and foot. Everyone in town knows it."

"He's fooled everyone in town."

"But I was in that house. I heard her voice!"

"You heard his sister's voice. They work scams, Whiskey. The FBI is going to find that For Art's Sake doesn't exist!"

"I've been to the store! I knocked on the door—"

"How much did you see? Keogh has a few good antiques and a few decent paintings. But the store's a front for the art he forges and fences. Nobody who dresses that badly could survive in retail."

"Let's talk about your Cumulus," I said.

"The real thing. Painted in October '79. A parting gift from the artist. I have the provenance, including Warren on videotape asserting that the Cumulus was his gift to me. I made sure no one could later claim I stole it."

That raised a good question. "So who buys a forgery? Doesn't every buyer require provenance?"

"If the price is right, some people ask no questions. My art is my investment portfolio. Warren gave me several lesser paintings, too. From his pre-Cloud days. And a few Cloud studies."

"He did studies? Of clouds? What for?" Keogh had said that clouds weren't hard to paint.

"You don't know much about art," Rico sighed.

"I know that your 'portfolio' is soaring in value, thanks to Matheney's mysterious death."

"Warren couldn't have lived much longer, the way he was living. And, yes, I have assets. But not enough to buy me the home of my dreams."

Odette said, "I can show you several stunning alternatives! Buy now; move up again soon. Why not start looking this afternoon?"

My best agent arranged to pick up Rico at his gallery. I said, "What do we have to satisfy a man who wanted a château?"

Odette's eyes twinkled. "Be prepared to be amazed, Whiskey." And she was off.

Almost immediately, my phone buzzed again. Acting Chief Jenkins on line one.

"A realtor I know thinks it's her place to solve crimes, and not just in this jurisdiction! What the hell were you doing in Angola?"

As I began to recap my adventures, Jenx interrupted. "I know what you did. I want to know why you did it."

"You convinced me Keogh hadn't told the whole story, so I went back to spy on him."

"Think you got the whole story now? He's gone, you know."

"He's . . . missing."

"And so's his sister, who's got a sheet as long as her legs. But I didn't call to pick on you. I called because somebody here wants to see you. You don't have to see her if you don't want to. In fact, this is highly irregular."

"Who is it, already?"

"Your favorite ex-client, or one of them: Ellianna Santy."

"I thought she was in jail!"

"I'm looking at her through vertical bars right now. She's on her way from Angola to Chicago, in police custody. The lady wants to talk to you. How about it?"

At the police station, Jenx confided, "Ellianna Santy's not the priss we took her for first time around."

The Chief led me down the hall to Magnet Springs' one and only holding cell. Inside sat a woman I didn't at first recognize. Her skin was pasty, her eyes small and dull. Her hair, so carefully tended the last time, was no longer blonde or even combed. It was now the over-dyed, over-permed hair of a woman who wished to be anonymous.

"How did it feel to kill my husband, eh?"

"How did it feel to kill Holly Lomax?" I countered.

"I've never killed anyone! That's why I wanted to see you. I didn't think you were made that way."

"Then who killed Lomax?"

"Gordon. First, he got her drunk, and then he dyed her hair so her corpse could pass for mine. Told her she'd be sexier as a blonde! He's also the one you saw with the wings. And the one who blew up your propane tank. If he'd whacked you, like he was supposed to, he'd be alive today. I can't fucking believe you got him first."

"Watch the language," Brady said. I hadn't seen him come in.

228

"Fuck you and the dog you rode in on," Mrs. Santy replied.

Officer Roscoe growled.

"What's with the dogs in this town? They're all big and crazy. Must be the water."

"It's the magnetic fields," Jenx corrected her.

I asked Mrs. Santy, "How could your husband have killed Holly Lomax? He was in the bar at Mother Tucker's."

"He killed her and then went to the bar. It's called creating an alibi, bimbo!"

As if on cue, a sugary voice sang out: "Chief Jenkins—Marilee Gallagher to see you! Hellooo!"

Jenx and I locked eyes. "Do you want to talk to this one or that one?" she asked me.

Such a choice: I picked the crook.

"How did your husband kill her husband?" I asked Mrs. Santy.

"Gordon didn't kill him."

"Then who did?"

She faked an innocent expression. "I thought the official ruling was 'natural causes.'"

"Not anymore," said Brady. That's when I noticed he had a manila folder in his hand. "Crouch's toxicology report." He nodded in the direction of Marilee Gallagher's disembodied twittering. "That's why she's here."

"I'm intrigued," Mrs. Santy said, cupping her chin in her hand. "What does he say now?"

Brady gave her a look so cold that it didn't belong on his sweet young face. Then he opened the folder and read, "Cardiac blood: Positive for cocaine—"

"We knew that," I said impatiently.

"And Digoxin."

"What's that?"

Mrs. Santy said, "Ever heard of digitalis?"

Ignoring her, Brady flipped a few pages. "Crouch made an amendment to his original autopsy report: 'Abnormal findings include the presence of Digoxin, a digitalis derivative—'"

"Told you," Mrs. Santy said.

"'—prescribed in cases of congestive heart failure or atrial fibrillation.'"

"'A-fib.'" This time we both looked at her. Mrs. Santy smiled. "My first husband was a doctor."

Brady cleared his throat and resumed reading. "'Its presence in the quantity indicated in the blood of a healthy thirty-four-year-old man suggests a deliberate overdose leading or contributing to fatal arrhythmia. Immediate cause of death: Asystole due to Digoxin overdose. Possible contributing factor: Cocaine. Manner of death: Homicide.'"

Three distinct handclaps. Mrs. Santy was applauding.

"Not bad. For Hoosiers."

"Wolverines," I corrected her. "People who live in Indiana are Hoosiers. You should know that." To Brady I said, "Gallagher was about to get a massage from Noonan. Before that, he was with Lomax. How did he get the Digoxin? And from who?"

Mrs. Santy said, "Your report doesn't tell you that, does it? Dear, oh dear, how will they figure it out?"

"Why don't you shut up!" roared Brady. As if on command, Officer Roscoe threw himself against the cell bars, howling, his hackles raised. I jumped back.

"Sorry," Brady said to me. "Roscoe and I are taking a good cop/bad cop seminar in East Lansing. My bad cop needs a lot of work."

Roscoe continued scrabbling against the bars and barking viciously, his teeth bared. Pale as parchment, Mrs. Santy huddled against the back wall of her cell.

"Enough!" Brady boomed. Roscoe immediately stopped, turned in a circle, and lay down.

"When we do good cop/bad cop for real," Brady said, "Roscoe's always the bad cop. He's got a gift for it."

Brady tapped the report and looked at me. "We need to go see Noonan."

The sarna bells on her front door tinkled, and Noonan parted the curtains to greet us.

"I knew that was you," she said. "I've been meditating on it. And I'm going to feel so much better after we talk."

I wasn't sure that I felt better afterwards. But we did learn a few things. Brady brought along a tape recorder, which Noonan allowed him to use. Here's her complete account of Dan Gallagher's visit to the Star of Noon Massage Therapy Studio:

Brady: First, can you state for the record what you do?

Noonan: I'm a certified massage therapist and tele-counselor for the Seven Suns of Solace. It's a New Age Healing School based in Taos, New Mexico.

Brady: Okay. And what does a New Age tele-counselor do?

Noonan: I counsel those seeking enlightenment. Over the phone.

Brady: Why not in person?

Noonan: I do that, too, but that's not tele-counseling. Most of my clients are tourists who take a couple massages while vacationing in Magnet Springs. I tell them about the Seven Suns of Solace, and they start the program here. Then they complete it at home, over the phone.

Brady: Can you explain what you do, exactly?

Noonan: I help people discover their inner and outer realities and re-shape them for maximal karmic resonance.

{Long silence punctuated by Officer Roscoe's yawn.}

Brady: Did you offer the Seven Suns . . . to Dan Gallagher?

Noonan: He was dead before I had the chance.

Brady: You never started the massage?

Noonan: Oh, I started it. At first I just thought he was relaxed. Then I noticed he didn't have a pulse.

Brady: That was when you called 9-1-1?

Noonan: Yes.

Brady: Let's back up. What happened from the time Mr. Gallagher arrived until the time you started the massage?

Noonan: He came in alone. He said he had a stiff neck.

Brady: Then what happened?

Noonan: I showed him into my studio and asked him to get undressed. Then my Seven Suns of Solace phone rang. See, I have a dedicated line for my tele-counseling clients. It has a distinct ring—and also Caller ID—so I can prepare for a client's special needs.

Brady: Who was calling?

Noonan: It was my newest client, Kimba Reitbauer. She was having a crisis.

Brady: What kind of crisis?

Noonan: I don't think I can tell you that. Client confidentiality.

Brady: That applies to physicians and attorneys—not massage therapists.

Noonan: But I took a vow of confidentiality during my Seven Suns of Solace tele-counseling training—

Brady: Worthless in a court of law. Why did Mrs. Reitbauer call?

Noonan: Well, I could hardly understand her, she was carrying on so. Something about her husband and how mean he was. Ordinarily, if a tele-counseling client calls when I have a massage therapy client, I arrange to talk as soon as the massage is over. But Kimba was hysterical. By the time I calmed her enough to schedule a call-back, we'd been on the phone for thirteen-point-eight minutes.

Brady: How do you know that?

Noonan: My dedicated line has a meter on it. For billing purposes.

Brady: So you left Dan Gallagher alone for almost fourteen minutes while you talked to Kimba Reitbauer?

Noonan: Yes. And there's something else. My dedicated line is back here in my office, not out in the lobby where I make massage appointments. While I was on the phone, I thought I heard my sarna bells ring. Twice.

Brady: Meaning?

Noonan: Meaning someone came and went, but I don't know who.

Brady: How long between rings?

Noonan: Almost six minutes. I checked the meter. When I say that Kimba was hysterical, I mean she was sobbing. She was so loud I could hardly hear anything else. But I thought I heard Dan Gallagher say something. I couldn't make it out, though.

Brady: What happened when you went in to give his massage?

Noonan: I apologized for the delay and asked if he'd tried to talk to me. But of course he didn't answer.

Brady: And you didn't think that was odd?

Noonan: Clients fall asleep on my table all the time. I play Cassina's CDs. Her voice puts people right out.

Walking back to the police station, Brady was stoked. "Witnesses saw Gallagher with Holly Lomax. They probably did coke together. Later Lomax suggested he get a massage to help him unwind. She and Mrs.

233

R. had a plan. After Gallagher went into the studio, Lomax called Mrs. R., who called Noonan. Then Lomax slipped in and told Gallagher she had another good drug. I'm going to guess she administered it intravenously, probably between his toes where no one would see the mark. He may have protested, but Noonan couldn't hear him. Then Lomax planted the fake ID in Gallagher's wallet. We'll have to subpoena phone records, but I'm betting on a Lomax-Reitbauer connection."

"I am, too," I said. "Is Noonan in trouble?" I hoped not.

"Legally, I don't think so. Ethically, she should have spoken up sooner. She put business before honor and protected the wrong party. Speaking of party, did you see that sign on her bulletin board? She's hosting a psychic party on Saturday night. Does that mean no invitations are necessary? And do they show up by car or by teleporting?"

I said, "Do you think the Cook County coroner will find Digoxin in Matheney's blood, too?"

Brady thought they might.

Back at the station, Mrs. Santy was gone, but Marilee Gallagher was still there. She dabbed at her eyes with an embroidered hanky.

"I went over Crouch's report with her," Jenx said, taking Brady and me aside. "And I had her look at some photos. She recognized both Holly Lomax and Kimba Reitbauer from the homeless shelter where she volunteers in Grand Rapids. They used to come in together. Mrs. Gallagher thought they were—you know. . . ."

"Hookers? Druggies?" I offered.

"Much, much worse." Jenx's eyes twinkled. "Like our good coroner, she prayed for them. One day they stopped coming. She hadn't seen them for at least eighteen months, maybe longer. Then, a few weeks ago, Holly showed up again, just to say hi. Without Kimba. She said they were in Chicago now, doing just fine. But Marilee wasn't satisfied. She sat Kimba down and lectured her about the joys of het-erosexual love."

"Oh no!"

"Oh yes. Mrs. Gallagher showed her a picture of her wonderful husband. Somehow Holly managed to take it with her. Mrs. Gallagher didn't notice it was gone until much later."

"That's the photo that showed up on Gordon Santy's fake New Brunswick driver's license!" I exclaimed.

"Which Holly Lomax planted in Dan Gallagher's wallet right after she killed him," said Brady. "She and Kimba were working for the Santys, who needed the world to believe that Gordon Santy was dead."

I frowned. "Remind me why, exactly."

"The Santys were wanted for art fraud and art theft—and likely to be implicated in Warren Matheney's death if Lomax stayed alive. Both Santys needed to disappear. So they did, using the bodies of Gallagher and Lomax."

"But what was in it for Kimba Reitbauer?"

Brady said, "She goes way back with the Santys. Probably used their contacts to meet her tycoon-sugar daddy. You can take the girl out of the criminal element but not the criminal element out of the girl."

Jenx said, "The Digoxin fits, too. Marilee says Kimba used to brag that she could get her hands on any kind of prescription drug."

"Excuse me!" trilled Marilee Gallagher. "Could I have a word with Whitney?"

"Be my guest," Jenx said and led Brady from the room.

Marilee limped toward me wearing only one shoe.

"What happened?" I asked, pointing to her naked foot.

"Ingrown toenail. So I took it off. Never liked these pumps anyway because the heel's too high, but Dan said they made my legs look thinner."

She stopped suddenly and stared at the remaining shoe. Then she kicked it off with such force that it cracked against the wall, narrowly missing Officer Roscoe, who ducked.

"Sorry!" she called out.

"You wanted to see me," I reminded her.

"Yes. About something personal."

Inwardly I groaned, hoping she didn't want to be my friend now that we'd both admitted being widows.

"It's about being widows," she began.

"Hey, I'm comfortable with that," I said. "You'll get there, too, I promise. It just takes time."

Her blue eyes widened. "Oh, I'm sure that's true. But that's not what I'm talking about. Have you heard of WUMPERs?"

"Pardon?"

"*Widows United for Mutual Power and Energized Renewal.* We're a national Christian support organization about to found a branch in West Michigan."

"No, thank you," I said, trying to sound flattered. "I'm a joiner but not a self-helper."

"You haven't even heard my question."

I began to explain that I don't do organized religion except on major holidays and my mother's birthday. Comprehension flashed across her face.

"I'm not recruiting you, Whitney, although, of course, you're welcome. We're Interfaith, so anyone who accepts Jesus Christ as their Lord and Savior can join. I'm just asking if you'll show us some real estate. This is a big organization, and I expect to do big things with it. Did I mention I'm running for president? They'll elect me. I'm famous for my enthusiasm, and frankly, I need a new cause. I'm sick of homeless shelters. Anyway, I plan to enlist thousands of women on this side of the state, so we'll need a meeting place and office space by the end of the year."

"In Grand Rapids," I ventured.

"Why not Magnet Springs? It's a resort community. And you and I both know the Holy Spirit's here among us."

THIRTY-ONE

I GAVE MARILEE GALLAGHER my card and promised to call. Then my cell phone purred. It was Odette, offering to buy me dinner at Mother Tucker's.

"Are you feeling sorry for me, or do we have something to celebrate?"

"Both. I'll be waiting at the bar with Walter and his best red."

I'd never sampled a finer Pinot Noir.

"What's the occasion?"

Odette and Walter exchanged glances. He began. "I for one am relieved to be alive, and I'm glad you're still here, too, Whiskey. Even though your home is inclined to become a crime scene."

"Don't get sentimental on me!"

His eyes crinkled. "Life is tenuous. But we're halfway through leaf-peeping season, and we're all getting rich."

He hoisted a glass in salute.

"*Who's* getting rich?" I said. Then I took in Mother Tucker's Bar and Grill, once again packed with tourists. "Congrats. You and Jonny must be very pleased."

"We're exhausted. Now it's Odette's turn to share."

"Make me a toast!" she cried. "I've sold the Schlegels' house! For cash!"

I stared. "To who?"

"Our very own bad boy, Richard Anderson. He fell in love with it! Offered the asking price while we were still on site. The Schlegels accepted with alacrity. We close in two weeks!"

"To the best real estate agent I know!" We three clinked glasses. "Who's Richard Anderson?"

"Rico Anuncio! He's no more Hispanic than you are. We knew that couldn't be his real name. Turns out he never legally changed it. That's his Big Secret. We're supposed to help him keep it."

"Or what? He'll sue us for negligence?"

"I doubt it now that he's into Apocalyptic art. He was entranced by the Schlegels' paintings. You won't believe what he paid for the lot." She whispered an improbably high number in my ear.

"For screaming souls and open graves?"

"And other horrors. The Schlegels are moving to Sun City, Arizona, so that Mrs. Schlegel can have a prickly-pear prayer garden. By the way, Gil Gruen was at Shadow Play, replacing his FOR SALE sign. Drive-by geeks keep stealing it. You should have seen his face, Whiskey, when I added *Under Contract* to ours."

Odette and I ate at the bar—Alaskan king crab for her, angel-hair pasta with white clam sauce for me. At some point, Walter switched us from red wine to white, and then to club soda with lime. Although I'd been tempted by the crab legs, I knew I couldn't manage them with only one good arm. Jonny's white clam sauce satisfied completely. Walter said he makes it with chopped littleneck clams, sweet butter, sweet onion, fresh garlic, Chardonnay, and heavy cream. I didn't need the recipe since I never planned to cook again. But it was tasty, my first feast in days.

So I was verging on happiness as I drove home that night. The real estate business was booming, Abra was still boarding with Wells, and the bad guys I knew about were either in jail, on the lam, or dead. Then I remembered that hostile Avery Mattimoe and her ticking double-occupancy womb awaited me. I would have inhaled deeply to calm myself if I hadn't had two broken ribs.

I heard the siren about a quarter-mile from home. Seconds later an ambulance passed me en route to the local hospital.

What were the odds that another emergency vehicle had been dispatched to Vestige? But the next sight was not encouraging. Every light in my house was on. Either Avery was scheming to bankrupt me via the electric company, or something had gone seriously awry. As I parked in my driveway in front of what used to be my garage, my porch light blinked on. It must have been the only lamp left to ignite. *At least there's no crime scene tape*, I thought. Then the front door flew open and out leapt Chester. He was flailing his arms and jumping about in his signature dance of high drama.

"Did you see the ambulance?" he cried.

Instantly I assumed that something had happened to Cassina. Chester must have dashed over to my house screaming for help. He'd searched every room for me and finally I was here.

"Is she all right?" I said, rushing toward him.

"She's having two babies!" he announced. That's when I knew we were talking about Avery.

"Already?" I felt my strength ebb away.

"I came in by the usual way to see if Abra was back. Avery freaked when she saw me." He looked ashamed. "How could I know she'd be in the kitchen? Nobody uses that room!"

I wondered if she'd found any food, but Chester's stricken face stopped me from asking.

"She started screaming," he said. "I tried to calm her. Then she grabbed her big belly and yelled that she was having two babies. So I called 9-1-1. I think her water broke. There's kind of a mess on your floor."

That was an understatement. Gathering my cleaning supplies, I gave silent thanks that I'd missed the event. Chester assured me that Avery had "settled" once the EMTs arrived.

"They told her, 'You're doing great.' It helped her relax. I offered to ride along in the ambulance, but they wouldn't let me because I'm not related." He sighed. "I'm hardly related to anybody."

"You're related to people! You have a family. Don't you?"

"I don't have any aunts or uncles or cousins or grandparents."

"You don't?"

He shook his head. "Cassina was raised in foster homes, so she never had a family."

"What about your father?"

"Rupert? Who knows."

"I thought you were going to visit him and get acquainted—"

"Look!" Chester's tone changed suddenly. "I've seen them!"

He was pointing at the wall-mounted kitchen television, whose drone I had ignored since entering. Two faces stared down at us: Darrin Keogh's and Kimba Reitbauer's.

"—the missing brother and sister," said a newscaster. "Mrs. Reitbauer is the wife of Chicago cement baron, Robert Reitbauer. Authorities believe that Darrin Keogh witnessed Wednesday's freak bicycle accident near the shore of Lake James, which claimed the life of international fugitive Gordon Santy. His wife Ellianna was later arrested in a condo leased by Mrs. Reitbauer. But the search continues for Keogh and his sister. Both are wanted for questioning by the FBI and local law enforcement agencies in three states. An unnamed source told Channel Six that the two may have information concerning the sudden death of world-famous artist Warren Matheney, also known as Cloud Man."

"I've seen them!" Chester said again. "They were at Bake-The-Steak when I was there with Abra! The night she stole the purse with the finger in it. They were behind us in line. Everybody turned around and looked at them."

"Why?"

"They were fighting. When she saw me watching her, the lady stopped talking and smiled, real fake-like."

"What about the man?"

"He just looked sad. I don't think he wanted a steak. Don't worry, Whiskey. They couldn't have heard what I told Abra."

"I know," I said, putting my good arm around him.

Then my mother called. She had been watching the same newscast.

"That missing person is the man I met in your hospital room!"

"What man?"

"He was the nervous one. The *only* one!"

I feigned a lapse of memory.

"Don't play games with me, Whitney Houston! I know all your moves."

I sincerely hoped not. "Hey, Mom, I need some advice about babies."

Silence filled the phone line. "Hello?" I said.

"Oh, Whitney." She sounded tearful. "I'm happy for you! But why didn't the Judge use a condom?"

Of course, I would set her straight. Eventually. First I wanted to envision one of those credit-card commercials where they tally the value of personal experiences.

"Messing with your mother's mind: Priceless."

What would Leo do? What would he want me to do?

I asked myself those questions often over the next few weeks. On my drive to Coastal Medical Center the night Avery gave birth, I could think of nothing else.

I had loved Leo more than life itself. I still loved Leo, but life was going on without him. Although I had no idea what my own life might yet hold, it seemed promising. I kept meeting memorable people, and they weren't all criminals.

I wanted to live my life fully right through to the end; I knew Leo would want me to. But that meant living as though Leo were gone. Not as if he'd never been here; not as if he hadn't left a mark. But as if he were truly, irrevocably gone. There was no point waiting for him. Abra and I could both watch the kitchen door forever; Leo Mattimoe would not walk back into our lives.

I was deeply conflicted about his only child. From the start, Avery and I had disliked each other. I knew enough about motherhood to predict that she wouldn't be nicer after she'd had her babies. She'd be exhausted, protective, and suspicious of my every move. On the other hand, her children were innocents and Leo's only biological heirs.

"So you'll join us for Thanksgiving?" Over the phone Odette sounds more impatient than usual. I hear water running and wonder if she could be cooking. "Whiskey? Are you listening?"

I should confess that I'm not. Instead I say into my headset, "Of course. Looking forward to it. What day is that again?"

Odette huffs. "Thanksgiving! Next Thursday? You're not listening, as usual."

I shift the baby from my right shoulder to my left and burp her successfully. I've only just learned how to do this, and it's surprisingly satisfying. For me.

"There's something else, Whiskey. I was going to ask you at the office, but I didn't want anyone to overhear. How would you feel if I invited Jeb?"

"As in Jeb Halloran, my ex-husband?"

"That would be the one."

I've skipped ahead a little, to the middle of November. Amazing, isn't it, how life accelerates? Before Leo, my days and nights passed at a mostly predictable pace. Then we met, fell in love, and got married, and life started zooming. We were a rocket ship. When Leo died, I clicked off the ignition. The rocket crashed, I survived, but nothing moved for months. Then along came leaf-peeping season, like it does every year. This year it triggered events that reshaped my life. Now the trees are bare, winter sports season is a few weeks away, and I'm still gaining momentum. I'm also healing.

When I walked into Avery's room at Coastal Medical Center and found her holding Leo and Leah, something inside me gave way. Driving over, I'd rehearsed a speech about finding her a place to stay and paying for a part-time nurse. But as soon as I saw those babies, I knew I wanted them at Vestige. For a while.

So we struck a deal. I hired the nurse and invited Avery and babies to stay through the holidays. Then they have to go. That's not as harsh as it sounds. I'll keep paying for the nurse. And I'm helping them find a house in Magnet Springs; I'll even make the down payment. Moreover, I've offered to train Avery in real estate. If she inherited her father's sales potential, she could make a million instead of suing me for it. I'm still waiting for the first sign of Leo's charisma to shine through. Maybe she has a knack for some other real estate-related career. Like demolition.

Wells Verbelow insists I should hire an attorney. Not a paper-pusher, but a protector. New house and new job aside, Wells predicts Avery will refuse to leave Vestige. My mother, on the other hand, thinks I'll be too attached to the babies to let them leave.

I'm neither as naïve as Wells fears nor as maternal as my mother wishes. If things don't go the way I want them to, I'll find a way that works. I've learned that I can do that, and losing Leo was not my only lesson. There was also the matter of Abra in heat. She's pregnant. Like Avery, she won't tell us who the father is. We know it's neither Mooney the Rott hound nor Officer Roscoe. Wells fears it might be a border collie who gets loose in town a lot. If so, no one will ever contain those pups. We'll know more soon enough; she's due in early December. If Avery was a bitch during pregnancy, Abra is in a class of her own. She insists on eating in bed. My bed. The up side is that her extra weight has temporarily grounded her. For now, anyway, she's not streamlined enough to slip through windows, sail over fences, or steal handbags.

After delivering the twins, Avery was still too angry at her mother to call, so I looked up Georgia's number in Belize and told her about her grandchildren. I didn't want her to think I was usurping her role. Silly me. Georgia's having much too much fun with her boy-toys to envy me changing diapers.

Avery hasn't mentioned Darrin Keogh. About once a week, though, when I answer our home phone, the caller disconnects. Sometimes I find Avery in a whispered conversation with someone she won't name. In either case, it could be Keogh. Or the babies' father. Or someone else entirely. She hasn't explained what happened to her CRX, either.

I find myself wondering if she lent it to a former antiques dealer and art forger who's now a fugitive.

I gave Avery the photo of Leo that she wanted, and I made copies to put in the scrapbooks that I've started for his grandchildren. While Avery was still in the hospital, I cleaned out Leo's closet. In the tote bag he'd never unpacked from Brazil, one pocket bulged with travel brochures. Presumably for us.

I cancelled Leo's voicemail accounts. That means I can no longer dial up his essence, although I can still hear him, when I want to, on the soundtrack of several home videos. There have been no more crank calls since the night Avery broke in. Although I lack hard evidence—and telephone telepathy—I suspect Rico Anuncio of playing that wicked phone trick on me. I'm willing to let bygones be bygones, provided it never happens again.

Kimba Reitbauer is still at large. Her husband, age fifty-six, died in a Chicago convalescent home on Halloween. I suppose that means Kimba inherited a fortune although she'll have to come forward to claim it. He died of heart failure. Or so the papers said.

I've heard nothing more about Warren Matheney. Brady assures me that the general public does not know what we know about a lost finger, a found ring, a questionable heart attack, and some unfortunate dogs.

The Angola Police recovered six healthy, well-trained Afghan hounds from Darrin Keogh's house. The dogs were promptly sent to the local animal shelter, where, after a few days, all but one was adopted. When the wire services picked up the story of an abandoned one-eyed Affie, Pashtoon also found a good home.

That brings me to Jeb Halloran, who's home for the holidays. I hadn't seen my first husband since the year I married Leo, when Jeb went off to save the world with his bluegrass tunes. In the right light, he could pass for James Taylor with hair. Yesterday Jeb showed up at my office. I suspect one or more of my friends have been emailing him, although none will admit it. Jeb knows a lot about Leo, Abra, Avery, and Chester. He asked about them—and about me. Then he showed me the web site for his new Celtic band, Skye Song. They have a CD.

Jeb has less hair now than he did six years ago, but still more than James Taylor. He looks good. Too good for an ex-husband. Let me put it this way: I'm no longer worried that my "equipment" has failed.

Odette says she might invite Jeb Halloran to Thanksgiving dinner. I tell her she can if she wants to. It's her party.

Chester's high-pitched voice floats down the stairwell into the family room, where I'm holding Leo and Leah. Avery is out. She's at her twice-weekly non-telephonic counseling session with Noonan. Avery says it helps her forgive the Universe for cosmically screwing her. That's the *Fifth* Sun of Solace, out of Seven. I wonder where it will end.

"Whiskey! It's starting!" Chester cries.

For an instant, I think he means that Abra is going into labor. Then I realize that it's time for Cassina's VH-1 special. She's broadcasting live from Sri Lanka. I relocate myself and the babies to the recliner in Chester's room upstairs, where a very swollen Abra occupies his bed. This is another part of my ongoing education: watching over Chester while Cassina and Rupert do the world. I'm relieved that his father is finally in his life. Or, in his mother's life, at any rate. Rupert is managing Cassina's tour and accompanying her on the piano. If all goes well—and since we're dealing with two divas, that's a big if—Rupert will return with Cassina to Magnet Springs and get acquainted with his son.

Meanwhile, Chester has agreed to be keeper of Abra and her brood. Free of charge. We signed the contract this morning. It's the best deal I've done yet.

~The End~

If you enjoyed this book, you'll want to read our next
Whiskey Mattimoe mystery

Whiskey Straight Up

by

NINA WRIGHT

ONE

"Whiskey, there's a guy from your past here to see you."

Tina Breen, my nasal-voiced office manager, intercepted me before I could stomp the snow off my boots.

"From my past?" I echoed, mildly interested. "Professional or . . . romantic?"

"Uh. . . . " Tina slid her eyes toward the nearest cubicle.

"Does the name Roy Vickers ring a bell?" The resonant voice came first, then the trim, tastefully dressed form of Odette Mutombo, top producer in my real-estate agency. Riding her desk chair into the foyer on cue, she smiled slyly. "He may have changed your destiny."

Odette, who was from Zimbabwe, had a syncopated accent and an unnerving way of inserting herself into other people's conversations.

"I doubt it," I said.

Odette and Tina exchanged glances. Never a good sign.

"Okay. Spill it," I began as my overloaded briefcase did just that. Tina dove to retrieve the contents. Since she's usually not helpful, I knew for sure something was up.

"Leo would remember him. . . ." Odette teased.

I ran the name Roy Vickers through my usual mental filters. The one with Leo's name on it still occupied most of my brain. Dead nine months already, my late husband was never far from my thoughts. Leo had been a wise and wonderful partner in both business and the stuff that really mattered. Despite everything that had happened to me since his sudden death, my first reaction was often to go tell Leo. Only I never could again.

"I'm drawing a blank," I said.

"Think about it," insisted Odette. "Roy Vickers. You must remember him."

"Maybe we should let Jenx tell her." Tina sounded nervous.

"And let our new police chief have all the fun?" Odette made a rude noise. "Here's a clue, Whiskey: Roy Vickers is seventy."

"Then he's not my old lover," I said. "He's just old."

"There's a real-estate connection. Sort of. . . ." Tina said, handing me my newly alphabetized files.

I was already bored with the game. "Was he an agent?"

"No."

"A former client?"

"Leo's former client. Before you were married."

"Then he's from Leo's past, not mine." I yawned and started toward my office.

"It's not that simple," Tina called after me. "He's a handyman, and he needs a job."

"We have a handyman. And seventy's way too old."

Tina followed me down the hall. "But what can he do? He just got out of jail!"

"Jail?" I stopped cold.

The name Roy Vickers suddenly illuminated a dark corner of my mind. Repression is an underrated gift, one that I'm proud to cultivate. But it's a challenge in the company of Tina and Odette, who never met a disturbing fact they wished to forget. Especially in someone else's life.

"He went to jail nine years ago," Odette said, rolling her desk chair toward me. "For stabbing Leo in a rent dispute."

"Leo was married to Georgia then," Tina added. "But you know what happened, don't you?"

Indeed I did.

Although Leo never discussed the incident, other residents of Magnet Springs, Michigan, weren't so reticent. When it happened, I was twenty-four and on the road with my musician husband, Jeb Halloran. My role in his entourage wasn't musical. It was to remind his groupies that he was married. The point is that I wasn't around at the time Leo Mattimoe was stabbed. I hardly even knew him. But the event became part of our local lore, and the story goes like this:

Town drunk Roy Vickers, a carpenter reduced to catch-as-catch-can repair work, opened his mail to find a rent-increase notification. Although it was a bitterly cold January afternoon, Roy was too incensed and too intoxicated to don a coat before staggering the two blocks to his landlord's office. Leo Mattimoe listened to Roy's bourbon-scented complaints. Then he explained his reasons for raising the rent. Roy wasn't interested in logic; he called Leo a slum landlord with the heart of a robber baron. Leo pointed out that Roy was free to find another place to live. Roy blubbered that he had very little reason to live because his wife had left him.

Then he seized Leo's letter opener and began waving it around. Worried that Roy might try to kill himself, Leo grabbed for the blade. In his whiskey fog, Roy mistook the action for a counterattack.

Moments later, he stumbled outside and knelt in the snow to wash away Leo's blood. The snow turned bright pink, and his frozen-raw hands darkened to purple, but—like Lady Macbeth—Roy couldn't stop rubbing. A passing tourist spotted the moaning, blood-spattered man without a coat and detoured to the police station.

Our then-chief, Big Jim, strode directly up to Roy and asked what he was doing. Roy shook his head and cried, "Better go tell Georgia she's a widow."

Georgia was Leo's first wife. She left him a year later. Two years after that, Leo married me, and then I became his widow. But that's getting ahead of the story.

Big Jim found Leo on the floor of his office, blood pouring from his chest wound. A few more minutes, and Leo would have died.

Now I stared at Odette and Tina. "Give me one good reason why I should hire Roy Vickers."

"Karma." The response didn't come from Odette or Tina. Noonan Starr, massage therapist, New Age guru, and my best tenant had entered the lobby. Brushing invisible snowflakes from her spiky white-blonde hair, she added, "Plus, Jenx thinks it's a good idea."

"Then Jenx should hire him," I snapped.

"But that wouldn't close the circle," Noonan said. I braced myself for metaphysical metaphors. "Only by restoring balance with Leo's heirs can Roy make himself whole again."

"I'm not Leo's only heir," I said as I pictured his daughter Avery, a chronically unhappy young woman who had arrived on my doorstep in time to deliver twins and was now using my home as her nursery. Housing her and her babies and providing a nanny was less traumatic than I'd expected. Still, I wondered if Avery would ever leave. Or look for work. Or smile. And she steadfastly refused to name her babies' father.

Leo had another heir who could use Roy's help: his blonde Afghan hound, Abra, a diva dog if ever there were one. She was as difficult as Leo's daughter, only faster on her four perfectly pedicured feet. Unlike Avery, Abra had a criminal record. She used to steal purses. Like Avery, Abra had a new brood, father unknown. That was mostly my fault since I'd neglected to have her spayed. In the months following Leo's death, I'd been distracted. First I had to recover from the injuries I sustained when Leo's heart failed and he crashed our car. Then two people were murdered in properties I managed. To put it mildly, life got complicated.

"You're a good person, Whiskey," Noonan reminded me. "You'll think of ways to help Roy free his karmic flow."

"He can send me a greeting card," I suggested. "They make them for every occasion: 'Sorry I stabbed someone you loved. I did the time for my crime. Wish me well.'"

Noonan's dewy eyes darkened. "He needs a job. You can hire him."

"But why should I?" My question was a whine.

"Because Leo would have wanted you to."

I hated to hear that because it was true. While Leo wasn't perfect, he was generous to a fault.

Odette re-entered the conversation. "I hear prison reformed Roy Vickers. He's a new man."

"He sobered up and found a community," confirmed Tina. "Jenx says the inmates called him Pop. They looked up to him."

Probably because he was tall, I thought. Although I hadn't known Roy Vickers, I'd seen him on the streets of Magnet Springs when I was young. Back then, he must have been six foot four, a rangy, loose-limbed alcoholic who did odd jobs, mostly for people who pitied his wife. I couldn't remember her name, but I recalled folks wondering why she stayed with him as long as she did.

"He lost his community when they released him from prison," Noonan pointed out. "Now he faces the challenge of his life: building positive relationships where he destroyed relationships. It's what will heal Roy Vickers."

Noonan spoke with such passion that the room fell silent. Everyone was waiting for me to do the right thing.

"I'll talk to him," I mumbled.

Odette clapped her hands together three times. Tina cheered. Noonan hugged me. I realized that my twice-broken ribs no longer hurt, which meant I was healing, too. At least my bones were.

"Your goodness will help Roy Vickers open his soul to the light," Noonan said.

I didn't know about Roy Vickers's soul, but the rest of him looked damned fine. I'm not sure what I expected, but what I encountered blew me away. My first thought when he strode into my office: The guy doesn't look a day over fifty. My second thought—and this one's embarrassing: He's buffer than any man I've slept with.

Then again, I'd mainly slept with musicians and desk jockeys. And it had been a long time since I'd slept with anyone. Thirty-nine weeks and two days, to be exact. I'm only human. And still only thirty-three.

Roy Vickers had sun-punished skin, military bearing, and bulging muscles. His steel-gray hair was cropped close to the scalp, but he seemed to have most of the hairline he'd started with. His electric blue eyes were clear and calm.

"Thank you, ma'am, for seeing me without an appointment," he said. We shook hands. His large paw was calloused but warm.

"Please. Call me Whiskey. Everybody does."

He chuckled. "That was my nickname, too. Once upon a time."

"Oh, but I'm not a—." I stopped myself just in time.

"Didn't think you were," he said pleasantly. "Any more than Cokie Roberts is a cokehead."

"You know Cokie Roberts?"

"Sure. I listen to a lot of public radio."

I nodded, thinking I didn't know a thing about this guy.

ABOUT THE AUTHOR

NINA WRIGHT is a professional actor turned playwright and novelist. When not at her keyboard, she leads entertaining workshops in the creative process. In addition to the Whiskey Mattimoe series, Nina writes a wide range of fiction for adults and younger readers. She loves big dogs and beaches.

WWW.MIDNIGHTINKBOOKS.COM

From the gritty streets of New York City to sacred tombs in the Middle East, it's always midnight somewhere. Join us online at any hour for fresh new voices in mystery fiction, book club questions, author information, mystery resources, and more.

Midnight Ink promises a wild ride filled with cunning villains, conflicted heroes, hilarious hazards, mind-bending puzzles, and enough twists and turns to keep readers on the edge of their seats.

MIDNIGHT INK ORDERING INFORMATION

Order by Phone:
- Call toll-free within the U.S. and Canada at
  1-888-NITEINK (1-888-648-3465)
- We accept VISA, MasterCard, and American Express

Order by Mail:
Send the full price of your order (MN residents add 7% sales tax) in U.S. funds, plus postage & handling to:

> Midnight Ink
> 2143 Wooddale Drive
> Woodbury, MN 55125-2989

Postage & Handling:
Standard (U.S., Mexico, & Canada). If your order is:
> $49.99 and under, add $3.00
> $50.00 and over, FREE STANDARD SHIPPING

AK, HI, PR: $15.00 for one book plus $1.00 for each additional book.

International Orders (airmail only):
> $16.00 for one book plus $3.00 for each additional book

Orders are processed within 2 business days. Please allow for normal shipping time. Postage and handling rates subject to change.